Penguin Books
Jerusalem the Golden

Margaret Drabble was born in Sheffield in 1939 and went
to Mount School, York, a Quaker boarding school. She
won a Major Scholarship to Newnham College,
Cambridge, where she read English and received a double
first. She won a travel award in 1966 from the Society of
Authors and received the E. M. Forster Award from the
American Academy of Arts and Letters in 1973.

She has written several novels: *A Summer Birdcage* (1963),
The Garrick Year (1964), *The Millstone* (1965, filmed as
A Touch of Love in 1969), *Jerusalem the Golden* (1967),
The Waterfall (1969) and *The Needle's Eye* (1972), all of
which have been published in Penguins. Her latest novel is
The Realms of Gold (1975). She has also written a short
critical book on Wordsworth, a television play, and
various articles, as well as *London Consequences* (1972,
edited with B. S. Johnson) and *Arnold Bennett, a
biography* (1974).

Margaret Drabble

Jerusalem the Golden

Penguin Books

Penguin Books Ltd, Harmondsworth,
Middlesex, England
Penguin Books, 625 Madison Avenue, New York,
New York 10022, U.S.A.
Penguin Books Australia Ltd, Ringwood,
Victoria, Australia
Penguin Books Canada Ltd, 2801 John Street,
Markham, Ontario, Canada L3R 1B4
Penguin Books (N.Z.) Ltd, 182–190 Wairau Road,
Auckland 10, New Zealand

First published by Weidenfeld & Nicolson 1967
Published in Penguin Books 1969
Reprinted 1969, 1970, 1973, 1974, 1975, 1976, 1977

Made and printed in Great Britain by
Hazell Watson & Viney Ltd,
Aylesbury, Bucks
Set in Linotype Times

For Judith Landry

Chapter 1

Clara never failed to be astonished by the extraordinary felicity of her own name. She found it hard to trust herself to the mercy of fate, which had managed over the years to convert her greatest shame into one of her greatest assets, and even after years of comparative security she was still prepared for, still half expecting the old gibes to be revived. But whenever she was introduced, nothing greeted the amazing, all-revealing Clara but cries of, 'How delightful, how charming, how unusual, how fortunate,' and she could foresee a time when friends would name their babies after her and refer back to her with pride as the original from which inspiration had first been drawn. Finally her confidence grew to such an extent that she was able to explain that she had been christened not in the vanguard but in the extreme rearguard of fashion, after a Wesleyan great aunt, and that her mother had formed the notion not as an unusual and charming conceit, but as a preconceived penance for her daughter, whose only offences at that tender age were her existence and her sex. For Mrs Maugham did not like the name any more than Clara and her school friends did, and she chose it through a characteristic mixture of duty and malice. When Clara explained this to people, she found that they merely laughed, and the thought of people laughing, however indirectly, at her mother's intentions, gave her a deep and secret pleasure.

The reversal of fortune was in fact so complete that Clara sometimes found herself wondering whether she had not gone so far as deliberately to seek a world in which her name could be a credit and not a shame. Her social progress had certainly taken her far enough from her starting point. On the other hand, time had converted liabilities other than her name into assets, and things surely more integral to the nature of her progress.

Her intelligence, which was considerable, must for instance have played some more significant and guiding role: the name question was merely a piece of luck. Her intelligence, like her name, had been as a child a source of great trouble to her, for it too had singled her out, when her one desire had been to be inconspicuous. It made her an object of ridicule and contempt from the earliest age, and some of her most frightful memories were of her mother, grim-faced, ill concealing her resentment, as she flipped through those predictably shining school reports. She wished at such moments that she could fail examinations as other children did, and her most cherished subject was geometry, in which her marks were sometimes quite comfortably low. And yet at the same time she doubly resented her mother's resentment, for her mother herself was no fool, she had never herself possessed the lovely blessing of stupidity: she had merely crushed and deformed and dissembled what gifts she had once had, in deference to what? To a way of life perhaps, to a town, to a suburb in a town in the North of England.

But Clara, try as she might, found it hard to dissemble. And always, at the back of her mind, there was some faint hope that some day it might pay off, that some day she might find herself somewhere where she might win. So she cultivated, stubbornly, discreetly, her inclinations, and in the end it was this same intelligence which in her home town was so sourly disowned, so grudgingly deprecated, that got her out of it and transported her incredibly, mercifully, to London. When she received her first term's cheque for her State Scholarship Allowance, she stared at it for some time as she contemplated the fact, the printed fact before her, the final vindication of her lonely belief that there was more than one way of life in England. And see, there was, for somebody somewhere had thought that intelligence was worth paying for. Even her mother could not annihilate ninety pounds by mere disapproval: the cash payment spoke to Clara's industrial heart decisively. Money was there, and in her hand, and moreover money would continue to arrive at settled intervals, being the gift of a settled politic faith, and not a mere whim of authority. At times she felt a certain shame about taking the money, as though she were being paid for displaying or exercising some horrific deformity, like the dwarf in the circus, like the fat lady, like the woman with the hairy chest. And she never learned to take a simple pleasure in her own abilities; they remained for her a means, and not an end, a bargaining power rather than a blessing. Yet nevertheless, as the years rolled by, she grew more bold about the power, for if intelligence were a deformity, then it was certainly not as rare or as disfiguring a one as she had expected, and there were plenty of people who found it acceptable. As with the name, it was simply a question of finding the people to take it; all she had to do was seek a place, a place other than Northam, where her eccentricities might go unmarked, where indeed, more hopefully, they might be greeted with delight.

And as far as people went, she had not done too badly. She had to make do with some unsatisfactory substitutes at times, for it took her some time to learn her way about, and she was in her third year at University before she met the Denhams: but then she had to acknowledge that if she had met them earlier, at the age of eighteen, straight out of Grammar School, raw, uninitiated, desirous, she might not have been capable of seeing them for what they were, for at that age all people who were not from Northam seemed at first sight equally brilliant, surrounded as they were by a confusing blur of bright indistinct charm. Moreover, even if at that age she had recognized their distinctions, her recognition would have been of no use to her: she would have admired, silently, in servile envy. Whereas when she did finally discover them, at the age of twenty two, she had at least learned words and signs and gestures; she knew at least the outlines of their world. Sometimes she wondered what would have happened if she had missed them, and whether a conjunction so fateful and fruitful could have been, by some accidental obtuseness on her part, avoided: she did not like to think so, she liked to think that inevitability had had her in its grip, but at the same time she uneasily knew that it had in some ways, been a near thing.

For the truth was that her first sight of Clelia had not impressed her. In the light of future impressions, she found it hard to credit this disturbing historic recollection: it seemed to convict her of such gross insensitivity. Nor did she like the implications of accident that this initial blindness carried; she felt, looking back, like a lover who had met and passed by, indifferently, without recognition, the one love of his life, distracted from his destiny by the need for a drink, or a fixed intention to have an early night. Though it was not as though she had missed her for long; the time lag, between meeting and recognition, had been infinitesimal. Infinitesimal, but sinister. Clara would have found it more satisfactory if, upon vision, upon the instant of meeting, a sudden lightning had descended: if she could have said then, this is the kind of thing I have been looking for, and if this is not it, then it is nowhere else.

But in mercy to herself, to her own perceptions, she had to acknowledge that the circumstances of their meeting had been colourful and confusing enough to excuse a good deal of distraction. For she had first seen Clelia in the dressing room of a theatre, and she had never been in such a room before. She was so amazed by the novelty of finding herself there at all that it took her some time to distinguish its various occupants, though she was solicitously introduced to each in turn by her escort, and introduced, she later assumed, to Clelia too, though she could not remember even a smile or a handshake; that first contact dropped from her memory as though it had never happened and she would look for it sometimes, and sometimes she and Clelia would try to recall it together, sadly, pleasantly, nostalgically, but it had gone forever. Her main pre-occupation at the time, she remembered, had been a desire to recognize the people whom she had just seen, ten minutes earlier, upon the stage, so that she could say to the right people that she had much enjoyed the evening. Although she was quite ignorant of the etiquette of such occasions, she rightly took this to be her duty; she could tell that she was right by the way that Peter, after introducing her, politely echoed her sentiments, although he had expressed quite other sentiments whilst sitting beside her in the auditorium.

She had confidence in Peter, for he was familiar with such places, and it was under his guidance that she was there; she admired him for being able to conceal his views, but she admired him even more for the sophistication of having them, as she herself had no views whatever about the spectacle which she had just witnessed; an evening's reading of modern English poetry was not an event that she felt herself competent to judge.

She had listened, she had paid attention, but she had no opinions, either about the poems themselves, or about their delivery. She could tell that some of the poems were long and some short, some simple and some obscure; she could even tell which were descriptive, which erotic, and which political, but beyond that she could not go. She was always baffled by that ready phrase, so common in her home town, 'I don't know much about it but I know what I like,' for she herself was so perpetually aware that without knowledge she had no means of liking or of disliking. Of French literature she knew something, and might have ventured, after hesitation, to prefer Zola to Hugo, but of English literature she knew little. She was aware that she might nevertheless, despite this ignorance, have had some attitude towards the readers, but she had not; their skills were as alien to her as the skills of football players, and she would no more have dreamed of preferring the one called Eric Harley to the one called Samuel Wisden than she would have thought of making comments about Danny Blanchflower and Stanley Matthews.

She had, however, found plenty to watch. Being in a theatre at all was in itself a rare amusement, and she had stared with curiosity at the four readers, who were all real poets in their own right, though they did not all read their own poems; for some reason more subtle, she assumed, than mere perversity, they had shuffled their works amongst themselves, with a few quite extraneous additions. Margarita Cassell's written works were, she noticed, sparsely represented, though she had more than her fair share of the declamation; the reasons for this were fairly evident, as her talents clearly lay more in the spoken than in the written word. Clara liked watching Margarita Cassell, because she was beautiful, and because she wore a nice dress, and because she was wholly audible, and yet she had a lurking suspicion that she was the soft option, that she was there expressly to amuse such people as her own uninitiated self, and this suspicion effectively undermined her pleasure. She liked to like things, if at all, for the right reason. And all in all, she was glad that she had Peter and his views to back her up, in the desert wastes of her own interested indifference. She even found that his views did in some way give some slight shape to her own

11

vestigial parched buds of inclination, for when he had whispered to her that he thought Denham was superb and Harley awful, she noticed in herself a slight but unmistakable flutter of surprise; for was not Eric Harley so well-articulated, so clear, so strong, and Denham so monotonously even and undramatic? Though that in itself was, she saw, quite possibly the point.

Peter, unlike Clara, had the advantage of being upon home ground, for he himself wrote poetry, and he also claimed the honour of being acquainted with Samuel Wisden. It was this acquaintance that had drawn him to take Clara to the poetry reading in the first place; he liked the idea of appearing by her side as an intimate of published writers. And he knew that Clara, unlike some of his other girls, was susceptible to such impressions, and that she would be suitably affected by his claims to a foothold in the poetic world. And she had been impressed: she had even gone so far as to look up some of Samuel Wisden's works before attending the reading. They were shy, lyrical, lower middle class pieces about young men in cheap suits in parks and on railway stations; she had pictured some plain and sensitive man, given to riding bicycles, and was agreeably surprised when she found that a motorbike was more the image that he evoked, for he was flamboyant, leather-jacketed, and he had a fancy hair cut. She liked such floutings of expectation. Eric Harley, whose poems were highly sophisticated, obscure and ambitious, turned out to look far more like the Samuel Wisden of her imagination; he had an accent which she recognized as northern, though well overlaid by American, and he was wearing a very old suit. Margarita Cassell, the only one whose fame had filtered through to the regions where Clara lived, looked just as a poetic actress ought to look; she was middle aged and beautiful, flippant and intense, strident and informal. Her dress was of pale shining embroidered silk, and she read with great emotion, and when Peter said, finally, in Clara's ear, that she was not good, Clara knew that she had known it, for how could anything so pleasant be good; and yet she was nevertheless grateful, for such colourful badness, for the drab empty stage, with its bleak abstract backcloth, and its ill-rehearsed lighting changes, demanded such relief.

12

Of the four performers, Sebastian Denham was the only one to exude real authenticity. He was, for one thing, the oldest; the programme said that he was in his early fifties. He was also the most famous, though Clara could not have known this had she not looked him up in various works of reference, because before she had been invited to the Poetry Reading she had not so much as heard of him. As she looked through the list of his published works in the library catalogue, and read the comments on him in the Penguin Guides, and inspected his career in the programme notes, she felt ashamed that someone of such evident distinction could have eluded her consciousness so entirely. His reputation was clearly as firm as a rock; adjectives such as 'classic' and 'masterly' abounded in the vicinity of his name. And when she stopped to consider that she could name, offhand, no living English poets other than T. S. Eliot and Robert Graves (and was not Eliot dead?) she had to concede that there was room in the literary world for other fixed stars. She noted that he was the only poet (apart from Miss Cassell, whose virtues were non-poetic) to be represented on other evenings of the national Poetry Week, and that he had top billing. His very appearance was a kind of guarantee, because if he was not a real poet, in such a place, he was nothing, for he clearly had not been selected on decorative grounds like the embroidered Margarita. He was not ugly: he was dull. No ulterior motives, no ephemeral yearnings, nothing more than the gift itself could have placed him there, upon that wooden platform. He wore a suit and glasses, and the programme said that he was a lawyer in his non-creative life. He looked so unlike a poet that Clara felt that he could be nothing else, that he was unmistakably the real thing, and she found in his solid, impassive cultured countenance a guarantee of worth. His poetry she could not understand. It was about subjects of which she knew nothing, and the scansion of it was regular, and it rhymed. She could not have said more about it, and luckily nobody asked her to do so.

And when she came face to face with Mr Denham, in the large and shabby dressing room, she found it surprisingly simple to shake his hand and to say that she had so much enjoyed the evening. He replied, unremarkably, that he was glad; clearly he expected and hoped for no more original a salutation. He stood quietly, with his back to the wide dusty mirror, smiling affably, mild, adult, dissociated. Margarita Cassell, on the other hand, though her age might have equalled his, seemed genuinely anxious for opinions: when Samuel Wisden introduced Peter and Clara to her, and when she had made polite inquiries about Peter's mother, with whom she had once been at school, she turned about the subject of the past evening with an eager greed. 'Well then, what *about* it?' she said to them, and the rest of the assembled company. 'Whatever did you think of it? Was there anybody *there*? I just kept my eyes shut and didn't look, I was so afraid there wasn't going to be *anybody* there at all.'

'Of course there were people there,' said Samuel Wisden. 'There are always people at these things. God knows why they go to them, but they do. The poetry lovers of England, you know.'

'It was quite a good house, actually,' said Peter. 'The front stalls were a bit thin, but the rest was almost full.'

Clara listened to this and to the ensuing discussion with pleasure: she liked to hear people use phrases like 'quite a good house'. She knew them all, all the right phrases, but some deeply excluded modesty prevented her from using them. And she liked the way they talked about poetry and about poetry readings, and audiences, and whether people understood it or not, and whether people liked it or not, and whether people who went to poetry readings liked whatever they heard anyway, simply because they were the kind of people who liked going to poetry readings and hearing poetry: and she could tell from the tone and the pattern of the talk that everyone there had expressed similar views in similar conversations a dozen times before, but was nonetheless ready to express them yet once more, for all that: and it was this sense of trivial, gossipy familiarity and repetition that most pleased her, for it convinced her that she was listening to real professionals. Even Peter, who could be intense and zealous enough when on his own, was managing to affect a finely nonchalant contempt about the problems of communication; she liked the cosy way they all seemed to assume that the evening was a wash-out, inevitably, and that the whole job of writing and reading poetry was somehow fundamentally ill-conceived. And yet, at the same time, they

14

wanted to think they had done it well. The mixture of general cynicism and personal vanity was peculiarly appealing; Margarita at one point, perched most delicately and leggily upon Sebastian Denham's dressing table, said, 'Of course the *most* depressing thing is the way they all grow instantly silent for the *worst* possible poems, like that one I did of Reggie's, and no offence to poor darling Reggie, but it really is *nothing* but a bit of sophisticated *jingle*, and yet it always goes down marvellously at readings, haven't you noticed?' Clara, who was often depressed by her own observations, found herself merely enchanted by such emphatic indulgent transparency.

And while they talked, Clara found time to watch, and to check up on who was there. Apart from herself and Peter and the four performers, there was a man from the BBC called Lionel, who was connected in some way with the show – director, she thought, or producer, or possibly both. There was another man whose name she had not caught, but who might have been Margarita Cassell's husband. There was also an astonishingly pretty boy, who was quite clearly an actor; she worked this out for herself and felt clever, and then reflected that in the circumstances the deduction was not truly brilliant. He too seemed to be connected with Margarita Cassell. He was so pretty that Clara could hardly take her eyes off him, although it would clearly have been more profitable to pay her attentions to Samuel Wisden, who was handsome enough, without being excessively, exclusively so. And then there was Sebastian Denham's daughter. In view of all the other men in the room, Clara paid no attention at all to Sebastian Denham's daughter, apart from wondering whether she had heard her name aright, for she seemed to be called Clelia: the name, at first hearing, was so uncannily like Clara that Clara dispensed with the notion that she might have misheard the initial consonant, and that the girl might be supposed to be called Dahlia. Clelia was a name with which she had no acquaintance. She did not think it likely that she would ever need to use it, so she was not unduly uneasy about her ignorance.

On the other hand, as time wore on, she did begin to feel mildly uneasy about her claims to existence in that dressing room. She wondered, in short, if she and Peter ought to go.

Nobody else seemed to be going, and Peter's friendship with his poet seemed to be, fortunately, at least as intimate as he had claimed, but she did feel that they ought not to spend the evening there. She wondered if anyone might want to put the room to its true purpose, and undress in it. She did not see why anyone should want to undress, as everyone was quite respectably clothed; nobody was wearing anything outlandish and embarrassing, like a dinner jacket. The only person who might have been thought to be uncomfortably or unsuitably dressed was Miss Cassell, whose dress was even more amazing off stage than on, but then it was not even her dressing room; her dressing room was next door. Moreover, she showed no inclination to change her dress; she clearly enjoyed its extravagance, and leaned right forward from time to time to make sure that no one missed the magnificence of her bosom. And Clara, whenever she managed to wrench her gaze away from the beautiful young man, found it resting itself inevitably upon those two tight pale mounds, and the deep powdery yawning cave between them. She had never before seen such a dress upon anyone with a right to wear one, and the combination of natural and unnatural gifts was quite startling; she suddenly saw what all those other women had been aiming at in their strapless gowns and their deep cleavages with their large chests and their thin collar bones. And she understood the other women, because it was an effect worth taking a few risks for.

She did not want to go. She wanted to stay there, and hear them talk about poetry and money, and about how Eric Harley got more for being on The Spoken Word series on I T V than he'd made out of a year's writing. After a few minutes, somebody suggested opening a bottle of champagne, and then somebody else said that it might be better to go down to the pub before closing time, and she hoped that they would go to the pub, because she did not feel that she could stay and drink their champagne, even if it was offered to her. Although it would have been nice to have been obliged to drink a glass of champagne in a dressing room. She could not recollect that she had ever tasted champagne, and she liked the thought of its spiritual flavour. However, as so often happened, the gathering, threatened with action, started to show signs of breaking up; Margarita Cassell said that she had to go to the pub anyway as she had to meet a friend there, Eric Harley also claimed a friend in the pub, and the Lionel man said he had to go home, and put on his coat and went. Then Clelia Denham, who had hitherto spoken not a word, rose to her feet and said, 'I'll be off too.' Clara began to feel slightly alarmed, not because she had any interest in Clelia, but because she did not like this desertion of the evening and she was afraid that if enough people went Peter would decide to go too. She thought she could rely on Samuel's inclinations, but then on the other hand he might have other fish to fry. So she was quite relieved when Clelia's father said, 'Don't go, Clelia, come and have a drink. I'll give you a lift home if you hang on for half an hour. And I promised to have a word with Maurice. Not more than half an hour.'

Clelia looked at her watch. She appeared to be slightly, very slightly annoyed. 'Oh, all right,' she said. 'I'll see you down there.' And she went.

Clara was also relieved by the universal assumption that there was only one pub to be visited; she had always had a horror of ending up, by some misunderstanding, in the wrong and empty and unfashionable place. She could not quite see why the pub, relentlessly nameless, should be so clearly recognized by everyone there as an obvious destination, as she had not yet grasped the principle that nearly every theatre has its own pub. There was no reason why she should have grasped it. She had no experience of such things. But when she and Peter and Samuel and Eric made their way down the wooden, broken staircase, and through the dark warren of small rooms full of light switches, and out through the stage door, she could see that it would have been difficult to miss the correct pub. Because it was part of the theatre: the other half of the theatre. And it was full of the theatre audience, and the stage management, and of unmistakable actors and actresses; even the Lionel man, who had departed so resolutely, was there having a quick whisky. And Clelia was there, leaning on the bar snapping her fingers at the barman. She ordered herself a drink. Clara was impressed; she had never in her life dared to buy herself a drink. Somewhere, in the depths of her heart, she feared that if she were to ask a man in a public house for a gin and tonic, he would spit in her

17

eye or call the police or laugh at her or rape her on the spot. She could not overcome this fear, and it was too shameful to confess. She did not mind drinking, and accepted Samuel Wisden's offer of a drink with pleasure, but she looked at Clelia Denham's back with initial stirrings of respect.

Eric's friend, after a few moments, turned up; he was a high-powered school teacher, and he provoked a new and somewhat repetitive discussion of the poetry reading. Clara listened, but she spent more of her time watching. She noted, with satisfaction, the lovely entrance of Margarita Cassell, who arrived with one arm through her husband's and the other through the arm of the pretty young man; in the sombre Victorian gloom her dress and her wide cold neck shone with a pale and striking colour. And her voice preceded her and welled out from her, deep and vibrant and delightful: an instrument of sound rather than of communication. She and her entourage established themselves within speaking distance of Samuel's group; they talked, and from time to time a remark was flung across the gap between the two parties. Clara could not help noticing that although Margarita relinquished her husband's arm fairly promptly (as soon, in fact, as he had been dispatched to order drinks) she instantly took hold of the boy's hand, and kept a firm though flippant grasp upon it, almost as though she did not dare to let him roam loose upon the pub floor. Clara found this sight cheering, disturbing, and exciting. She wondered if in such circles such an act meant something or nothing, and then concluded that nothing, anywhere, in any circle, meant nothing.

After a while, it occurred to her to wonder what had happened to Clelia Denham and her independent drink. She looked round for her, and there she was, talking to a completely disconnected man, and looking, from time to time, at her watch. There was still no sign of her father. Clara looked at her more closely, and wondered, as soon as she did so, why she had not bothered to look at her before, because she repaid inspection. She still looked rather restless and annoyed – sullen, almost, Clara might have thought, if the word had not implied a heaviness that was not there. She was listening very intently to the disconnected man, with her head on one side; from time to time she would nod, or speak, but not at length. Her face, though not noticeably beautiful, had a hard, fine outline, and a shape very much its own; wedge-shaped, one might have called it, though it would have been hard to say which part composed a wedge. And her hair fell in a solid heavy piece, straight edged, stopping sharply midway between chin and shoulder; it was dark, and it had a weight that made it look as though it were well cut, though it was not. It looked, as the hair of Japanese children looks, as though it might be composed of wood and not of hair, so distinct were its outlines, so uniform and massy its swing. She seemed to be wearing no make-up, and her clothes were bizarre, though in no way ostentatious; her skirt was very short, and made of black velvet, and over it she wore a long maroon jacket with brass buttons and epaulettes. They were not fashionable garments, but they spoke of confidence; Clara felt, suddenly, that her own outfit, though quite becoming and unexceptionable, lacked nerve. She was in truth so unsure of her own taste that she restricted herself to wearing the most negative, unassertively simple things that she could find; the principle was, she knew, sound in itself, and her face quite good enough to appear to advantage above a grey wool jersey, but nevertheless, watching Clelia Denham, she felt that there were fashionable flights quite within her style that she had never yet had the courage or the knowledge to attempt.

When Clelia abandoned her stranger and joined Clara's own conversational cluster, Clara was pleased, and would have liked to have spoken to her, but could not think of anything to say. So she listened. Samuel Wisden seemed to know her quite well, for when she arrived he embarked upon some complicated discussion of some third party called Robert, who had, it emerged, recently pulled off some coup of some deeply obscure nature. The point was whether this would be bad or good for Robert. Samuel seemed to think that it would be bad for him, but Clelia took the line that without this unexpected stroke of success poor Robert would merely have gone from bad to worse. 'Look,' she said from time to time, 'don't think I'm saying he *deserves* it, God knows he's the last person to deserve anything, I know quite well what ought to happen to him, I really think he's quite shocking, and quite, quite indefensible, but I really can't help liking him, I keep telling myself how awful he is, and then every

19

time I see him I can feel this stupid great smile spreading all over my face. Because he's so nice, he really is nice, you can't deny it. And now this has happened he's even nicer. And since *all* he is is nice, then he might as well be it, don't you think?'

'I don't agree with your basic premise,' said Samuel. 'I don't think he's nice.'

'Oh *well* then,' said Clelia, spreading her hands in eloquent yet modest emphasis, 'in that case I can't see why you even bother to think about him.'

'Well, one can't help thinking about him,' said Samuel. 'Especially in view of this new thing ...'

And so they went on. Clara was highly impressed by the way in which the plight of Robert was gradually turned into a public discussion; Peter, Eric Harley and his friend, and finally she herself were all drawn into the debate, and found themselves talking at some length about the psychological and philosophical basis of the plight, which Clelia had somehow managed to convey to them in a classic structural sense, as a case far removed from the contaminations of the inconveniently unknown personality upon which it rested. Clara thought such transpositions implied a high intelligence, as well as a hopeful generosity of communication, and she watched with increasing attention. She began to realize that she was in the presence of the kind of thing for which she had been searching for years, some nameless class or quality, some element which she had glimpsed often enough, but which she had rarely at such close quarters encountered. A kind of excitement filled her, not unlike the excitement more frequently experienced, of love. And rarer than love. Because Clara had always supposed that such people as Clelia, so strange, so lovely, so clever, so undismaying, must somewhere exist, but she had never yet seen quite such a promising, hopeful example: and she had begun to think that she had created herself, through her own imagination, the whole genre. She had wanted such people to exist, so dressed, so independent, so involved; she had needed them, so she had presupposed them. And here, as she slowly realized, was a woman who was the thing that she had presupposed. She stood, and watched the felicity of her own invention, and experienced the satisfaction of her recognition.

Sebastian Denham did not turn up. When closing time was announced, Clelia broke off in mid-sentence, looked at her watch, and said, 'Oh hell, what about my father, he's forgotten me.'

She said it very crossly, but to herself. And as though she had expected to be forgotten.

'I'll drive you home,' said Samuel.

'I thought you lived in Dulwich,' said Clelia.

'Yes, I suppose I do,' said Samuel.

'What's the point of saying you'll drive me home then?' she said.

'Well, I would,' said Samuel.

'You know you wouldn't,' said Clelia. 'Anyway, I'll go on the bus. As a matter of fact I'm rather glad he forgot me, he gets horribly depressed by these readings. And since he's forgotten me, I can call in on Colin on the way back.'

'How *is* Colin?' said Samuel, eagerly, implying heaven knows how many possible afflictions; Clara thought they were in for another elaborate dissection, but Clelia seemed not to be interested in Colin, for she said very absent-mindedly, 'Oh, he's fine, thanks. More or less fine.' Clara was disappointed. But Clelia immediately made up for this reticence by a far more enticing comment; she started to tie her black head square on, and said, 'Well, I must go, I must get back to the baby. They simply have no idea about that baby, I've got into such a state that I hardly dare leave the house.'

'How *is* the baby?' said Samuel, with an eagerness only slightly less marked than that with which he had greeted the names of Robert and Colin.

'Oh it's all right,' said Clelia. 'But it's teething. And nobody else wakes up for it in the night. So I never like to stay out after they've gone to bed. And Mama's taken to going to bed at nine o'clock these days, she hates Martin so violently. It's pathetic, really. Excuse me, I must go to the Ladies.'

'I'll go to the Ladies too,' said Clara. She had been wondering where it was for the last hour, and had been unable to see it; she was as diffident about asking for Ladies' rooms as she was about ordering drinks. So she followed Clelia into the varnished depths of the pub, her mind full of a host of suppositions about

Robert, Colin, Martin and the inexplicable baby; she was aware of an emotional situation of unparalleled density and complexity, of some dark morass of intrigue. And she had been, over the last few years, rejecting simplification after simplification solely in the hope of discovering just such a spirit of confusion. She was surprised by some of the elements of the confusion: she had never suspected that a mention of a vague baby could cast such a strange light upon a person. Nor had she expected that mothers and fathers would feature in any profitable way. Babies, mothers and fathers had hitherto been for her the very symbols of dull simplicity. She saw that she had been wrong about them, and possibly therefore about other relations of life.

The ladies' room was through two doors, down half a flight of stairs, through a yard, and up another half flight of stairs. She would never have managed to find it alone, as it was inadequately sign-posted. She envied Clelia her certainty, and wondered whether knowledge or instinct had led her directly there. There were two water closets; Clara hurried, because she did not want Clelia to leave before her, but when she emerged Clelia was still there, dragging a comb somewhat roughly through her thick hair. The comb was encountering some resistance. Clara combed her own hair, and powdered her nose. She wanted to speak, but could not think what to say. Clelia did not speak. Finally, seeing the moment evade her, in some misery, Clara said, 'And do you write poetry too?' because it seemed an interesting question, and one that must at least be answered. And it was answered. Clelia, staring at herself with some dislike in the mirror, said, 'I certainly do not.' And her tone, as she said this, could only have been called, and in quite simple, inescapable terms, rude. She spoke rudely.

Clara was taken aback. Rudeness was somehow not what she had expected. Flippancy perhaps, coolness more possibly, disinterest almost certainly, but not rudeness. She was dismayed: half of her, more than half of her wished to withdraw quietly and quickly away from such offence. But at the same time, she was saying to herself, really, I did not deserve it, there *was* nothing wrong with my question, there is no reason why I should not ask her a question, she does not know me, I am younger than she is, she has no right to be rude. And she heard herself saying, to her own surprise.

'Why did you speak to me in that way?'

And she was surprised because for once she had said exactly what she had been thinking. She did not usually do anything of the sort. She waited to see what would happen.

Clelia turned round from the mirror, and looked at her, and said, 'What?'

Clara repeated her question.

Clelia said, 'I don't know what you mean, how did I speak to you? What was wrong with it?'

Clara, thinking that she had after all nothing to lose and everything to gain, said, 'You were rude.'

Clelia stared. She looked amazed, but no longer annoyed.

'Oh hell, was I really?' she said.

'Yes, you were,' said Clara. 'I asked you a perfectly ordinarily stupid question, and you were rude. And anyway, it wasn't such a dreadfully stupid question. I mean, why shouldn't you write poetry? A lot of people do. Your father does. It might run in the family. Why shouldn't I ask you if you write poetry?'

Clelia began to look rather upset. She even began to comb her hair again, fretfully, at a loss. And then she said,

'Well, really no reason at all. No reason at all why you shouldn't ask me. But no reason why I shouldn't be rude, either, was there?'

'I thought you ought not to be rude to me,' said Clara, deciding it was worth taking a risk, deciding, in fact, that a risk was bound to pay off, 'because I was at a disadvantage. And I don't think people should be rude to people who aren't in a strong position.'

Clelia thought this over.

'I quite agree with you, in principle,' she said. 'But why do you imagine yourself to be at a disadvantage? What was it about you that I should have noticed, and shown mercy to? Why shouldn't you instead have been merciful to me, and not asked me such a bloody silly question?'

'You're older than me,' said Clara.

'Not much,' said Clelia.

'And you belonged here and I didn't,' said Clara.

23

'What did they say your name was?' said Clelia.

'Clara,' said Clara. 'Clara Maugham.'

'Clara,' said Clelia, 'what a pretty name. Almost as nice as mine. Rather like mine, in fact.'

'I used not to like it,' said Clara.

'I can't see that my coming with my father means that I had any right to be here, that I belonged here, in any spectacular way,' said Clelia. 'And why shouldn't you belong here even more than me? I never come to this theatre, I hate this theatre, I hate experimental plays.'

'Does it do experimental plays?' asked Clara.

'Of course it does,' said Clelia. 'How ever did you manage not to know that? You must have known it.'

'I didn't know it,' said Clara. 'And now you see that I can substantiate my disadvantage.'

'I should call such ignorance a positive *blessing*,' said Clelia. 'But I take your point. Wherever can you come from?'

'I come from Northam,' said Clara. 'It's a town in Yorkshire. But at the moment I'm at the University. At Queen's College.'

'Ah,' said Clelia. 'I see. You're reading English.'

'No, I'm not,' said Clara.

'Then whyever, if I may ask without being rude, did you come to this thing? I can never understand why anyone comes to these things.'

'I came with Peter. Peter de Salis.'

'Oh, I *see*,' said Clelia.

'I don't suppose you do,' said Clara, feeling that she should make her relationship with Peter clear, and not quite liking the tone which Clelia adopted towards her escort.

'Oh,' said Clelia, correcting herself, delicately correcting her intonation, 'Oh yes, I see.'

'He just thought I would be interested,' said Clara.

'And were you?'

'Yes, I was interested. I was interested to meet you,' said Clara. Clelia put her comb back in her bag and pulled her skirt straight, but not disinterestedly, on the contrary, as though something had been settled between them.

'I must be going,' she said. 'The buses take so long. And the baby really does wake. Though I was lying when I said Martin doesn't hear it, he always hears it, but he can't kind of do anything with it when it wakes.'

'It isn't your baby?' said Clara, following her back through the corridors towards the bar.

'No, it's not really,' said Clelia, 'but I feel kind of responsible for it. Sometimes I pretend it's mine. But if it were, I wouldn't call it it, would I? Poor little thing. It's a he, really.'

'How old is he?' said Clara.

'I'm not exactly sure,' said Clelia. 'Somewhere in the nine month range, I imagine. Look,' she added, 'if you give me your address when we get back there, I'll give you a ring, and you must come and see me and I'll tell you about it.'

And when they got back to the bar, Clara did indeed inscribe her name and address and Common Room telephone number upon a page of Clelia's unbelievably occupied diary; they had no time to exchange further intimacies, as Sebastian Denham was there and waiting to drive his daughter home, and ready to be annoyed by the delay that she had caused him.

'I haven't got your number,' said Clara, as she departed. 'Oh, mine,' said Clelia, 'it's in the book.'

And Clara, living as she did, in the floating insubstantial bed-sitter student world, had not so much as thought of the book. It seemed very wonderful to her, that people could live in London, and live there long enough to have a number in the book.

And as she went home that night she knew that she was sure that Clelia would at some point ring her. She knew, moreover, that she had found something that she had been looking for, and that events would prove the significance of her discovery: she wondered only at the means of her recognition. The fact of it never ceased to astound her, and she would return over the ground constantly, searching for marks, for tracks and breaths and sighs and trodden grass and names and cloudy indications, because she could not forget that she had not recognized it at once, that it had required on her part some keenness of perception, some chancy courage, to see it: and she breathed perpetually an air of terror, a cold air of chance, an air in which she might for the whole of her life have missed it, marginally perhaps, but missed it and forever.

Chapter 2

Because there was nothing in Clara's past that would seem to have fitted her for such recognitions: she was not bred to it. And when she reflected, as she frequently did, upon what she had been bred to, she was profoundly puzzled by her own origins. Her birth, as far as she could see, had been accidental; no careful well-intended deity could have selected for her her own home. But she did not like to admit the accidental, for if her birth was the effect of chance, so then was her escape; the same arbitrary law that had produced her might well have blinded her at the most crucial moments of her life, and left her forever desiring, forever missing, never achieving, an eternal misfit. She had seen people like this. She had no confidence that time would bring with it inevitable growth: she grew by will and by strain. As a child, she was always deeply affected by the story of the sower who sowed his seeds, and some fell by the wayside, and some on stony ground and some fell among the thorns, and some fell upon good ground and bore fruit. This story was a favourite of the headmistress of her primary school, so she heard it often at Morning Prayers, and long before she could see it as a parable, she already felt shock before its injustice. The random scattering of seeds, and how much worse, of human souls, appalled her. As she grew older, she looked upon herself, tragically, defiantly, with all the hopelessness of fourteen years, as a plant trying to root itself upon the solid rock, without water, without earth, without shade: and then, when a little older yet, when conscious of some growth, she had to concede that she must have fallen happily upon some small dry sandy fissure, where a few grains of sand, a few drops of moisture, had been enough to support her trembling and tenacious life. Because she would live, she would survive.

It always amazed her to see that other people could live so

comfortably upon such barren territory. Northam was to her the very image of unfertile ground, and yet other people lived there and stayed there when they had money in the bank and legs to walk away on. She hated her home town with such violence that when she returned each vacation from University, she would shake and tremble with an ashamed and feverish fear. She hated it, and she was afraid of it, because she doubted her power to escape; even after two years in London, she still thought that her brain might go or that her nerve might snap, and that she would be compelled to return, feebly, defeated, to her mother's house. She was so constantly braced, her will so stiff from desire, that she could not sleep at nights; she feared that if she fell asleep she might lose her determination and her faith, might wake up alone in her narrow bed, in the small back bedroom, overlooking the small square garden, backing onto the next small square garden, where for so many years she had lain and dreamed her subversive dreams. She was frightened of this : and also she was frightened of her mother.

Her father was dead. He was killed on a pedestrian crossing when Clara was sixteen. Those who took an interest in Clara might have seen in his death the loss of an ally, because outwardly at least he appeared to be more intelligent than his wife; at least he did not scorn in public, as she did, all efforts of the mind, and all the aims of education. But in fact he had never been particularly sympathetic towards Clara, and paid but a feeble and superficial attention to her progress. He did not like children; he did not much like anything. He took slightly more interest in his two sons, Arthur and Alan, but not through any natural preference for them; it was simply that with them he knew better what questions should be asked. His work, which he pursued at the Town Hall, was never mentioned in the house, and as far as Clara could gather it was mathematical, highly respectable, and highly dull. When people asked Mrs Maugham where her daughter got her brains from, she would sniff and shrug her shoulders and say, as though disclaiming a vice or a disease, 'Well, she certainly didn't get them from me, she must have got them from *him*, I suppose' – a remark which Clara took years to place, in all its ambiguity, for the truth was that Mrs Maugham had done well at school, she had shone and prospered, and the evidence of her distant triumphs still lay around the house in the form of inscribed Sunday school prizes. But whatever talents she had once had, she had now turned ferociously against them, whereas her husband did still pay a curious self-willed homage to the intellectual virtues; he possessed an 1895 edition of the *Encyclopaedia Britannica* which he would, from time to time, read. He would also exhort his children to read it, and laid great stress upon the utility of information. His own father had been a skilled mechanic (a phrase which conveyed little to Clara) and as he himself had managed to purchase by his own labours a three bedroomed semi-detached house in a pleasant suburban district, he might have been thought to have cause to feel fairly content with life. But he did not. He was perpetually in the grip of some obscure, niggling, unexplained bitterness, which led him to repudiate most of the overtures which Clara would from time to time make towards him; she made these attempts because she was less frightened of him than she was of her mother, and she did on one or two occasions – the purchase of a bicycle, permission to go to the cinema – manage to enlist his sympathies. But she could see that his heart was not in it. And truly, she could not blame him. She could hardly bear to think the thought, but it did seem to her that anyone who had lived for so many years with her mother could be excused for a certain lack of *joie de vivre*.

When he died, she felt no real grief. The only reality of the event had been her mother's reaction, which was silent, grim, and grudging to the last; not a tear did she shed, and after the funeral, as she turned away from the graveside and started to walk slowly through the cemetery mud she set her mouth in that prophetic way, and straightened her thick body, and then, as she passed a gravestone announcing that death is but a separation, she opened her mouth and said, 'Well, he's gone, and I can't say I'm sorry.' And Clara, walking by her side and hearing these words, burst suddenly and at last into loud hysterical weeping, and as the tears flooded down her hot cheeks she knew that they were not for her father, but for the meanness and the lack of love, and for the fear that she would die in so ugly a hole, and so unloved. Nobody comforted her, for weeping was not necessary, but it was on the other hand permissible, and when she

28

got home the aunts and uncles were kind to her and offered her cups of tea. Even her brothers were kind, though embarrassed, and Clara, as she sat there picking endlessly at the fringe of the tablecloth, had a vision of some other world where violent emotion could be a thing of beauty, where even tears could be admitted and not ignored, where good taste in tomb stones consisted not in cheap restrained economy of design, fabric, and word, but of marble angels wildly grieving. Anything, anything would make death tolerable, she thought, anything that could admit something of the grand somewhere, and not this small cramped sitting room, this domestic duplicity, this pouring of cups of tea, these harshly unaltered faces. One tear would have sufficed her, one murmur of regret, but there was nothing; the family were not even in mourning, for they found the wearing of mourning a false and hypocritical extravagance. They would admit nothing; they sat there like stones, and their one aim was to sit there like stones, so that no one could tell if they cared or did not care, so that there should be no difference between caring and not caring.

The funeral itself had been a grotesque manifestation of Mrs Maugham's opinions. She had refused to have her husband cremated, not because she had anything so fanciful as a religious objection to cremation, but because she quite erroneously considered cremation to be a new-fangled idea, and she objected to the new. She had been brought up as a chapel-goer, and two generations back her family had been staunch Wesleyans, but she herself had long since dropped any pretence to faith of any kind, and now considered all religious observance as ridiculous frivolity. However, she maintained the moral impetus of her early years, although she had quite cast off its derivations and turned her back upon its fraudulent source; the narrow fervours and disapprovals were there, but their objects had subtly altered over the years. So that the wearing of mourning, fifty years earlier a sign of virtue, had now in Mrs Maugham's generation become a habit to be scorned and condemned; it was ostentatious and therefore it was insincere. And her dislike of the insincere ran so deep that she would rather publicly disclaim all grief for her dead husband than be accused of insincerity. But it took a trained observer to follow her through the quicksands

29

of her disapprobation; a false step on the part of one of the aunts, for instance, could have reversed her attitude, and led her into a eulogy of black, into a martyred position whence the garments of all the others were an insult to her lone and exclusive widowhood, into a position where she alone had the right to flout the weight of tradition. She was, as Clara had discovered at an early age, colossally inconsistent; and sometimes Clara thought that it might have been easier to live with a true religious fanatic, whose fads and fancies would be at least predictable and well-marshalled, with the backing of some kind of external authority, from which there could be some appeal.

As it was, it was impossible for even the most servile and well-meaning to avoid offence. For what Mrs Maugham thought one week to be wholly disgraceful, she was praising the next, and with no apparent consciousness of discrepancy. For instance, there was the question of the coffin. Clara could not count the times she had heard her mother declare that when she died she would be dead, and she wouldn't care what happened to her body, and for all *she* cared they could put her out for the dustman to collect – sentiments which from the first had filled Clara with a vague alarm and horror, for they were clearly reasonable enough in their own way. And yet, when her husband died, the price and quality of the coffin became topics of obsessive interest, and the precise balance of economy and decency a subject for endless dissertation. Clara heard again and again of Mrs Hewitt, who buried her husband in an economy coffin of some inappropriately cheap and porous wood, and claimed a rebate from the insurance, and of the equally wicked and abandoned Mrs Duffy, who had squandered a fortune on black crepe and gilt handles, through a sheer love of ostentation. In the end, Clara, exasperated beyond endurance, brought up once more the possibility of cremation (not daring to mention, even in her own mind, which had not quite forsaken filial tenderness, the possibility of the once-praised dust cart) and Mrs Maugham, square, immutable, said quite astonishingly for her, and invoking sanctions she had been deriding for thirty years, that ashes must go to ashes and dust to dust. Clara forebore to point out that cremation did result, precisely, in ashes, because she took, expertly, her mother's meaning, which was that cremation was an unnatural practice and that bodies ought to rot quietly at their own leisure. And moreover Clara had even seen in the phrase some dim, far-off flicker of comfort, because, harsh though it was, it was not without a consoling figurative literary beauty.

The world of the figurative was Clara's world of refuge. The literal world which she inhabited was so plainly hostile that she seized with ardour upon any references to any other mode of being; she came across few direct ones, in that suburban and industrial spot, so she had to make do with the oblique. Even a turn of phrase could affect her, however worn and faded in its application, and one of her mother's favourite sayings – 'What can't be cured must be endured,' never failed to give her a certain thrill, partly because of the grim inevitability of the rhyme, and partly because it almost managed to lend a little spare dignity to her mother's stoic outlook. Similarly, she would turn to the quotations from the Bible, which appeared on church notice boards, and on certain hoardings in the town centre, and which would declare. 'I am the Way, the Truth and the Life', or 'Straight is the Gate and narrow is the way which leadeth unto life, and few there be that find it', or 'Man shall not live by bread alone'. These comforted her, not because she had any faith in their message, but because they were phrased with some beauty; they were made up of words that seemed to apply to some large and other world of other realities, and they bore witness, also, to the fact that somebody had thought it worth his while to put them up. Just as some would pay for intelligence, so would others pay for the spirit. Even if the messages were not true (and she had no hope that they might be true) at least somebody believed sufficiently in their truth to pay cash for them, to rent hoardings and to put up posters for them, and that in itself offered some kind of alternative: Christianity meant nothing to her, but she was glad that in despite of her mother's defection, it existed.

Of hymns, too, she made her own use. She was not alone in this, for most of the girls at her school managed to infuse a certain erotic passion into their rendering of various appeals to the Creator, and there was one girl, who fancied herself in love

31

with a naval cadet, who could actually produce real tears during the singing of

> Eternal Father, strong to save
> Whose arm doth bind the restless wave.

She was a truly wondrous sight: her prestige for this feat was enormous. Clara never managed to do anything nearly as impressive, but nevertheless she had her own private favourites; she was not without a vulgar inclination towards

> Jesu, lover of my soul,
> Let me to thy bosom fly

an inclination which she shared with every other girl in the school, but her own particular choice was a hymn by J. M. Neale, the first verse of which ran:

> Jerusalem the Golden
> With milk and honey blest
> Beneath thy contemplation
> Sink heart and voice oppressed
> I know not, oh, I know not
> What social joys are there
> What radiancy of glory
> What light beyond compare.

The combination of the words and the music of this hymn could unfailingly elevate her to a state of rapt and ferocious ambition and desire; she pictured, even at a most tender age, not the pearly gates and crystal walls and golden towers of some heavenly city, but some truly terrestrial paradise, where beautiful people in beautiful houses spoke of beautiful things. It must have been the word 'social' that created for her this image, a word judiciously expunged from later versions of the verse. And it seemed to her that that broken line, 'I know not, oh, I know not', expressed a level of passion as high as any the English language could achieve; the interjection and the repetition and the archaic inversion were to her the exhaled breath of yearning.

She also sought, of course, the more usual and natural means of escape and fantasy, such as the watching of advertisements, the reading of fiction, and the spinning of self-indulgent romances, but her experience of life as a child was so narrow that she had no way of telling the possible from the absurd. And even as a child, she wanted things to be possible. She read with avidity the endlessly cosy adventures of wealthy children on farms and in smugglers' caves and country houses, but she found built into them a warning against too much belief. They did not sufficiently approach the reality that she knew, whereas the threat of the straightness of the gate seemed unfailingly significant. Moreover, children's stories and advertisements never offered any true complication, and it was complication, in the absence of conviction, that she was seeking. She did not believe that the wicked could be caught by ten-year-old children and returned to the police station in exchange for a pony, any more than she believed that constant hot water would make young mothers smile constantly with relief and proud love. Her mother had constant hot water, and she did not smile. She searched in vain in these golden childish worlds for the true brittle glitter of duplicity, for the warm shine of wider, more embracing landscapes; she looked for half-truth, for precious qualification, for choice, for possible rejections, and she could not find them. The advertisement life was better than her own, but it was crude, amoral: it lacked both virtue and vice.

The books about children with ponies were books from the library. The books which were in the house were of another kind and pursued a different and more old-fashioned simplification; some of them were indeed Victorian in fact as well as in tone, relics of her grandmother's childhood. Nobody read them but Clara, and she read them only because she read everything. They preached the lessons of moderation, cleanliness, simplicity, self-denial and humility with an admirable thoroughness, low-church to the core; not an angel or a lily disfigured their pages. Their only appeal to Clara lay in their austerity, which sometimes reached a point where it bordered on the dangerously extreme; there was one sad tale, for instance, of a little girl who cared for her cruel stepmother with unfailing devotion, and who died of pneumonia after running out in her nightgown to look for her stepmother's cat. But her favourite was a book called *The Golden Windows*, a Sunday School prize of her mother's. This was a book of fables, most of them pointing in the inevitable direction; the title story told, with some charm, of a little boy who saw from a hillside while out walking a house whose windows were all of gold. He searched for this wonderful house, but could not find it, and was returning home disappointed when he realized that the house was his own house, and that the gold was merely the reflection of the sun. The moral of this story, was, she assumed, that one must see the beauty in what one has, and not search for it elsewhere; but it carried with it, inseparably, the real sadness of the fading windows, and the fact that those within the house could never see them shine. There was another story about a blind mother, whose son did not return after the battle; she wept when he did not return, and asked the survivors if they had seen a young and lovely boy lying slain, dressed in delicately embroidered garments of fine silk, and the survivors said No, they had seen no boy, but they had seen a great bearded man dead, and he had worn tied about his waist strange garments, torn and faded and old, which had once been embroidered with flowers. Clara did not understand this story, but it seemed to her to tell of an emotion a size larger than pathos. The most interesting story of all, however, was called *The Two Weeds*. In this tale, two weeds grew on a river bank; one of them conserved its energy, and grew low and small and brown, with its sights set on a long life, while the other put forth all its strength into growing tall and into colouring itself a beautiful green. During the summer, these two weeds reviled each other, as fabulous creatures will; the lowly weed accused its brother of grandiose, spendthrift ambitions, and the tall weed called the low weed mean and miserly. At the end of the summer, a beautiful girl passed, and she saw the tall weed, and plucked it and put it in her dress, where it blushed a glorious red and died content; the weed on the bank saw it die, and laughed, and reflected that it would live till the next year. And it did.

The curious feature of this tale was its moral ambivalence. By every law of the genre, the death of the tall weed should have vindicated the life of the other, as the death of the grasshopper vindicates the ants, but the story somehow did not end that way. Incredibly enough, it seemed to end with a choice. It would hardly have been possible for it to support beauty and extravagance and pleasure at the expense of mere survival, but it did at

34

least hint that such a view could be held, and its mere admission of this possibility was to Clara profoundly satisfying. Each time she read the story, she experienced a new shock; it was the shock of finding the new contained and expressed in the framework and the terms of the old. In such context, between such gilt-lettered cloth-bound boards, the concession was nothing less than munificent.

When she was eleven, Clara, like her brother Alan before her, acquired a Grammar School place. Her mother, although of the mentality that refuses such places because of the price of the uniform, was luckily not in a social or financial position where she could reasonably do so, and although she was often unreasonable enough, she did not like to appear to be so in the eyes of the whole neighbourhood, so she constrained her parsimony and her innate distrust in education into selecting the less distinguished of the schools available, on the grounds that the bus fare was cheaper. It was a large, rather forbidding and gloomy building, called Battersby Grammar School, and it was on the fringe of that decayed, desolate, once-grand grey fringe that surrounds the centres of most cities; the houses in this area, large and terraced and of some dignity, had been long abandoned by the middle classes, and were now occupied by families who could not afford to live anywhere else. An occasional member of the fugitive genteel stuck it grimly out until death; once Clara was accosted by an old lady, battered and ragged and bent, who said as she walked along, and in accents of refined madness, that once the people that lived there had held their heads up high. Clara, a poor audience with her twisted knee socks, did not know what she meant.

The shabbiness of the district and the dingy gloom of the school itself meant nothing to Clara. To her, the building was endlessly exciting, and she liked it for all the reasons that most people would specify as particular causes for dislike. She liked its huge, barn-like, inhuman bleakness, its corridors shoulder-high in dark green, shoulder-to-ceiling in pale peppermint, its vast lukewarm radiators, its muddy echoing boards, its tall, high, dirty windows. She liked the cloakrooms and the lockers, the sense of institution, the rows and rows of washbowls and lavatories, the accessibility of the drinking fountains. She liked the way it stood, distinct and certain, rising out of the level muddy waste of grass and tarmac that generously surrounded it: a bomb had fallen during the war, on a neighbouring chapel, and the site had been levelled out and was now an unofficial part of the school's playgrounds. The whole area was of a bleak airiness, and a cold wind seemed to blow incessantly upon it, turning the knees and knuckles of the girls pink and blue, and snatching away their obligatory berets the moment they emerged from the school porch. Clara did not mind the cold, for she liked anything that was not small and cramped and heartlessly cosy; she liked the nameless multitudes that tramped mud on the cloakroom floors and left hairs in the cloakroom basins, and liked them because they were nameless, because they were not her mother and Alan and Arthur. Domesticity appalled her, and she nourished in it, despite a yearning for the comfortlessly grand.

She liked, too, the work. She found it easy: to begin with, she found everything easy, as her memory for facts was remarkable, and it was only as she grew older that she began to notice in herself slight doubts about her ability to pursue higher physics and mathematics. The subject known, broadly, as Science, was at first her favourite, because she liked playing with Bunsen burners: at home she was not allowed even to switch on the gas fire. She liked it also because of the power which she most rapidly acquired over Mrs Hill, her science teacher: the first power of her life.

Mrs Hill was a small, plump, middle-aged woman, with fine frizzy hair which she encased in a fine frizzy hair net; she always wore a purple and blue flowered pinny, a garment more in keeping with an aunt or a cleaner than with a lover of science. She handled her apparatus with the efficient familiarity with which other women handle their baking boards and rolling pins; years of housework had left their mark on her. She had no children, but unlike most of the staff, she had a husband, and the girls could detect in her manner a faint abstraction, a slight absence from the ingrown matters of school life. She was set apart, by her overall and her laboratory and her marital status, which was lucky for her, as her position otherwise would have been truly grim. For she was one of those born failures as a disciplinarian, one of those teachers whose classes know they can do anything they want. If she had been an ordinary teacher, trying to teach an ordinary sedentary subject like history or Latin, she would have been mercilessly flouted and mocked, but as it was she managed to get by. For one thing, her subject was in itself appealing to most of the girls, or at least intermittently so; they enjoyed watching crystals grow, and weighing small things on small scales, and making little bits of sodium whizz round saucers of water, so they quite voluntarily offered her their attention from time to time. But her great quality was a capacity for being genuinely impervious to inattention. She did not really care whether people listened or not; she was interested herself in what she was saying, and she was quite happy to potter about from bench to bench watching people writing their diaries when they should have been writing up their experiments. Her blackboard technique was also extremely idiosyncratic; she would write up equations, get them wrong, mumble to herself, rub them out, look them up in a book, and all this without any suspicion that she might be forfeiting the confidence of her pupils.

The girls, although they did not know it, found her relaxing. They affected to despise her, but they did not find their contempt a strain, whereas the other really bad disciplinarian in the school, a Geography mistress, one Miss Riley, inflicted on them an intolerable suffering, for they felt themselves compelled to torment her, and she would sit before them, thin and pretty and anguished, making vain attempts to restore order, miserably transparent in her misery, and unable to conceal the depths of her humiliation – depths which frightened them, but which they could not leave unplumbed. Mrs Hill, on the other hand, with her vague indifference, did not rouse their cruelty, so their behaviour in her classes left them unashamed. Their behaviour was at times appalling; when little they would spend long stretches of each class on the floor behind the benches, playing with bits of mercury, pricking it with needles and pen nibs, watching it slip into the coarse splintery cracks of the dusty floorboards, and forcing it out again, marvelling at the way it shrugged the dirt off its rounded shoulders. When older, bored

37

with such simple pleasures, they sought new diversions, such as burning holes in the benches with the Bunsen burners. On one occasion Clara's class purchased a pound of sausages, took them in with them, and roasted them on one of the burners, and ate them, in full scent and in fairly good view; Mrs Hill appeared not to notice, and talked quietly on of Boyle's law. Clara did not enjoy her sausage, for it was burned black on the outside and raw in the middle, and her mother had told her that it was impossible not to get worms from raw sausage meat, but the taste of the damp mince with its bitter crust remained a strong reminder of illicit pleasure.

Mrs Hill took a fancy to Clara. Clara, when she became aware of it, was not displeased, because although the other girls laughed, she knew enough of the world to know that no affection, however oddly won or placed, is laughable or negligible. Other teachers and other girls were forever taking fancies to each other, but there was something strangely eccentric about Mrs Hill's fancy, just as her whole position in the school was eccentric. It was in no way intense, and indeed coming from such a figure it could not help but appear a little maternal; Mrs Hill did not seem to discover anything odd in her own attitude, and would consult Clara's opinion without any attempts at subterfuge or bravado; she would defer to Clara's position in the class by outrageously open remarks such as 'Now, Clara, you're the only girl likely to remember what I said last week', or 'Well, I suppose I'm wasting my breath on all but Clara Maugham.' This frankness was so unprecedented that the girls could not resent it; they could not, in the context of school behaviour, take it seriously enough to resent it. They giggled about it, and Clara giggled too, and that was that. Clara even grew quite fond of Mrs Hill, and proud of herself for feeling fond of one so odd.

The case of Miss Haines was a different question altogether. Miss Haines too favoured Clara, but being young and honourable she made every effort to conceal it. French was her subject, and she was potentially the classiest teacher in the school. She liked Clara because Clara was bright, and for no other reason: she had no need to like her for any other reason, as she was well equipped with a busy social life and a lover. The girls respected her because she had nerve and a good front of confidence, and because she possessed a very smart line in jerseys and fancy stockings, and wore shoes so fashionable that to the untrained eye they looked positively orthopaedic. Clara was not fully aware of Miss Haines' interest, because it was hidden by a sharp and brisk demeanour, and by an almost excessive severity, so she worked all the harder in her efforts to impress. It was not until she reached the age of specialization that she realized how well she had succeeded, although she had had her suspicions: but at the age of fifteen, at the moment of choice, the moment from which the Arts stretched away in one direction and the Sciences in another, never to meet again, she realized that Mrs Hill and Miss Haines had actually been fighting over her. The knowledge gave her an inexplicably profound satisfaction. She never for a moment thought of deserting French for Mrs Hill, having encountered amongst other things some nasty problems about the nature of electricity, but she did enjoy the sensation of flirtation: she spent a long time making her mind up, and finally was summoned by the headmistress, who told her she ought to stick to Sciences, because they offered better prospects. Whereupon she came out into the open and said she would choose Arts.

On the way out of this interview, she came across Miss Haines, clad in a thin ribbed sweater in a very nice shade of mustard, with a very nice matching skirt. And Miss Haines, as Clara suddenly realized, with a curious tremor of conviction, had actually been hanging around in the corridor waiting for her to emerge.

'Hello, Clara,' said Miss Haines.

'Hello, Miss Haines,' said Clara, giving nothing.

'I hear that Miss Potts asked to see you about next year's work,' said Miss Haines.

'Yes, she did,' said Clara. There was a slight pause, while she relished to the full her own desirability as a pupil.

'I hope you didn't change your mind about taking up languages,' said Miss Haines, finally, and with a slight constraint.

'Oh no, Miss Haines,' said Clara, mercifully, smiling now. 'Oh no, of course not. I told her I was frightfully keen to carry on with French. And she said I was to think it over, but I've thought it over already, really.'

And Miss Haines, who had been smiling too, as she heard this, abruptly stopped smiling, and assumed once more her brisk air of challenge, and said, 'Good, good,' and stalked most coldly off. But Clara was not perturbed by this change of manner: she knew now what it meant.

On the bus home that day, she wondered what her parents would have to say, if she were to ask them about it. She wondered if there was the faintest chance of impressing them with the significance of her position. It was a pleasant summer afternoon, and the rows and rows and rows of houses looked unusually bright and gay in the sun; the city, like Rome, was built on a series of hills, and there were several impressive long-distance views of hillsides covered with serried networks of roof tops and chimneys. This helped to alleviate the dreadful nature of the houses, which looked shocking from nearby, but which looked oddly bright and distinct and well-intentioned when glorified by mass and distance. Indeed, Clara knew from first hand experience the moral truth of the story told in *The Golden Windows* about the house with the golden windows, for she had once admired from a friend's house the whole dazzling, distant, smoky lay-out of her own hillside. It was hard, travelling home in that bus, and surrounded by the immense, evident, and varied liberties of people and land, to believe in the small impossibilities of her own home, and she felt, as she so frequently felt, the will to believe it to be different: the truth was too grotesque and too unnatural, and her hopes were so strong that she carelessly let them wander a little, giving them a little leeway, letting them sniff and pry and explore. When she got off the bus at her usual stop, even the moderate leafiness of the district contributed to her hopes, and she saw, fleetingly, the features that caused it to be described by others as a desirable residential area. She walked down Chestnut Drive, and as she picked a leaf off a privet hedge here, and ran her hand along a row of railings there, she thought that it was not so bad after all, and that she would tell them about it: they always said, when accused of indifference, that they were interested, so she would jolly well try to make them show a bit of their interest.

Even the sight of their own front garden could not quite depress her. It consisted of a small oblong patch of mown but weedy grass, in the centre of which stood a small green flowerless shrub with dirty leaves. The path to the door, like the path of the other half of their semi-detached building, was made of crazy paving. Mrs Maugham did not like crazy paving, because the stones worked loose, and she wanted it done in asphalt; Clara did not like crazy paving either, but felt obliged to defend it. The front door was painted blue, and had a coloured glass panel, which Mrs Maugham did not like. Over the porch was a wooden pointed hood with scalloped edges, to keep off the rain, presumably from the heads of visitors waiting for the door to be opened. Mrs Maugham did not like this either, on the principle that it was neither use nor ornament.

Clara, naturally, did not approach the front door; she went in by the back, and into the kitchen. Her mother was there, checking over a grocery order. She did not look up as Clara entered the room, but said, 'I put down large, and they go and send me outsize'. She always accompanied her unpackings by such comments, always with the same indignant implication that the grocers did their best to defraud and anger her with every item. Nevertheless, Clara could tell from her tone that she was pleased about something, and, as she took off her blazer and hung it in the cupboard, she waited to hear what it was. Information, however, was not proffered at once; Clara was sent upstairs to change out of her uniform. When she got down again her mother was setting the table for high tea; Clara, mutely, began to help, thinking that she might either find some opportune moment for introducing her own problems, or that she might be treated with news of her mother's latest triumph. Usually she tried to evade such duties, by hanging around in the bathroom or in her bedroom; she loathed the tedious, repetitive business of the house.

'Mrs Hanney came in today,' said Mrs Maugham, as she passed the tea cosy through the hatch to Clara.

'Oh yes?' said Clara, in the grip of a horrible, bored fascination.

'She wanted to use the telephone,' said Mrs Maugham.

'Yes,' said Clara, beginning to understand the nature of her mother's satisfaction; the lack of telephone of Mrs Hanney had been for some years a subject for discourse in a vein of amazed contempt.

'Her television had gone wrong,' continued Mrs Maugham. 'She wanted to ring the service men.'

She paused, dramatically, allowing this statement to speak for itself, which it sufficiently did, for the fact that Mrs Hanney had a television and no telephone was the focal point of the Maugham household's scorn. Such flouting of values, such wanton disregard for respectable priority, had often been re-marked upon; Mrs Maugham was wont to enlarge upon the theme by describing situations in which a suddenly-paralysed Mrs Hanney, unable to reach a phone to ring for a doctor, would expire before the inane cacklings of her own television set. It was true that Mrs Maugham's moral fervour had had slightly more edge in the days before she herself acquired a television set, but even now she managed to retain sufficient cause for indignation, and the quality of her feeling for Mrs Hanney had changed not at all, though her attacks had been somewhat restricted in scope. Clara often thought that Mrs Maugham's attitudes towards the television typified her whole moral outlook; before acquiring it, she had considered it in-finitely vulgar and debased; after acquiring it she considered all those without it as highbrows, intellectual snobs, or paupers, while still managing to retain her scorn for all those who had had it before the precisely tasteful, worthy and perceptive moment at which she had herself succumbed to its charms.

'She wanted,' continued Mrs Maugham inexorably, 'to have it put right before that dreadful serial thing, whatever it's called, that thing about the family.'

And Clara saw that Mrs Hanney's ignominy was complete, for this programme, the name of which her mother so evidently did not forget, was considered by her mother to be the very lowest form of entertainment available, designed for the excep-tionally stupid and depraved.

'I told her,' said Mrs Maugham, handing her daughter a plas-tic butter dish, 'that I'd never seen it.'

And with that, her recital appeared to be ended.

'Did the service men come?' asked Clara, feeling some word

required of her, and yet not daring to comment upon the story's true import.

'I wouldn't know. I told her she should have it serviced more regularly. She said they only got the men in when it went wrong.'

This remark she delivered with the immense complacency of the wise virgin; Clara could not help but feel that having men in only when things went wrong was not as wildly eccentric as her mother supposed, but as she knew no other way, no other world, she could not be sure. She was continually amazed and depressed by the way that the neighbourhood accepted and appeared to respect her mother's self-erected authority; none of them did as her mother did, and yet they all deferred to the solidity of her principles. She had no friends, for she repelled intimacy as though it were an insult, but she had a position: her manner imposed itself relentlessly upon the indifferent and the unconcerned. Clara could never understand why others did not repay her contempt with contempt – why, for instance, the church-goers and novel-readers and fillers in of football coupons and motorbike owners in the area did not possess the courage of their convictions and gang up on Mrs Maugham's massive disapprobation. But they never did. They appeared to apologize for their pitiable weaknesses, instead of forming themselves into a counter attack. Clara had actually heard one constant church attender, caught out donating a small charitable sum to the Vicar, defend herself to Mrs Maugham by saying that she hadn't really meant to give it, and that she never would have given it if it hadn't been that her little boy had just given up Sunday school. There was something in Mrs Maugham's solid air of conscious rectitude that threw a faint shadow of guilt over everyone who approached her, though as often as not people did not know why they were guilty: her disapprovals were so vast and public, her approvals so private and ill-chartered that all immediately cast themselves as goats in the discrimination of her gaze. Occasionally a cheeky shop girl in town, caring nothing, and with nothing to lose, would face her out, but Clara on these occasions felt such anxiety and associated shame that she dared not rejoice. The local shop girls never risked her wrath. They were afraid of her.

And Clara too was afraid. Although she fully intended to profit from the soothing exposure of Mrs Hanney by a judicious introduction of her own concerns, she found herself, when the moment came, quite unable to do so. She stood staring at the yellow-flowered table cloth, as phrases formed and re-formed inside her head, but she said nothing. She did not know why she should feel such fear, because she felt for her mother not respect, but contempt: and why should she lack courage before someone whose attitudes were to her so transparently, pettily contemptible? She loathed her mother's loathing of Mrs Hanney; it made her shiver with horror. Even the sight of the table, laid there before her, filled her with disgust, for it bore witness to so many foibles, so many fixed and rigid rules. There was not an object on that table that was without its history of contention; every implement lay there in the pride of hideous superiority. And everything was ugly. Clara could have forgiven the things their ugliness, if that very ugliness were not such a source of pride. The cloth was linen, for Mrs Maugham held that plastic table cloths were the last resort of the working classes, and had said so often and at length; but it was adorned with place mats of plastic. There was no need for place mats as the meal was to be cold, but place mats were invariably laid. The rest of the objects were more in keeping with the plastic table mats than with the linen cloth, for Mrs Maugham was in practice a sworn friend to the synthetic; to her, utility was a prime virtue. And yet her views of utility were far from strict. The house was crowded with mock-useful objects, like push-button ashtrays (and in an un-visited house of non-smokers) and gadgets for watering plants and killing flies and dispelling odours and concealing rolls of lavatory paper and dicing potatoes and dispensing sugar. Mrs Maugham was a great shopper in large department stores, and she could not resist their sillier notions; if anyone had accused her of extravagance, she would have roundly rebuffed the accusation as fantastic and perverse, and yet she must have spent many useless pounds in her pursuit of useful acquisitions. Similarly, she always maintained that she hated clutter-clutter, implying, in her tone, the dense decorative drawing-room knick-knacks of Victorian England – and yet clutter reigned in all her rooms. But she could not see it as such,

44

and indeed it could be said, on her behalf, that not a single object had been purchased or positioned for its decorative value. Clara calculated that at least a third of the objects laid on the table, by regulation, were not used during the course of any single meal, and yet their function was certainly not one of gracious adornment. There was a particular slop basin that Clara regarded with particular dislike. It was decorated with purple tulips, and it was hardly ever used, for Mrs Maugham was not unaware that it was something of an anachronism. And yet, every meal time, it stood there. To Clara, it was always painfully conspicuous, an indictment of a way of life; she knew nothing of the history of slop basins, nor of the society that evolved them and their joyless name, but the sight of one affected her like some shameful family secret. In no other household had she ever seen a slop basin, and she hated to see an eccentricity erected into a symbol of the traditionally correct.

As so often happened, she deliberated too long about the introduction of her own affairs, and when she finally found the courage to speak, she chose a bad moment. She waited until tea time, and listened in silence while Mrs Maugham recounted her adventures with Mrs Hanney to the rest of the family: they were received in silence by Alan, Arthur and her father, who did not waste their speech. Then Clara, into the lull that accompanied the pouring of tea, said sullenly,

'I saw the headmistress today. About what to do next year. I'm going to do French.'

Her mother poured the last cup of tea, stirred it vigorously, picked up her slice of bread and butter, took a mouthful, chewed it, and then, 'Suit yourself,' she said.

Chapter 3

Long before she left school, Clara discovered that whatever negligent indifference might greet her in the bosom of her family, she was capable of arousing strife in breasts other than those of Miss Haines and Mrs Hill. The bosomy metaphor is appropriate, for Clara developed young, to the astonishment of her contemporaries, who had convinced themselves that sexual and intellectual precocity never coincided. Clara regarded her own development with unreserved satisfaction, for she knew that it promised well. By the time she was fifteen, her stock in the school rose enormously by virtue of the fact that she was a constant recipient of billet-doux from the boys of the neighbouring Grammar School. The girls in her class, who had hitherto regarded her as relatively plain, and as a non-starter in the fashion stakes, with no notion of how to twist a school beret or hitch a school skirt, quickly reconsidered their assessment of her, and she found herself elected to an honorary membership of the fastest, smartest slickest coterie. She was naturally gratified by this change of front, and drew the appropriate moral – the possession of big breasts, like the possession of a tendency to acquire good examination results, implies power.

She never came to take her membership quite for granted: she had admired the in-people for too long ever to feel herself to be truly one of them. Most of them had been in from the start, born survivors, born leaders: amongst these lucky few were numbered Rosie Lane, an athletic, pretty, small-faced girl whose father owned a large grocer's, and whose primal popularity had been cheaply purchased by the judicious distribution of dried apricots and jelly cubes, which the girls devoured whole. Another was Susan Berkley, a bossy, self-willed creature, whose natural vigour went, as adolescence progressed, the natural way. Then there were Heather and Katie, inseparable friends, who bolstered each other by their mutual devotion; never had they known a moment's shame of friendlessness, never had they had to look for a partner in dancing or in gym, never had they walked alone from classroom to classroom, and their confidence overflowed and imposed itself upon all beholders. These four, in Clara's year, were the hard core of self-satisfied splendour, and to them others had been added. Isabel Marshall had been added at the age of fourteen, when her gawky, bony clumsiness had suddenly transformed itself into dazzling beauty, and Clara, her especial friend, was added a year later when her breasts grew. And then there was the odd case of Janice Young, who was, if anyone ever was, the doomed and unalterable scapegoat – she was not pretty, she was not clever, she was not good at games, and yet, during her fifteenth year, she managed to make herself acceptable as one of the inner ring. The inner ring itself could never quite understand her arrival there, and concluded finally that she made it through sheer cheek. She was irrepressible, shameless, brazen; she ran after the boys, and the boys, to the amazement of the other girls, meekly succumbed, and took her out, and bought her presents. She talked about her boyfriends in a tone of most frightful, spine-chilling, whimsy determination, and they took it. She threatened them, she menaced them, and one day in this vein she would marry one of them. She was not to be resisted. And Rosie, Susan, Heather, Katie, Clara and Isabel could not resist her either; they let her join them, weakly, unable to refuse such primitive intention. They showed, from time to time, a faint suspicious desire to force her to provide her non-existent credentials, but every time, just as their forces gathered for the attack, she would produce out of her hat some new and dazzling boyfriend, all ready to pay tribute to her elusive powers.

Clara felt herself to be extremely fortunate in her membership of this group, and the insecurity of Janice's position in it fortified her, for she knew herself to be more secure, less irritating, less tactless in every way than Janice. So she was especially kind to Janice. She was also rather surprised by the way in which she took her own newly-acquainted charms, for she was almost as determined as Janice to make the best of herself, and she had more to make the best of. Some of the girls – and even, oddly enough, the dashing, heavy-lipped, inviting Susan – were a little nervous about their developing selves, and a little alarmed by their own powers. Clara, on the other hand, was not at all alarmed. She did her best to stimulate a constant flow of love letters, and found the collecting of admirers a very satisfying pastime.

The chief scene for amorous exchange was the entrance to the boys' swimming baths, for the girls had no baths of their own, and were obliged to use those of their brother school for their weekly afternoon's lesson; here, on the steps, small red messenger boys would collect, proferring envelopes from their elders. The girls enjoyed their swimming lessons, titillated by the well-known fact that some of the more daring boys used to watch them changing through an easily accessible sky light. This well known fact was somehow never discussed in public by the girls, for public admission of it would have destroyed and inhibited its oddly private thrill, and would have shamed the vain ones into cowering in their cubicles, as the timid and modest already did. As it was, such girls as fancied themselves would leave their cubicle doors open, in the hope that tantalizing glimpses of leg and breast and buttock might be seen through the high and smoky glass, and once Clara, taking advantage of the convention that they were unobserved, walked the whole length of the changing room draped only from the waist down by a small towel, on the pretext of borrowing a safety pin. The other girls, knowing quite well that she had done it for the benefit of one Geoffrey A. Machin, were shocked and admiring, but the convention restrained them from expressing either shock or admiration. On another famous occasion, Clara, stark naked, drying herself in her cubicle, caught sight of her own image in the wet tiled floor: 'Good God,' she cried out, 'just look at me, how weird I look from underneath,' and all the girls had cried out, 'Ssh, ssh, Clara, somebody might be listening.'

'Whoever could be listening?' cried Clara loudly, knowing that Geoffrey A. Machin and Peter Hawtrey had cut Geography in order to do just that, and the other girls clucked and murmured and veiled themselves, thinking such deliberate flouting of the conspiracy of shame to be in doubtful taste.

But Clara had not cried out, originally, through vanity, nor for the benefit of her friends on the roof. She had been truly moved by herself, by her own watery image, by her grotesquely elongated legs, her tapering waist, and above all by the undersides of her breasts, never before seen. She stood there and stared at herself, seeing herself from that unexpected angle, as though she were another person, as though she were a dim white and blue statue on a tall pillar, a wet statue, a statue in water, a Venus rising from the sea, with veined white marble globes for breasts. She had never expected to be beautiful, and she was startled to see how nearly she approached a kind of beauty.

She had never expected to be beautiful because nobody had ever suggested that she might be so. Some mothers assume beauty in their daughters, and continue to believe it to be there, in defiance, often enough, of the facts, but Mrs Maugham was not one of these mothers. She assumed plainness, and she found it. She was so devoted to the principle that beauty is a frivolity and a sign of sin that she would have been ashamed to have it in the house. Nevertheless, her conviction of its absence was not wholly generous, nor wholly without malice. (On one occasion, with magnificent inconsequence, she had remarked after staring at one of Clara's dazzling reports, 'Well, handsome is as handsome does'; this was the only occasion on which she had ever said anything complimentary about Clara's looks.) Clara as a child had fully supported her mother's attitude, for she was in no way a pretty child; she was sullen, dirty, and her features were too big for her face. As she grew older, however, her face grew as well as her hips and bosom, but her way of looking as though she were about to burst out of her clothes became an asset rather than a disadvantage. She had not expected to be such a kind of girl; she had watched this kind of girl for years (the lips discreetly reddened, the loud laughter on the school bus, the tossing of long hair beneath rakish berets, the swinging of hips, the whispering in the garden) but she had never expected to become one. She had expected to be one of the others.

Although she was pleased with what she had become, and saw some future in it, there was one aspect of it that she did not like. She did not, could not like the boys. She persevered with them, in the hope that a taste for men, like a taste for the other desirable sophistications of life such as alcohol and nicotine, could be acquired through hard work. But it was hard work. She often shrewdly suspected that they found it hard work too, and that for all their signatures of fondest love they did not really like her; they wanted her, they thought that she would do, but they did not really like her. The difficulty was increased by the fact that she wanted good-looking boys only, and for some reason the really good looking boys were quite impossible to cope with. For one thing, they could pick and choose, and they usually chose somebody else. And when one of them did choose her, she found herself quite unable to talk to him at all. There was one particularly disastrous episode with a boy of startling beauty; he was called Higginbotham, but even such a name could not dim his lustre nor silence his eclat. This Higginbotham, the admired of all beholders, honoured Clara with a note one day, delivered at the door of the swimming bath by a small minion; it said:

Dear Miss Maugham,
 I have observed you several times coming and going. Perhaps you have observed me, I am often around, if you are not fixed up at the moment what about me waiting for you at the bus stop tonight? I can go your way.

Yours faithfully,
J. R. Higginbotham

The receipt of this letter threw Clara into ecstasy, for she had indeed observed his comings and goings, and had been suitably taken by his solid, rocky, regular features and by the dashing abandon of his hair style. She flashed the note around, proudly though covertly, and looked for him at the bus stop, but she could not look for him without some misgiving. She hated to admit it to herself, but there was something in the style and appearance of his note that would not do. The looseness of the syntax was a familiar symptom enough, but coupled with the handwriting it took on a more sinister light, for the writing was one of those faint, regular, carefully-looped hands which indi-cate an underlying antipathy to the written word. She knew, from looking at it, that they would not get on. But she pas-sionately wanted to get on with him; she made every effort to entertain and to captivate, for in proximity he was even more dazzling than from a distance. Her excitement, as she sat next to him on the narrow dirty furry seat of the bus, was almost too much for her. But it would not do. He did not find her amusing, and she found him quite disastrously dull. She could not have said that she found him dull, because she did not know it, and was conscious only of her own failure, and her misery at her own personal inadequacy quite drowned any sensation of boredom. When he asked if he could see her again the next day, she would not have dreamed of declining; they saw each other for about a fortnight, and her enthusiasm for him increased with each meeting, though he said not a word of any interest in the whole two weeks. They had no level of communication at all, and a bus ride with him was an ordeal rather than a pleasure, for she had to rack her brains to reply to his remarks about the weather, the town's football teams, the cinema, his headmaster, and so forth, but nevertheless when he wrote her a note saying:

Dear Clara,
    I think it would be better if we stop seeing each other, I find I have a lot of work to do with my Alternative Maths,

Yours ever,
                        '
James

she burst into floods of horrible tears, and cried for a whole day.
    It was on the rebound from Higginbotham that she took up with the first boy that she came near to liking. He was not nearly as beautiful, but on the other hand his preliminary note promised other qualities. It read:

Dear Miss Maugham,
    I have had my eye on you for some time. Now that Higginbotham has been given the brush off, may I venture to approach you? I hope that you won't think I am *rushing in*, for I assure you that I am no *fool*, unlike certain other people. Nor am I an angel, exactly, you will find that out for yourself, that is if you give me a chance. There is a good film on at the Rex. This is a hint. I await your response.

Yours in hope,
Walter Ash

51

Clara knew quite well who Walter Ash was, and therefore did not flash this letter around the classroom, as she knew he was not a great prestige catch; on the contrary, he had a reputation for being rather a bore. Nevertheless, she thought his note had possibility. The syntax was not perfect, perhaps, but it was a great deal better than Higginbotham's, and the use of such lengthy phrases as 'venture to approach' and 'await your response' showed some acquaintance with the useful cliches of the language. The handling of the 'Fools rush in where angels fear to tread' theme, though not wholly elegant, showed ambition, and the assumption that Clara was responsible for the dismissal of Higginbotham showed courtesy, though she would have preferred his name to be left out of it altogether. All in all, she thought she would give Walter Ash a try, despite the fact that people said he was very conceited, and despite his appearance, which was slightly against him, as far as his ears went. Only slightly, however. There were girls who were prepared to put up with far far worse than Walter Ash's ears.

The evening at the cinema proved to be rather successful. The film was a Western, and without guidance Clara would have dismissed it as a childish frivolity, a glorified version of *The Lone Ranger*. However, Walter Ash said it was a classic, and talked knowledgeably about the genre, and so she permitted herself to enjoy it. She had not even known that Westerns were a genre of their own; it was exciting news to her. He talked, it was true, with a little too much self-confidence, and she could tell that his views were not entirely original, but she did not really care, because they were interesting, and it was something to be interested. She was tremendously impressed by a casual comparison which he drew between the victorious hero of the film and Corneille's *Le Cid*, and all the more impressed because *Le Cid* was one of her set texts for A Level, whereas he was taking physics, chemistry and mathematics. 'It's all a question of the difference between the epic and the tragic,' he said, when she expressed a preference for heroes that die. 'In this kind of film they're not supposed to die, they're supposed to win.' His chief failing was a habit of cracking heavy pedantic jokes; he was unable to let a good idea drop, and remarked several times during the course of the film that the heroine looked like she ought to be playing the horse. The comment had some truth in it, in that the heroine did indeed have an equine cast of feature, but he made it too often, and with too little variation; however, she was willing to forgive him, in view of his evident tolerance of her own social errors, such as an inability to say whether or not she wanted an ice cream.

This outing was a prelude to many more. She went out with him faithfully for several months, and as time went on she found that she liked him both less and more. He annoyed her in many ways – mostly by his incurable facetiousness, which went down very badly with her girl friends, and by his desire to undress her at every possible opportunity. Although only sixteen, she was not much shocked by his attempts, but she was alarmed by her own lack of response, for she did not fancy him nearly as much as she had fancied the infinitely tedious Higginbotham. What she liked in him most was the sense which he gave of being connected to and aware of other worlds; he promised connexion. He was aware of things which she had known only by hearsay to exist, and he possessed sophistications which were most unusual in one of his age. For instance, he took her to a newly opened Greek restaurant, and introduced her to the delights of something called Baklava Syrien, which, having a sweet tooth, she very much enjoyed – although he managed simultaneously to annoy her by various highly irritating remarks about the way in which West Indians eat Kit-e-Kat, and by a joke about a man in a Chinese restaurant who found a finger in his Chinese soup. His taste in films, plays, books and music was far more decided than her own, though she would not admit that it was superior: she thought that, given time, she could outdo him, but as he had a good start on her in time, she was glad to listen to him. What impressed her most of all was his knowledge of the town itself, and of the way a town functions. She had no knowledge of the town; her impressions were confined to the bus ride to and from school, and to various coffee bars and shops in the centre. But Walter was well on the way to knowing his way around. He knew which cinemas occasionally showed good films, and which cinemas never; he knew about a painter who had been born in Northam, and whose work could be seen in a room at the Public Library. He knew the name of the Mayor, and he knew why Battersby was not the best Grammar School. He was sufficiently well-informed to be able to declare that it was a scandal that the town lacked any kind of orchestra, whereas Clara would have taken the lack of it as a simple act of God. He even ventured, once, a remark on the architecture of the Town Hall, but he would not elaborate upon it. (She found the remark, years later, in Betjeman.) The other girls laughed at this erudition, but Clara did not laugh, for she could imagine a scheme of events in which such knowledge might be an asset.

One of the moments which remained most strongly in her memory took place in the town's most learned book shop, a charming building that dated, almost alone in the town, from a pre-industrial epoch: it was tall, and narrow, and its windows were so small that it could display only ten books at a time, and those ten were changed but once a month. Clara had visited this shop many times, and had stood for hours surreptitiously reading C. P. Snow, Tolkien, D. H. Lawrence and the poems of T. S. Eliot. She regarded it as an unofficial library, as remote and as municipal as the library itself. And then, one Saturday morning, she went into it with Walter Ash, to look at (not to buy) the text of Anouilh's *Ring Round the Moon*, which was being currently performed at the local rep. While they were there, an elderly man came down the stairs from the upper floor (with its second hand books and books of local interest), and started to wander around, absent-mindedly. Clara could tell from a certain straining of attention on Walter's part that he was trying to catch the old man's eye, and eventually he succeeded in doing so; the old man nodded and smiled, with a bare minimum of recognition, and Walter said 'Good morning, Mr Warbley.' When the old man had wandered upstairs again, with a book under his arm, Clara whispered 'Who was that?' and even as she whispered she realized that it could be no other than the book shop's owner, and added hastily, 'That must be A. J. Warbley, I suppose?'

'No, it's his son,' said Walter, shepherding her out into the street. 'The old man founded the book shop, and that was his son. Don't you know about the Warbleys?'

'Well, not much,' said Clara, wisely unwilling to betray her total ignorance. 'How do you know them?'

'I don't, really,' said Walter. 'My parents know him, though. He used to come round to the house, a few years ago, before he took up so much with the Labour Party.'

And Clara, who could see no elegant way of enlarging this tantalizing scrap of information, had to make do with it – she dared not ask any further, for she knew nothing about the Labour Party, nor about the elder Ash's political views, nor about A. J. Warbley himself, beyond the fact that his name was written up in black Gothic letters over his son's shop door. But the hints and intimations which it conveyed to her stretched far, far away, into the past and the future, and she had a sudden, piercing, painfully beautiful vision of a life where men with book shops called upon friends for the pleasure of society, and quarrelled with those friends upon topics as elevated, as unworldly and as magnificent as the Labour Party. Her desire for such a life was so passionate, and her gratitude to Walter for this glimpse of it was so great that she could have kissed him in the street, and later that day she did in fact allow him to undo her brassiere strap without a word of protest.

For her parents had no friends. Nobody ever visited their house except through obligations, and such family celebrations as still persisted had been transformed into grim duties. Christmas came, and the family groaned, and dourly baked its cakes and handed round presents; birthdays came, and useful gifts were unfailingly proffered. Nobody ever dropped in, and her parents never went out, save to large and joyless civil functions, or to the cinema. Clara could feel her friendly spirit choking her at times; she had affection in her, and nowhere to spend it. Sometimes she dared to wonder at the causes for this way of life, for she could see that it did not represent a normal attitude towards society, though it was so deeply bred in her that all aberrations from it were for the rest of her life to seem to her perverse: but when, occasionally, she glimpsed some faint light of causation, she recoiled from it and shut her eyes in horror, preferring the darkness to such bitter illumination. Once her mother, talking of Christmas, had said that as a child she had herself received no presents, as it had never occurred to anyone to buy such things – but that one year her elder brother, think-ing to tease her, had hung at the end of her bed a stocking, and that when, excited, she had sprung to open it, she found it con-tained ashes from last night's grate. This story was recounted as a warning to naughty children. Clara, having heard it, lay in bed and trembled, too frightened to cry, and counted herself lucky for her share of lip service.

The worst moments of Clara's domestic life were not in fact those moments at which domestic indifference fronted her most blankly and sheerly, for they could be faced by an equally stony frontage – they were those which bore witness to hidden chinks and faults, deep within the structure. One of the events which shook her most of all was the occasion upon which her mother gave her permission to go on the school trip to Paris. This school trip was not an annual event, but a newly-organized affair, to which the school's attention had been drawn by the tireless Miss Haines; it was to take place in Clara's last year, when she was seventeen, a year after her father's death. All those who were doing Advanced Level French were encouraged to go, and most of them were only too glad to do so, because the trip was both cheap and co-educational. Clara, when the idea was broached, declared instantly that it was not worth her while to ask her mother's permission, whereupon the school embarrassingly said that if it were finance that were in question, then help might be forthcoming. Clara could not explain to the school that it was not so much a question of finance, as of her mother's instinctive opposition to any pleasurable project – and anyone could see that a visit to Paris could not possibly fail to entail more plea-sure than instruction. Finance was not, in fact, particularly in question, as Mr Maugham had provided for his family with a thoroughness that bordered upon the reckless – in so far as a man may squander upon insurance, he had done so.

The school's offer of support put Clara in a difficult position, because she felt obliged to make the project known to her mother. She did not feel she could turn down such charity with-out proof of the necessary conditions of rejection. She had, at first, absolutely no hope of consent, and for a week or so she tossed in bed at night preparing to brace her spirit against the

56

inevitable refusal. And then, under pressure from Walter Ash, she allowed to slip into her mind the faint, faint hope that by some quirk of reasoning her mother might be persuaded to agree. Once she had admitted the hope, she was inundated by whole floods of desire; the project took life in her mind, the trees grew leaves, the cathedrals grew towers and arches, the river flowed beneath its bridges. A whole week in Paris at Easter seemed to her something for which she would willingly have sold her soul. She tried, bitterly, to resist this fatal colouring; she tried to reduce the trip to words upon a notice board; but the mind had gone its own way, and she could not force it back into its grey and natal landscape. She turned on Walter Ash and reviled him for allowing her to hope, and indeed, despite the final outcome, it was his dangerous encouragement of this scheme that prefaced her final disillusion with him. She could not bear the sensations of loss with which she knew that she would be obliged to sit down and confront her mother. She hated the school for forcing her through the mockery of inquiry. She wished that the whole thing had never been.

And yet, when she finally, despairingly, screwed herself up and loosed the small words into the drawing room air, her mother said yes. Sitting there, knitting, watching the television, knitting, her lips pursed over some unimaginable grievance, she listened, and nodded, and thought, and said yes. Clara, who had phrased the question so deviously, flinching in preparation from a brutal negative, thought that she must have misunderstood, and repeated the whole rigmarole, and her mother once more nodded her head and said yes. Or rather, she did not say 'Yes' – she said 'We'll have to see,' but in her terminology this counted as a positive affirmative. Clara, perched nervously on the edge of her easy chair, was almost too overwrought to continue the conversation, but she managed to say, 'You mean you really think I might be able to go?'

'I don't see why not,' said Mrs Maugham, with a tight smile which seemed to indicate pleasure in her daughter's confusion. 'I can't say that I see why not. You say all the other girls are going, and if it's such a bargain as you say, then I don't see why not. Do you?'

Clara could hardly shriek at her, you know bloody well why

not, you know bloody well why I can't go, it's because you're such a bloody-minded sadistic old hypocrite, it's because you think Paris is vice itself, and so do I, and so do I, and that's why I want to go, and that's why you won't bloody well let me. She could say nothing. So she said nothing. But she was almost choking with emotion. And not with joy, either.

'I don't see,' continued Mrs Maugham, 'why you shouldn't have a bit of fun too. And if you say it'll be such a help to you, with your examinations, I don't see why you shouldn't go.'

Clara did not know where to look.

'Thank you,' she said, and then, with a fine instinct for disaster, she tried to think of something to say to avert her mother's next words, she tried to speak, but she could think of nothing, and her mother, shifting in her seat, said,

'After all, Clara, you've had a hard year. With your father. You deserve a change.'

And Clara sat there and endured it. Because the truth was that this evidence of care and tenderness was harder to bear than any neglect, for it threw into question the whole basis of their lives together. Perhaps there was hope, perhaps all was not harsh antipathy, perhaps a better daughter might have found a way to soften such a mother. And if all were not lost, what effort, what strain, what retraced miles, what recriminations, what intolerable forgivenesses were not to be undergone? And who, having heard impartially this interchange, would have believed in Clara's cause? Clara's one solace had been the cold, tight dignity of her case, and this had been stolen from her, robbed from her by an elderly woman's few words of casual humanity. She had learned a fine way of sustaining the role of deprivation, but gratitude was an emotion beyond her range.

She did not even thank her mother. She sat there in silence, and resentment made her cheeks hot; she resented the wasted hours of battle with her own desires, she resented her failed and needless attempts at empire, she was filled with hatred at the thought of lost anticipations. Now that she was to go, she knew that she might have had the pleasure of looking forward to going, instead of such long and cheerless debates and equivocations. Bitterly she thought, it is all spoiled, spoiled by consent, spoiled by refusal, it does not matter if I go or stay. By letting me go, she is merely increasing her power, for she is out-martyring my martyrdom. I die from loss, or I die from guilt, and either way I die.

It came to her later, as she started to do her homework, that Racine and Corneille appealed to her so strongly because their ways were hers. For one event, five acts of deliberation. But she played alone, because the other people would not play. And she thought, as she sat there translating a piece of Poly-eucte, that if ever she could find the personages for the rest of her tragedy, then her happiness would be complete. That would be what she would want from life; she would want no more than that.

Before the departure for Paris, Mrs Maugham fortunately forfeited her position by various gratuitous and irrelevant re-marks about the expense. Clara, grown careless and ruthless now that the struggle was over, did not fail to point out that the school would have helped upon request. Mrs Maugham countered this with contemptuous remarks about charity, and about the dignity of the family, and the lack of dignity of vari-ous families in the neighbourhood. Clara swore that she would pay for herself out of her Post Office Savings: her mother said that her dead father hadn't put that money away for her to squander on trips abroad. Clara pointed out that it hadn't been donated by her father in the first place, but by Aunt Doris, as birthday presents, over the past seventeen years. 'Well then, your Aunt Doris didn't give it to you to squander on trips abroad,' said Mrs Maugham. And she was right there, too, but Clara was beyond the rights and wrongs of the case, blissfully carried away into the angry, amoral world of combat, wonder-fully disconnected from truth and falsehood, freed from grati-tude by meanness, released from effort by knowledge of fruit-less impossibility.

And after no matter what contortions, it was upon Northam Station that she found herself, and with a ticket for Paris in her purse. And she thought, as she stood there with Rosie, Susie, Katie, Isabel, Janice and Heather, that none of it mattered, none of it had any importance, in view of the fact that she was going. What could those apprehensions signify, in the light of departure? What could the nearness of victory mean to Bérénice, after five acts, and at the moment of parting? Or the possible loss of Chimène? Excitement had for days so filled her that she could not sleep, and now at last she had embarked upon it; thoughts of loss and martyrdom paled before the facts. What she had wanted, she was to have. And she thought, guiltily, I do not even feel guilty.

Northam Station seemed to her a peculiarly lovely spot for such an embarkation. It was vaulted and filthy, black with the grime of decades, and its sooty defaced posters spoke to her of the petty romances of others, of Ramsgate and Margate, and she was going to Paris, albeit in a school raincoat, and with a beret on her head. The station had always been for her a place instinct with glory; its function beautified it immeasurably in her eyes. She felt herself to be of right there, to have a place upon its departure platforms, and the London train drew in for her with a particular significance. She had been to London once before only, and now she was going to Paris. As the train pulled out of the station, she watched the black and ridged and hard receding buttressed walls, travelling through their narrow channel into some brighter birth, and into some less obstinately alien world. And as they passed the rows upon rows of back yards, the grey washing on curious pulleys, the backs of hardboard dressing tables, the dust-bins and the coal sheds, it occurred to her to wonder why she should so suddenly feel herself to be peculiarly blessed, and a dreadful grief for all those without blessings took hold of her, and a terror at the singular nature of her escape. Out of so many thousands, one. Narrow was the gate, and the hillsides were crowded with the serried dwellings of the cramped and groaning multitudes, the ranks of the Unelect, and she the one white soul flew dangerously forth into some glorious and exclusive shining heaven.

Chapter 4

Victoria Station, when they arrived upon it, did not present a particularly exclusive aspect. It was crowded and swarming with school parties, hundreds of schools all gathered together, some in uniform, some not in uniform, some accompanied, some unaccompanied. Clara stared at them all hungrily, at the meek and the marshalled, at the loudly swearing, at the sophisticates, at the nervous and the panic-stricken ticket-mislayers. And she stared too at her own friends, who appeared to her suddenly in a new light, laughing and fiddling with their luggage labels, and casting their eyes around them as though unbalanced by the sudden variety of choice. The whole station was like some vast and awkward school dance, where need and constraint mingle in a heady, violent ferment of suppression. And Clara was glad that she was not accompanied by Walter Ash. She stood a better chance, she thought, upon her own: though a chance of what she would not have liked to have said.

The journey set in her a taste for such journeys that she was never to lose. The very sight of the sign at the head of the platform, shabby and tourist and third class though it was compared with that of the Golden Arrow at the other end of the station, was enough to raise her to a state she had never reached before, and as the train moved south, she sat in her seat and stared out of the window as though in a trance. The other girls in the compartment spent their time comparing their passport photographs, and commenting upon the rowdiness of some boys in the corridor, who seemed, to their disbelieving, priggish admiring indignation, to be drinking beer out of cans, but Clara, though she saw, was too rapt to speak. The boat too affected her profoundly; she had never been on a boat before, except for a rowing boat in the park, and she stood up on the top deck in the bitter grey April wind, and watched the foam

and the emptiness and the receding bar of Folkestone, and she
thought that she had never seen anything so wonderful in her
life. Later she explored, and the boat's possibilities seemed
limitless; she did not think that she could ever tire of it. It was
a rough crossing, and most people were rather quiet, and a
few were vomiting over the railings and indeed all over the
upper-deck, but Clara had never felt better, and the rough
lurching seemed to her an added attraction. She noticed that
several of the school parties were starting, tentatively to join
up; those of her own friends who were not suffering in the
Ladies' saloon were talking, intermittently, to a group of boys
from a school in Birmingham. But Clara did not join them:
she kept herself to herself. The only person that she spoke to on
the whole crossing was a young man who fell on top of her as
she and he were going down the stairs: he was following her,
two steps behind, when the boat gave a violent lurch and he
missed his footing and crashed into her, and she too missed her
footing, and they both sat down together upon the stairs. He
helped her to her feet, anxiously dusting her coat, apologizing,
undistressed, so courteous and unconfused that she felt that he
had conferred upon her a favour, and to her amazement she
heard her own voice answering, with equal, answering ease,
assuring him that no, she was not hurt, no, of course it was not
his fault, yes, it certainly was the roughest she had ever known
it. Then he left her, and she watched him go: he had yellow
hair, unmistakable yellow hair, and she said to herself, there
goes a public school boy. She was not familiar with the type,
but she recognized it when she saw it as she would have recognized the Eiffel Tower. Later, five minutes outside Calais, she
saw him drinking brandy in the bar, and he smiled at her, and
said, 'Why don't you have a drink?' but she smiled back, and
shook her head, and walked on.

Paris, unlike the journey, had its disappointments, though
she realized that what she principally disliked was the position
from which she was viewing it. The school trip was an example
of massive disorganized organization: every minute of every
day was officially occupied, and Clara wasted some time before
she realized that nobody in the whole world would care or even
notice whether she attended each event or not. She was not

used to laws so easily broken, authority so easily evaded. On the first morning, after a night in a Lycée bed, they all went to a preliminary reception at the Hôtel de Ville: Clara went, politely willing, but when she got there she found that it was a gigantic, milling, stifling insult. Thousands of school children, all of them well over sixteen, were crammed there into a large tall gilt room, and told not to insult the French, not to talk to Arabs, and not to go to Montmartre: then an English lady stood up and said that Paris had always been for her a *source inépuisable de* something, and everyone clapped, and then they were all turned out again, rather quickly, for the room was clearly needed for something else. Clara was not impressed, and amazed that she had the sense not to be impressed. But she still did not realize how unnecessary it was to attend such events, and she continued to go to all the scheduled treats. The Comédie Française did not impress her either, for it seemed to her a collection of posturing gabbling shadows, mocking at plays that she had studied in tranquillity and silence: the celebrated mirrors of Versailles were all spotty, Notre-Dame looked at her as though it had two spires missing from on top, and the famous intellectual cafés were full of old men and tourists. The lectures laid on at the Sorbonne were of an abysmal simplicity, and given by lecturers who grossly though understandably underestimated their audience: they bored her as she had not been bored by work for years.

In the end she decided that she did not like being a sightseer: the role filled her with an obscure rage. She could not recognize, did not dare to recognize the grandiose ambitions whence her rage sprang; it did not amuse her to sit in the Deux Magots, remembering that Sartre and Simone de Beauvoir had once sat there, nor did she wish to glimpse the exteriors of the houses of the famous dead. She wanted interiors. She could not admit this, not even to herself, for such an admission would have pronounced her mad, but it lay there, subtly underlining her enjoyment. She was not content to be insulted in cafés by waiters more rude than any to be found in Northam; she could not accept the lowliness of her status, for it seemed to pain her more abroad than it had done at home, and she felt that she should somehow have escaped it, that she should have been changed, somehow, into something new. Once she saw, sitting on the pavement before a café, drinking pale green drinks, and embracing, leaning over from their plastic chairs towards each other and embracing, the most beautiful couple; the man with a face angular and ravaged and tragic, the girl dark and thin, with pale lips in a dark tan face: and she was so moved that she said, aloud to Rosie who was walking with her, 'Look, Oh God, look at those lovely people': and Rosie looked and stared and laughed and said, 'Good Lord, what odd ideas you have, I wouldn't look like that if you gave me a hundred pounds.'

They ate, three times a day, in the Lycée where they were staying, and the food was the subject of much exclamation. Clara was glad that Walter Ash with his quips was not there to add to it. Drinking coffee from bowls was universally thought to be charming, but other eccentricities did not go down so well. Garlic was much disliked; the amount of oil was heavily frowned upon, and Clara was enraptured by the spectacle of the profound and shocked indignation which greeted a certain sausage that appeared for lunch one day. The sausage was extremely coarse and highly seasoned, full of solid lumps of fat and gristle, infinitely far removed from the smooth uniform bread-crumb paste of sausages in England, and it was received with a horror too deep for words. Silently, the rows of sixth-formers tasted, and chewed, and rejected; silently they pushed the food to the side of their plates. Clara, like the others, found that the sausage inspired her with a sense of violent disgust, but she ate it just the same. She chopped it up, and chewed it, and ate it. Her friends turned to her and said, 'You don't *like* it, do you?' and she turned to them with a smile of triumph, swallowing hard, and said, 'Oh, it's all right, really.'

It was not until the next to last day of the visit that she finally formulated to herself her secret desire, which was to see Montmartre at night. The fact that they had been warned off but made it the more attractive. She was not sure what it was, or what to expect should she go there, but she wanted to see it, because it had been forbidden. And on the penultimate day, emboldened by previous truancies, forays and excursions, she tried to persuade one of her friends to take the evening off from

Le Bourgeois Gentilhomme, and accompany her. But to her surprise, nobody would go. She had hoped that Rosie Lane at least, who was usually willing to try anything once, would have accepted the challenge, but she demurred, pleading a headache, and Janice told her, in mysterious tones, as though provided with obscene, private information, that she would be mad to go to such a place, that it was rough there, and wicked beyond all Clara's pitiful conceptions of wickedness, and that if she went there anything might happen to her.

'What?' said Clara. '*What* might happen to me?'

'Ah, anything,' said Janice, shaking her head darkly, as though she could have told, but would not.

So in the evening, after supper, Clara walked off by herself and caught the Métro and got off it at the Place Pigalle, for that was the only name on the Métro map that she recognized.

When she emerged, into the soft and dark and shining night, she caught her breath sharply, and tightened her grip upon her plastic shoulder bag. For here, in a sense, was what she had come to see. Here huge and naked cardboard women sprawled across the skyline, and red and green and yellow lights lit the blue air. The streets were full of people talking, walking and standing and talking, and the doors of the bars were open, and the pavements were like shops and the shops like pavements. The faint gay menace of music, issuing from juke boxes and radios, surrounded her, and it seemed that there was nobody, out of all those hundreds before her gaze, who was not there in the search of amusement – an amusement shallow, elusive, shapeless, all-embracing. She stood there, staring, immobile at first, before the riot of flesh and lights and people and advertisements, and she wondered what it was that she was supposed to fear, because she could not truly fear anything, in such well-lit company: and she wondered why she was not afraid, when they had all told her, all of them, the Party Organizer and Janice and her upbringing, that she ought to fear. She could see that nothing could harm her, that there was no danger, that danger in so far as it might exist was desirable, and she started to walk, slowly, up the street, looking at those who looked at her, exchanging glance for glance, shivering in the warm April air from a tremulous, hopeful, artificial apprehension. She shivered, and she walked as though she were naked.

She walked for ten minutes, and then she sat down, in front of one of the less dicey looking cafés, and ordered herself a Coca Cola. She wanted to order herself a drink, but she did not dare. Her courage had its limits. She watched the other people, and wondered how many years of observation it would take her to learn to distinguish the tarts from the students, for there were clearly some of each within her range. She opened her copy of Baudelaire, which she had brought with her, and started to look at it, and shortly she heard a voice say, 'Mademoiselle, je peux?' and saw a man looking at her.

She nodded, because for shame she could do nothing but nod, and he sat down at her table. He smiled at her, and she smiled back. He was young, and not at all bad-looking; she thought that it could well have happened in a much worse way. He asked her, in French, if she were German; she said no, she was English.

'Ah, ah, Anglaise,' he said, nodding his head knowledgeably, as though the word conveyed a wealth of information. She could tell, instantly, that he was stupid. He had to think for several seconds before he came out with, 'Moi, je suis Italien.'

'Ah, oui,' she said, politely, giving him time, 'Italien.'

He thought hard, and then said, 'Vous êtes étudiante?'

'Oui,' she replied indulgently.

'Vous venez de Londres?' he then asked, anxiously, solicitously.

'Non, non, du Nord de l'Angleterre,' she replied. The sense of effort in his conversation staggered her, and she watched him with pity, for he laboured as though he were to try to write a sonnet, and all the while the conversation was predestined, unnecessary, a mere coin of payment.

'C'est très grand, Londres,' he continued, unable to adapt to her last remark.

'Oui, très grand,' she agreed, and then asked him, politely, 'Et vous, d'ou venez-vous?'

'Da Milano,' he said, and added helpfully, 'Milan, c'est au nord de l'Italie. C'est amusant, moi je veins du nord de l'Italie, et vous venez du nord de l'Angleterre. C'est amusant.'

'Oui,' said Clara, and smiled benignly, while he laughed.

'Le nord de l'Angleterre, c'est L'Ecosse,' said the man, flashing his even teeth at her, showing them as though to compensate for the deficiences of his wit.

'Oui,' said Clara, thinking it not worth her while to draw the distinction.

'Une écossaise, alors,' he said, grinning. She did not correct him.

'Et vous, vous n'êtes pas étudiant,' she said, thinking that she might learn the difference between tarts and students sooner than she had imagined.

'Non, non, je travaille ici,' he said. She did not like to ask him the nature of his work, thinking that if he were something incommunicable, the effort of inventing a lie might crack him up completely. He did not look resourceful. On the other hand, she did not know what else to say, so she said nothing. He too had come to the end of his small talk. He sat there for quite a while, grinning at her, then looking away, then looking back and grinning at her again. Such behaviour, which always unnerved her when displayed by such as Higginbotham, did not unnerve her at all. The isolation of the moment, and its total disconnexion from all other moments, gave her a sensation of quite unfamiliar ease. Her hands, clasped on the iron table, grew limp.

After a while he offered her a cigarette. She took it, and he lit it for her. Her smoking experiences, hitherto, had been confined to a few borrowed puffs from Walter Ash's cigarettes, and some experimental moments, at the age of twelve, in the school bicycle shed. This cigarette tasted different; it was a Gauloise, and it tasted of France, as pungent, as unacceptably alien as that knotty sausage. She smoked it with delight.

'Comment t'appelle?' he asked, after a few minutes.

'Je m'appelle Isabel,' said Clara.

'Isabel. C'est jolie,' he said.

'Tu trouves?' she said. She did not ask him his name, for she did not wish to know it.

'Qu'est-ce que tu fais ce soir?' he said eventually.

'Rien, rien du tout,' said Clara.

'Tu veux m'accompagner au cinéma?' he said. And Clara,

67

overcome by the wonderful, felicitous acceptability of his offer, an offer so familiar to her, so marvellously manageable, trembled only most slightly as she said, staring down at the limp arrangements of her hands, 'Oui, surement.' She had been afraid that his suggestion, when it came, would have been too fraught with the unknown – his room, perhaps, or else, God knows, a naked nightclub – but as for the cinema, she could cope with that.

And so they went to the cinema. He took her arm, and held it firmly by its crooked elbow, propelling her so that she did not collide with the crowds of people, and she liked to have it held. They went to the nearest cinema: it was an American film, dubbed, from one of Hemingway's short stories. It was half way through, and she could not understand a word of the dialogue, and was surprised and rather indignant that she could not understand, for she had genuinely looked forward, with half of herself, to seeing a picture: as it was, she found herself obliged to concentrate on the other aspects of the affair. It was clear that he understood less of the film than she did, and cared less. She was glad that it was connected, however dimly, with Hemingway, for she knew about Hemingway, and she liked shockingly the sense of an operating corner in her inviolable mind.

After ten minutes, he took her hand. She allowed it to be taken, and it grew warm in his grasp. Their two hands lay warmly together upon her lap. Then he released it, and took a hold of her knee. She was used to this, and did not flinch. Her eyes firmly glued to the screen, she sat, and she endured and enjoyed. After a while, he withdrew his hand, put his arm round her shoulders, and pulled her towards him, and kissed her. She did not much like his way of kissing, for it was hot and suffocating, and she was glad when he stopped, and released her, and reverted to his grip upon her knee. He was more interested in her knees, and so was she. As the film progressed, he gradually began to hitch her skirt up, so that his hand was resting not upon skirt but upon stocking, and then his hand began to creep up the stocking. She had never had this happen to her before, and she was not expert, in this area, in the art of procrastination, and in no time at all he had managed to

68

slip his hand inside the stocking top of her offside leg. He was breathing heavily, and she was not herself unmoved. And she had to admit to herself that she was also faintly, dimly, desirably worried, for she could not tell when or if he would stop. She glanced, covertly, at her watch, and saw to her relief that the feature film had only ten minutes to run; she thought she could last ten minutes.

And she just about managed it. As his hand started once more to ascend the bare slope of her thigh, she tightened, immeasurably, her knees, and his hand halted. The film was nearing its climax: despite herself, and despite her incomprehension, her attention had been caught, and she was at last following it. Two assassins were cornered in a shabby hotel bedroom, awaiting inevitable retribution. And then, suddenly, one of them spoke a sentence which she understood. One of them said, grimly, sparingly, desperate, to the other:

'Il n'y a plus rien à faire,' and Clara, in the exquisite delight of understanding, relaxed the grip of her knees, and his hand, obedient, stirred itself once more. The assassins were shot, and Clara wrenched herself away, and the man murmured to her desperately, 'Laschemi fare, laschemi fare,' and Clara equally stricken, could not let him, and the credits came up, and the lights came up, and he let her go, and she straightened her coat and pulled her skirt tightly down over her knees, and that was that.

They walked out together, and stood there in the street, and Clara looked once more at her watch. 'I have to go,' she said, in English. 'Il faut que je m'en aille.'

'Oh, non non non,' he said anxiously. 'Viens. Viens boire quelqu'chose, viens avec moi. J'ai une chambre tout près, une chambre à moi ...'

'Non, je ne peux pas,' said Clara, realizing miserably that he did not believe that she would not go. She liked him, for all his heavy breathing; she did not like misunderstanding. And she had somehow thought that he would have known that she could not go.

'Tu peux, tu peux,' he repeated.

'Mais non, je ne peux pas, je dois partir. Tout de suite. Le Lycée se ferme à onze heurs.'

He had taken it, now, that she was not going; she expected to see resentment blossom, but he did not resent it. Hopeful, he said:

'Demain, alors?'

And she said no, she could not make tomorrow, she was going back to England tomorrow, which was not true, but true enough. It was a pity, she said. And he agreed that it was a pity.

'Je dois aller,' said Clara, losing grammar in urgency, beginning to be afraid that she might be late. 'Merci beaucoup pour le cinéma.'

'C'est moi qui te remercie,' he said simply. And then he shook her hand, and turned and walked away. Clara, as she ran for the Métro, was full of the greatest joy of her life, for she felt herself to be, at last, living; the thick complexity of what had happened satisfied something in her that had never before had satisfaction. She had dared, and she had not been struck dead for it; she had exposed herself, and she had not been raped, assaulted, or even insulted. Such contact had for her possessed beauty, and he had shaken hands with her upon it; he had not yelled at her for what she had not given. He had smiled at her, and shaken her hand. The bizarre absurdity of his action filled her with amazement and wonder, for it seemed to disprove so many meannesses and preconceptions. She would not have minded if he had yelled at her, for he would have had the right to. But she too had the right to leave.

She got back to the Lycée at five past eleven; the doors were not yet shut, and she crept in safely, under the protection of a large party returned from the Opéra. She went up to the dormitory, where she found her school friends, anxious and exulting over her delay, grieved and relieved that her sortie had escaped detection; they gathered round her, perched on the bed, drawing cosily round themselves the striped dusty coarse hooped curtains on their brass poles, and they listened to her story. Some of it they did not believe; some of it she did not report. But they were impressed, and she too was impressed by her own adventure. They whispered, and talked, and compared notes, and then Rosie, sitting cross-legged on the hard sausage of a pillow, said:

'Why didn't you go with him, when he asked you, why didn't

you go to his room? You should have gone to see what it was like.'

'I would have done,' said Clara, 'but they shut the doors at eleven.' And they said no more, because Rosie had been teasing, merely; it had not crossed her head that Clara might truly have stayed out.

But later that night, lying awake in bed, Clara found herself trembling, partly from fright, and partly from the knowledge that perhaps she ought to have gone. For there was no divine or moral key which turned the lock of the Lycée at eleven o'clock. She might have stayed out, and nobody would have known. And if they had known, what could they have done? They could not have raped her, or murdered her, or beaten her. They could not even have made her fail her examinations. And they would not have expelled her; they wanted her, and they could not afford to expel her. She might have stayed, and the truth was that the possibility of staying had not occurred to her. She sat for the evening with a strange man's hand inside her stocking, and yet it had not occurred to her that the laws of a disorganized school trip were not the laws of nature or of justice. She was ashamed of herself. She lay there, and her knees were trembling, but whether it was from running from the Métro, from past terror, or from shame, she could not tell.

On the last night of the trip there was a dance. Some of the girls had been looking forward to this as to the highlight of the trip, but Clara had been dreading it, and for a classic reason, which was that she had nothing nice to wear. Since her social life in Northam did not exist outside school, she had no evening clothes, and had had nothing resembling a party dress since the age of six, when she had possessed a fetching little garment of pink satin. All the other girls had at least a best dress, and some of them were burningly anxious to display clothes bought by extravagant parents especially for the occasion. Clara had had the sense not to try to ask her mother about a possible purchase, as she could only too clearly imagine the responses to which such a request would expose her, and the abuse which would be cast upon those girls fortunate enough to have a use for party dresses. Her mother tended to see all expenses as a sign of innate vulgarity, and had tried to instil into her children the view that the truly refined can manage without toys, clothes and entertainments. Nevertheless, Clara had been obliged to raise the subject of a best dress, because the brochure about the school trip had clearly stated that it would be expected. Her mother had reacted to the subject in a predictable way, and had expatiated at some length about the absurdity of taking a dress all the way to Paris and back for the sake of one evening's amusement, but in the end she had consented to do something about it. What she did was to go through her cupboards, where she discovered a dress which had once belonged to Clara's cousin, and which had been enclosed years before in a charitable parcel of hands-on. She came downstairs with this garment, triumphant, not unwilling to please with pleasure so cheaply bought. And at the sight of it, Clara's spirits faintly rose, because the colour – a blue-green – was one which, at that age, she rather fancied. But once she had tried it on, her spirits sank once more to unprecedented depths.

For the dress was quite impossible. Or worse – not quite impossible, but just about, just gently verging upon the impossible. It was not so ridiculously bizarre that it was unwearable, but it was bad enough. For one thing, the material was patterned, and Clara was going through a stage at which the uncertainty of her taste made her prefer the strictly plain to the figured. And the shape was all wrong. It fitted her in as much as it had ever fitted anyone, but the bodice hung droopily over her breasts, and the neckline gaped softly round her throat, and the hem dipped at the back, with a scarcely perceptible, ineradicable dip. And the material was shiny. Clara had a horror of the shiny. In vain did her mother insist that the material was expensive, and that anyone, looking at it, would know that it was expensive, for Clara knew in her heart of hearts that it looked cheap. As it happened, Clara was wrong, but she was not to know she was wrong, and she suffered as much as though she had been right. She stood in front of the mirror and in front of her mother, and she suffered, because she knew that there was no escape; the reasons why the dress would not do were reasons which could never be communicated.

As the girls changed for the dance, giggling, excited, she had moments when she thought that she could not do it, that she would prefer to go in her skirt and jersey. She knew she looked better in her skirt and jersey, but she had not the courage to wear them. Then she thought that she would not go at all, that she would stay behind and pretend to be ill. But she wanted to go. The only dances she had ever been to had been school dances, and she wanted to go to this one. So she put the dress on, and thought for a moment that perhaps it was not quite so frightful after all, and then, after looking at herself for a little longer, wondered if it were not in fact more frightful than she had ever imagined. She hardly dared to draw the curtains to show herself to the other girls, though she had warned them of the horrid sight in store for them. Pride always restrained her from describing her mother's attitudes in too much detail, and she tended rather to laugh them off, but nevertheless her friends had some shrewd notion of the situation. She had described the dress to them, haltingly, trying to make her account amusing, searching desperately for a tone that would make its existence plain and casual and innocent to them, but she had not quite attained it; 'My cousin Mavis,' she had said, laughing. 'You should just *see* her, you can't imagine, you would have to *see* her to know why she chose it,' and all the time, as she spoke, some more assured, sophisticated account underran her words, silently, in her own mind, an account by some other girl, some girl who could wear such garments, and laugh at them, and explain them, and not suffer – some girl so far above such things that nothing could pull her down. Some girl who would never need to make such explanations, some girl who had been bred in a world which did not admit such dresses.

And, when, finally, she did emerge from her curtain cubicle to face the other girls, they took it very well, for they could afford to be charitable, and they were secretly glad that Clara's style was cramped, for without some handicap she would have been a more serious threat. So they greeted her with comforts and praise, and said they liked the colour, and Janice lent her a necklace; Clara did not much like the necklace either, for it was made of large artificial pearls, and she secretly suspected the donor of malicious intent in offering such a loan, but she

73

put it on just the same, and ignored her suspicions, and allowed herself to be comforted, because she wished to be comforted, and because it was too late to get out of going. And when they got there, they found that both anticipation and anxiety had overestimated the occasion, for like the reception at the Hôtel de Ville, the dance was nothing but a stifling, uncomfortable, noisy, joyless crush. The rooms provided were far too small for the thousands of English scholars who were crammed into them, and the originally excessive numbers were heavily augmented by gate-crashing French students who had been hanging around the fringes of the course all week trying to pick up girls at the Lycée doors. There was a band, somewhere, but it could not be heard or seen. There were soft drinks, somewhere, but they could not be reached. The school parties stuck as rigidly together as they had done upon Victoria Station, lacking only their uniforms and labels, disastrously hampered by lack of space. Clara's contingent sized up the situation in a disappointed trice, and hunched itself together in a corner to confront the disorderly scene by a solid front of backs. Only Janice, eternally hopeful, kept her eye upon the possibilities; she perched herself, kneeling, upon a chair, so that at least her head could be seen above the crowd.

For three quarters of an hour they stood there, and bitterly complained and rejoiced in rumours of police intervention, faintings, and thefts – and then, slowly, the floor began to clear a little. They did not know whether it cleared because people had left voluntarily, or because people had been evicted, but clear it did, and a few couples from the co-educational schools ventured forth to dance. Janice, from her vantage point, managed to catch the eye of a boy to whom she had spoken on the boat, and terrorized, fascinated, he responded to her insinuations and oglings and came over to ask her for the pleasure of her hand. At this, Rosie, Katie, Heather, Isabel and Clara felt themselves put upon their mettle, and they swerved round, slowly, to expose their disdainful faces. The competition was, alas, horrific, as they had ill-advisedly placed themselves in a predominantly female quarter of the hall, where few boys were bold enough to venture. However, after a couple of dances had elapsed, Clara thought she spotted the civilized young man who had assisted her on the Channel crossing; once she had spotted him she turned rigidly away, so deep was her horror of imitating Janice's conduct, but she lost nothing by it, for within a couple of minutes he presented himself, courteously, at her elbow.

'Hello,' he said. 'I thought I saw you. Isn't it the most shocking scrum? Why do you imagine we all stay instead of going?'

'I don't know,' said Clara. 'Perhaps we just don't like to give up.'

'Do you feel like trying to have a dance?' he said.

'It looks,' she said nervously, 'a little difficult.'

'Oh, I don't know,' he said. 'If you don't mind your toes being trampled on . . .'

She hesitated, sadly, desperately anxious to accept, absurdly delighted that he had asked her, that he had so coolly bothered to cross the room to ask her, and yet at the same time horrified by the thought of displaying herself, by the thought of dragging her hideous dress from its hole-in-the-corner obscurity, by the thought of dancing at all, for she did not know how to dance. All the dancing that she had ever done had been at three school dances, and in sessions for instruction in the art of the polka, the mazurka, and the tarantella, and she did not think they would be much help to her now. On the other hand, she did not feel that she could refuse him, because if she refused him, by what right and for what purpose had she gone there in the first place? Such a false position was not for her, nor for her was the taunt of cowardice, so she smiled and assented, and allowed him to drag her into the sparsest area of the room.

It was not, as it happened, too bad. The floor was so thickly covered that there was no space for displays of skill; the most that the most expert could do was to shuffle feebly back and forth. Clara, clasped to the young man's bosom, reflected that he was in no position to notice her lack of grace. Nor could he possibly notice her dipping hemline. He held her quite tightly, and tried to prevent other people from banging into her. His hair was thick and shining and symmetrical like a yellow flower. She was proud of him, and of herself, but she was not too happy, for the strain was too great for happiness. He too seemed to feel some sense of strain, for he was too busy avoiding people to talk to her much; when he trod, helplessly, for the fifth time upon her foot, she stopped still, and said to him, lightly, and with a sense of great daring,

'It really is too bad, don't you think? Don't you think we might give it up?' The perfection of her tone, so perfectly deceitful and concealing, amazed her.

He stopped, and he seemed relieved.

'It's dreadful,' he said. 'I'm so sorry I keep treading on you, I just can't help it. Should you mind if we went to look for something to drink instead?'

'Is there anything?' she asked.

'I thought I saw something,' he said, 'in one of the other rooms.'

And so she followed him, in search of a drink. She was delighted by the success of her bravery, because she was far happier talking than dancing. She liked to be good at things, and she was not good at dancing. They found some drinks, eventually, in a small beleaguered ante-room, where he fought his way through to the bar and acquired some fizzy orange.

'Not much, I'm afraid,' he said, as he returned modestly with his two bottles and straws, 'but better than nothing.'

And they stood in a corner and drank them, and exchanged their names, at last: she much admired the clear way with which he presented his own. Peter Harronson, he said he was called. She thought the name faintly familiar, and faintly Scandinavian, but she did not like to ask where it came from, in case she should have known. Similarly, when they exchanged the names of their schools, she found herself immensely relieved when he declared that he was at Winchester, for she had heard of Winchester, she knew something about Winchester, she did not have to feign a non-existent knowledge of Winchester. Indeed, she was rather proud of the magnificent logic with which she countered his Winchester admission.

'Ah, then,' she said, sucking on her straw. 'Then you must have been to Paris before.'

He did not even query her reasoning; he took it, for what it was.

'Yes,' he said, 'once or twice, I have.'

'Well, then,' she continued, with what seemed to her to be

the very height of aware sophistication, 'why ever did you want to come here on this sort of trip?'

He seemed, strangely enough, to be very slightly disconcerted by her question.

'Oh, I don't know,' he said. 'I thought it might be amusing. And then, you know, the others were coming. And it gave one something to do with the holidays. And there were those lectures, too. They told me they'd be useful.'

'Did they really?' said Clara. 'I thought they were pretty dismal, didn't you? I mean, really.'

On this point, however, he did not follow her, for he clearly took her to be complaining of the endemic tediousness of all lectures, rather than of the inadequacy of this particular lot: he equally clearly did not wholly concede the point, for he said, faintly, falsely, without enthusiasm, 'Oh yes, I suppose they were.'

And she, warned off intellectual discussion by years of experience, withdrew, and could think of no more to say. And he too seemed to have exhausted his conversational store; she thought that they would both have liked to continue talking, but they could think of nothing to say. They were too young. And in the silence, she grew more and more conscious of the impossibility of her dress, and of her scuffed and inappropriately coloured shoes, and of her warm face. She wanted to get away, and she did not know how to get away. All explanations, all excuses were crude and deadly, and she could not bring herself to make them, but she could not sit there either, contemplating her own slow lapse from grace. She was immobile, cruelly transfixed, but in the very moment of immobility she saw most clearly a time when such moments need not be. It was left to him to move. He rose to his feet, and said:

'Should we go and see if there's any more room for dancing? It might have cleared a little more by now.'

And she too rose, and found herself saying, 'Thank you so much, but if you don't mind I think I'd better go and see what's happened to my face.'

'Of course,' he said, 'of course,' and he even showed her the corridor that led to the Ladies' room, and she escaped, and they escaped from each other. She stayed in the Ladies' room for a long time, amongst girls fainting, and weeping and grieving over laddered stockings, and when she emerged he had disappeared. She was wholly relieved that he had gone, for his absence enabled her safely to join her friends, to receive their questions and their anecdotes, and to hear of the brazen, wonderful audacity of Janice, who had not yet returned to the fold, and who had been seen leading, yes, *leading* her captive from the floor, in search of fresher air and darker night.

In bed that night, Clara thought of Peter Harronson and his fair hair. And she thought of the Italian's hand inside her stocking. And she thought of Walter Ash. Her life, she thought, seemed to be thickening up quite nicely.

The next morning, they left Paris. The station from which they departed was being cleaned, and she thought, what a strange thing to clean, a station. What would they say in Northam, if anyone proposed to spend money on cleaning Northam Station? And then, looking at the workmen, and the yellow emerging stone, she almost noticed that the station was not intended to be a station but a work of art, a building ambitiously decorated with scrolls and figures and carvings: ill-decorated, but decorated nonetheless.

That summer she gained a place at London University, and parted from Walter Ash. Her parting from him took place in a field of buttercups and small cows; they had gone there together on their bicycles one hot afternoon, she with the intention of reading her book, and he with the intention of persuading her to remove as many of her clothes as possible. They lay on his jacket, and she tried to read while he tried to kiss her. She won. After an hour the sun clouded over, so they picked up their things and started back towards the fence where they had left their bicycles. At the far end of the field, by the gate, there was a group of small cows, and as Clara and Walter approached, these cows turned round to face them. They were in a solid line, between them and the gate. There were about twenty of them. They did not move.

Walter and Clara slowed down. Clara was frightened, but on the other hand she could see that they were only small cows. They were not even small bullocks. And she thought it was

78

quite intolerable for Walter Ash to hesitate, even though she herself found it necessary to hesitate. She stood there, timidly, full of a most mordant rage. Then, pained beyond belief in some tender pride, she advanced alone upon the cows, and they parted softly and meekly before her and Walter Ash followed her, and they regained their bicycles.

And she thought, quite calmly: this isn't good enough for me, I shall get further if I'm pulled, I can't waste time in going first.

When Walter Ash rang her the next day she would not speak to him. She returned his letters unopened, and threw away his small gifts. She stayed indoors for the rest of the summer, lying on her bed, trying to read.

Chapter 5

Clara knew that Clelia would contact her, and she did. Less than a week after their first meeting at the poetry reading, she found a message waiting for her, asking her to ring Clelia's number, and she rang, and Clelia invited herself round to tea.

'I would ask you to come here,' she said, 'but there seems to be some kind of disturbance going on, and I don't want to add to it.'

'Oh, that's all right,' said Clara, 'do please come here, I should like you to come here.'

And she meant it, for she liked her college room, she was even mildly proud of it, and the thought of entertaining Clelia in it did not alarm her, though she had a deep aversion to the notion of entertainment, and had never in her whole three years at University embarked on the ritual tea parties or more ambitious sherry parties that mark the social life of such establishments. It was not so much meanness that restrained her, as a profound mistrust of her own organizations: and also she felt obscurely, that to invite people into her own room was to condemn them to boredom and unease. She recognized that this feeling was in part a hangover from her schooldays, when her occasional invitations to friends had invariably resulted in sessions of strained discomfort, presided over by the disapprobation, however concealed, of her mother; she had no precedent for successful hospitality. She had conquered this feeling sufficiently to allow her to accept visits from her friends, and had overcome the apologetic murmurs that used to assail her as she opened her bedroom door; she felt, in part, absolved by the wonderfully institutional shape of her room, which was on the third floor of a large block in the middle of Regent's Park. The room was what it was, one of many, it meant nothing, it spoke of nothing, it betrayed her in no way. She enjoyed its lack of significance, much as she had enjoyed the bleak and dirty corridors of Battersby Grammar School when she was eleven years old. She made no attempts to decorate it, to domesticate it, to possess it; she let it be, and her things lay in it. Some of her friends bought cushions and pictures and even, extravagantly, curtains, in an effort to make rooms look homely, and though she liked the results, she viewed the aim with contempt.

As she sat and waited for Clelia, she looked out across the park, at the spring trees, and tried to concentrate on her Spanish, and thought of what she should do next, without this view, without the solace of a yearly grant, without the irreproachable (or now, through custom, irreproachable) excuse of study. Her Finals were approaching, and she had no idea of what she should do next, and indeed did not dare to think about the future for she knew that it offered her little in the way of readily acceptable projects. Her friends, all equally indecisive, had no need to hurry their decisions, for nothing lay at their backs, pulling them, sucking them, dragging at their sleeves and at their hems. But Clara knew that her mother expected her to go home.

The thought of going home was for her the final impossibility, but she could not see any satisfactory way of avoiding it. She could not see why her mother wanted her, nor what she expected her to do in Northam, and whenever she mentioned the subject to others they exclaimed in horror, commiserating with her, telling her that she must be firm, never for half a moment assuming that she could or would really do it. She said to them, sometimes, but she's a widow, she lives all alone, she has no one, she seems to expect it of me: and they sympathized all the more, and said that they could see how hard it must be for Clara to break away. But nobody ever so much as hinted at the possibility that she might return. They all assumed, blandly, blithely, that she must stay in London, or go abroad; that the guilt must be endured, and no question about it.

Most of the time Clara assumed it too. Her years in London had merely strengthened her desire to live there for the rest of her life, and while she was there her mother seemed, most of the time, to be no more that a dreadful past sorrow, endured and survived. But then there were always the vacations. Clara dreaded the vacations, and tried to whittle them down as much as she could, by semi-obligatory study courses, and quasi-essential trips to the continent to learn the languages she was studying, but despite these nibblings and thefts, she still found herself obliged to spend a great deal of time each year in Hartley Road. She had neither the money, nor, finally, the nerve to stay away. And these visits managed to reduce her to exactly the same stage of trembling, silent, frustrated anxiety that she had endured throughout her childhood; she felt, each time, that she had gone back, right back to the start, and that every step forward must be painfully retraced. It was not so, at the beginning of each new term she found it was not so, but it seemed to be so, and the same mixture of guilt and hate and sorrow would strike her anew, each time as forcefully, each time she got off the train at Northam Station. She found that she was not alone in her vacational penances, and that many of her friends endured similar harsh shocks and grating transitions, but she was alone in the way she took it. For she found herself incapable of struggling against it, as others did; while at home, she made no efforts to alleviate her lot. She sought no friends; she shut herself off, in the old familiar world of bedroom and drawing room, and her only amusement, for weeks on end, was the reading of her set texts. She lived in the house, as though there had never been another world, and when a boy she knew, who lived in Doncaster, asked if he could come over and take her out, she refused him, although she liked him, because she knew that she could not bear to allow herself to emerge. And so she continued, through three years, through a series of such violent changes; she inspected herself anxiously from time to time for signs of manic-depression or schizophrenia, but she could find nothing but symptoms of increasingly quick recovery. In her first year, it took her a day or two to settle down to London, but in her last year she was there the moment she stepped on the train.

Nevertheless, she did not see that she could leave Northam for ever. She felt herself restrained from such freedom. And she sought, faintly, for compromise, for some way of life that would enable her to see her mother as often as a sense of duty obliged. She never allowed herself to suspect that duty might oblige her to return entirely, but the idea lay in the back of her head, as of some final, exhausting, bleeding martyrdom. She shunned it, she avoided it, but she could occasionally feel herself blench as she caught a rash and unguarded glimpse of it. She did not believe that she would ever do it, for she told herself that she was free; she thought that she would probably end by prolonging, in some way, her present situation, by returning for vacations and for long dead summers. Such a summer now stared her in the face, for she had, through indecision, failed to fix herself up any foreign excursions; she looked towards it and towards her approaching examinations, and felt sadly weak.

Clelia's visit, however, was all that she had hoped for. She arrived most promptly, sat down on the bed, and proceeded to tell Clara the story of her life. It was an impressive narrative, and impressively narrated; Clara found her craving for the bizarre and the involved richly satisfied. The picture that emerged was highly confusing, because she could not follow all its references, despite Clelia's efforts to explain herself; she found it impossible to sort out the complications of Clelia's family, which seemed to contain, as well as a poet father, an equally if not more famous mother, and a large number of strangely named children. The mother puzzled Clara particularly, for Clelia evidently assumed that she needed no description or definition, and spoke of her as one whose name is a household word. Clara, already familiar with children of famous parents, and with children who believed their parents to be famous, could not believe that Clelia's assumption was ill-founded, yet she could not even locate the field of Mrs Denham's distinction. She had more success with the identities of various names that had been puzzling her since their last encounter, and most satisfactorily of all, she placed the baby. The baby belonged to a man called Martin, who ran (or owned, or managed) the gallery where Clelia worked. Clara was not at all sure what a gallery was, but from the conversation she managed to deduce that it dealt in paintings, and unlike the

Tate and the National Gallery, dealt commercially. Clelia worked there because she painted: also because her parents pulled strings: also because she had been to art school: also because she had some highly inexplicit connexion with Martin. All these explanations were proffered, haphazardly, one on top of the other, and from the excess of explanation Clara concluded that a job in a gallery such as Clelia's must be something of a sinecure, and that Clelia's attitude towards it was not wholly happy. The nature of her job there was, to Clara, wholly obscure, but then the nature of most jobs was obscure to her.

Martin had managed to inspire some kind of admiration in Clelia, and had enlisted her sympathy in the cause of his dissolving marriage. 'It wasn't that I was in *love* with him, you know,' she said, from time to time, as chorus to her main argument, 'it wasn't as though I was in love with him, you know.' However, love or no love, Martin had arrived at the gallery one morning, with his small baby in his arms, and the news that his wife had left him, and the clear expectation of help of some kind from Clelia. Clelia had provided help, instantly, by holding the baby, and looking after it, and changing, with increasing expertise, its nappy, and then at the end of the day she had invited Martin and his child home. She seemed somewhat defensive about this stage in her narrative, and said, 'Well, after all, what on earth was I to do? He really is so peculiarly helpless, and I couldn't have let him take it home all by himself, could I? I felt I had to do something, he seemed to expect me to do something.'

So Martin and his abandoned baby had moved into the Denham household, and they had moreover stayed there. They had arrived before Christmas, and it was now May.

'We simply don't know what to do about them,' said Clelia. 'It isn't, after all, as though we had any reason for not having them, because now that Amelia and Magnus and Gabriel are all married there's plenty of room, and my parents are anyway worried, politically speaking if you know what I mean, about having so much empty house (though he's hardly the kind of tenant that *that* kind of consideration would provide), and he even pays some rent from time to time. But then, being so rich, he could easily go and live somewhere else. But he doesn't, and my mother won't tell him to go, because she's never in her life told anyone to go, it isn't in her, but he's grinding her into the ground, she can't work, she can't concentrate, he keeps talking to her all the time, and the baby cries, and it upsets her, for all that she keeps saying it doesn't, and that it takes her back to the happiest years of her life, when we were all in plastic pants, I suppose she means, except I think we all had to wear wet woolly leggings, she had this thing about plastic pants being unhealthy.'

'Why doesn't your father tell him to go?' asked Clara, for from what she could recollect of Mr Denham, she could not picture him suffering fools gladly.

'Oh, he just doesn't. He doesn't like to interfere. I think, truly, he thinks I must be in love with him, and he doesn't want to complicate things.'

'But you're not, are you?' said Clara.

'Well, it isn't exactly as though I'm *not*,' said Clelia. 'I mean, it isn't as though I wanted to get rid of him.'

'I see,' said Clara, feeling that maybe indeed she did. Her eyes were rapidly adjusting to such tones.

And then Clelia sighed heavily, and looked sadly at Clara's Japanese wooden egg puzzle, which she had been trying all this while to do, and said, 'How very dull for you, to hear all about my affairs, but I do so like to tell the story of my life, it makes me feel as though things have really happened to me, whereas otherwise they seem not to happen.'

'It wasn't dull,' said Clara, 'there is nothing, nothing that I wanted to hear more.'

'Is that true?' said Clelia, frowning intently at the egg, not risking the raising of her eyes, as though truly diffident, suddenly diffident. 'I am glad if you mean it. I think I must be like my mother, she is always letting herself be interviewed, my father says its vulgar, but she likes it, she likes people coming to ask her questions about herself and how she makes coffee and who she has to dinner and what kind of paper she writes on, she says it makes her feel as though she really has got somewhere in her life. It consoles her, without it she says she feels she hasn't moved. And she likes telling people things, she doesn't mind who she talks to, total strangers, interviewers, so long as its professional, so long as it's not personal. When it's personal, she gets confused. So perhaps I felt I must tell you all this, now, before I know you better, so that I can tell it you without too much confusion. And now I have told you, you must talk now, tell me about yourself.'

'There doesn't seem to be so much to tell,' said Clara.

'How can you say that, how can you say that,' said Clelia, 'by saying that you are condemning me, you're criticizing me, you're implying that I talk too much, God knows I do, but surely you could do better? Do tell me, believe me that in me you have the best audience of your life, you will never find as good an audience as me.'

And so Clara told Clelia, in return, some of her own history, and in telling it, she seemed to find, strangely and more securely than ever a tone that absolved her, a tone that redeemed her past from meanness and humiliations, so that she even found herself able to speak of her own mother without evasion. For Clelia was, as she had claimed, a good audience: she listened with an attention that picked up the faintest vibrations of meaning. And Clara, confident that she would meet with no misunderstanding, managed to relate episodes that she had never before related, and when, finally, she came to the subject of the future, she awaited Clelia's views as though they might even be of use. She even asked her for them; she asked her what she thought she should do.

'What a problem,' said Clelia, contemplating it. 'What about the rest of the family, what about your brothers, don't they help?'

'One of them went to Australia,' said Clara, 'and the other one is married, and lives right the other side of town. She has nobody, she really has nobody.'

'And she thinks you should go home?'

'She doesn't say so, but at times I think she expects me to although she knows I can't. We never talk about it: we never talk about anything though so the fact that we don't talk about that doesn't mean much. But I think, all the same, that she wants me at home, though she doesn't like me, and she could never admit that she might need me . . .'

86

'I know what you should do,' said Clelia, 'you should do a Diploma of Education or whatever it's called. And then you could go on going home for the vacations. They give you money to do those, don't they?'

'I thought of that,' said Clara, 'but I don't know if I would want to teach. And anyway, I don't want to go home for vacations.'

'Evidently not,' said Clelia, 'but evidently you feel you ought. And I consider it unadvisable to lay too great a strain upon one's conscience. Far better to compromise in my view.'

'How extraordinary to hear you say that,' said Clara, 'I was expecting you to say what all my other friends say, that I must clear out quick, be ruthless, cut all ties, leave her to it, live my own life. You know the kind of things that people say.'

'People are always telling other people to do that kind of thing,' said Clelia, 'it must give them a vicarious thrill. Because they never do it themselves, haven't you noticed? I never tell anyone to do anything. I haven't the nerve, I just encourage people to go on doing what they're already doing anyway.'

'But even if I did it,' said Clara, 'I would be stealing the state's money, wouldn't I? By doing a Dip Ed without meaning to teach?'

'Who knows?' said Clelia. 'You might even want to teach at the end of it. And you can't consider everyone, you know. You can't feel for both the State and your mother, can you?'

'As a matter of fact,' said Clara, 'I did put my name down to do a Dip Ed. I thought that anyway it would always come in useful. And kill time, if you see what I mean.'

'So you see,' said Clelia, 'you had made your mind up anyway. You're doing it in London, I trust.'

'Of course,' said Clara, 'where else?'

'Where else indeed?' said Clelia. 'I'm glad you'll be back. And I'm frightfully sorry, but I seem to have completely disorganized this egg. Have I ruined it beyond repair? I used to think I was quite good at that kind of thing . . .'

'It's just a trick, really, it's easy,' said Clara, and she took back the egg, and found that she could not put it together again either, so they decided to abandon it, and left it in little pieces in a glass dish on the mantelpiece with some dry and coloured gourds, and then they went downstairs and out into the park, and walked towards the bus stop, and Clara explained, lest the gourds and the egg should be thought to reflect in any way on herself, that they had been given to her by a friend the week before, to celebrate her twenty-second birthday. It was a dark cloudy day; there had been as yet no spring, and the grass was muddy from constant rain. They waited together at the bus stop for Clelia's bus, and as the bus approached Clelia said, confirming, 'Next Sunday, then, you'll come and see us?' Clara nodded and agreed.

And as Clara walked back towards her college hostel, she thought about Clelia, and wondered whether she dealt out all her friendships with so lavish a hand, or whether, once more in her life, she could count on some peculiar blessing. She had met people of this genre before – intense, smart, well-connected, impulsive, communicative, insatiably interested in the affairs of others – and she would, she supposed, upon interrogation, have classed herself, at least in aspiration, as one of the genre. But she had never before met such qualities so mildly and tactfully and decoratively combined, so settled and established, so kindly displayed. She looked back over her three years at college, now slowly approaching their close, and she thought of all the people she had known and all the friends she had made, and it seemed to her that most of them had been aiming with varying degrees of accuracy at just such an effect. She had, and she felt slightly uneasy about admitting it, she had sought the smartly intense, at the expense of the more solid and dowdy virtues; she had been attracted by surfaces, by clothes and manners and voices and trivial strange graces, and she had imitated what she had seen of these things in others. She was drawn unquestionably to the appearance of things, though she was aware that she had as yet much ground to cover, and that she had followed many a false trail; she remembered with particular regret the quantities of eyeshadow which she had once thought desirable, and the pendant earrings of the same epoch. She also knew that some of her preferences were base in the extreme, and that her affection for Peter de Salis sprang at the first most ignobly from his delightful name. She liked him, too, for being a poet, and for taking her out to things, but she often wondered whether her interest in his poetry were not as superficial as her interest in his name. She seemed to live by an instinct which drew her strongly and on the whole accurately towards such manifestations, such hints and echoes of a grander world, and which yet at the same time could not approve them. But Clelia, she could see, was secure beyond approval or disapproval: she was what she was, whatever that might be.

She looked forward to discovering what it might be, and how it might have been created.

When she got back to the college, she went to the library and looked once more at all the reference books pertaining to Sebastian Denham, in the hope of finding the nature of his wife's professional distinctions, but she was not successful. The biographies were terse and restrained, as far as his private life was concerned, and effusive only about the names and quality of his publications. She thought that she might ring Peter de Salis, and ask him about Mrs Denham, but she did not want to do this, in case Mrs Denham was a lady of such fame that ignorance of her would prove to be positively compromising. So she did nothing. She thought she would wait, and see what happened.

The Denhams' house, like the Maughams' house at 23 Hartley Road, Woodgrove, Northam, was semi-detached. But Clara, upon her first visit, could find no other possible point of resemblance, and even this point she missed, so different was the architecture and the attachment from anything she had ever before approached. It was a large, tall, four storeyed building, on one of the steep hillsides of Highgate; it had been built in 1720, but was deceptively flanked by scrappy houses and miscellaneous buildings of mixed and later dates, so that its lonely eminence had an air of somewhat tragic survival. In front of the building was a large paved double courtyard, which was level, despite the steep gradient of the hill; it was separated from the pavement by a high, elaborate, wrought iron fence, the gate of which stood fortunately open. Clara would not have liked to wrestle with its huge ornate metallic bolt. The building had two front doors, side by side, one for each house, and the steps up to each door were not divided; an urn full of some kind of greenery stood in the middle of the steps, but there was no attempt at distinction. It was this lack of division that most effectively concealed from Clara the basic, classic structure of the building, for she had been brought up with the notion that walls must be above eye-level, lace curtains impenetrable, bedrooms facing discreetly into the void. Once she had visited a friend who had a room in a house in North London; she had accompanied her friend into the small back garden, and had been deeply shocked to find that the walls dividing the row of small terraced gardens were only two feet high. A child could have seen over them: rows of small children were in fact busy looking over them as she stood there, and looking moreover without disguise at her. She retired quickly after her friend into the kitchen, overcome by a sense of invaded privacy; a garden, to her, was not meant for such intimacies.

The door of the Denhams' house was painted black, and it was solid, and heavily panelled; in the centre of the middle panel there was a lion's head with a brass ring in its mouth. There was also a bell, and Clara chose the bell. She had to wait for some time before the door was opened, and she hoped very much that it would be opened by Clelia, but it was not; it was opened by a thin, brown, balding, youngish looking man. He looked at her, and said nothing.

'I've come to see Clelia,' said Clara, standing on the door-step.

The man gulped nervously, and nodded, and said, 'Clelia, oh yes, Clelia, just a moment, I'll go and get her.'

And he disappeared. Clara, uninvited, thought she might as well step in, so she did. The hall into which she stepped was not a hall at all, but a large and very high room, with doors leading off it in most directions, and it was so full of unexpected things that she found it hard to know where to look first. The floor was tiled, in diagonal squares of grey and white marble, and the walls were so densely covered with pictures and looking glasses that it was hard to tell whether or how they were papered, but the general tone and impression was of a deep purple and red. At the far end of the hall there was a marble fireplace, and under it was a large pot of dying flowers and a very beautiful rocking horse. The petals of the flowers had dropped, and spilled brown and carelessly over the floor. There was also, she vaguely noted, in one corner a piano, and the windows had shutters of a kind that she had never seen in England.

After a while, Clelia appeared, from one of the doors at the far end of the hall. She was wearing glasses, and trousers, and a pink shirt with embroidered flowers, and she looked rather frightening, and Clara half wished that she had not come. As she approached, Clara thought that she still looked cross, but she could see that whatever annoyance was there was not directed against herself.

'Well, I came,' she said.

'So I see,' said Clelia. 'I'm glad you came. It's been a most shocking day so far, quite shocking. Let's go up into my room, the garden's full of Martin and my mother squabbling. Or not squabbling. We can watch them through the window.'

'Who was that that let me in?' said Clara, following Clelia meekly up the staircase, and up and up, to the second floor.

'That was Martin,' said Clelia. 'What did you think of him? He's rather lovely, don't you think?'

Clara could not think of any scheme in which the man she had just seen could have been described as lovely, but she instantly invented one.

'Yes,' she said.

'And this,' said Clelia, suddenly throwing open a high white door, 'is my room.'

And she said it with such pride and such display that Clara did not feel at all obliged to conceal the amazement and delight that she felt, as she might, if confronted with a more worldly modesty, have done: for Clelia's manner declared, this is singular, this is beautiful, this may legitimately amaze, you betray no innocence in admiring this.

And it was, by any standards, amazing. It was a tall, square room, facing towards the back of the house and garden, and it was full and overflowing with a profusion of the most diverse and wonderful objects, so full that the room's function – for it was, beneath all, a bedroom – was all but concealed. Clara,

91

when she looked hard, could just descry a bed, almost lost beneath a grey and pink flowered cover, a heap of books, and a large half-painted canvas. There were a good many books in the room; one wall was lined with them, and they lay in heaps on chairs and on the floor. There was a plant, which grew and blossomed along the picture rail, and climbed down a picture cord to embrace the frame of a small oil painting of naked nymphs; there was the end of a brass bedstead, upon which other plants clambered and flowered. There were photographs and postcards and letters pinned up and pasted on tables and walls, and amongst these more adult decorations, there was also a great quantity of carefully arranged and ancient toys, of a precise and coloured charm; there was a doll's house, a glass jar of marbles, a toy iron on a small brass stand, a heap of rag dolls, a row of painted wooden Russian dolls, a nest of coloured eggs, a tower of bricks, a weather house, a huge pendant snowstorm globe containing a small palace and a small forest with small ferny trees. Clara was staggered and bewitched; she had never in her life seen anything like it. Such a vision had never so much as crossed her mind. Some of her friends had fairly eccentric ideas of bed-sitter decoration, and had done far better than the Chianti-bottle, British Railway-poster effort, but none of them had ever conceived of anything like this: and the nicest room she had ever seen had been the drawing room of a friend's mother in Sevenoaks, which had been distinguished by a bare and gentle colour scheme, and some pretty Georgian furniture.

It was not for some time, and after some acquaintance, that she got round to thinking that one of the most charming features of Clelia's room was its sense of prolonged nursery associations. The childhood objects were not only lovely in themselves, they were a link with some past and pleasantly remembered time, a time not violently shrugged off and rejected, but a time to be lived with, in happy recollection, a time which could well bear remembering.

Clelia did not pretend not to be delighted by Clara's delight. 'I'm so glad you like it,' she said. 'I think it's so lovely. I like it so much. Some people think that it goes too far, but I don't see that it does, do you?'

'I don't see how you can go too far, in the right direction,' said Clara, not for the sake of saying it, but because, on some level, she profoundly believed it to be true.

They stayed in the bedroom for half an hour or so, talking, looking at the things, talking: and Clara remembered thinking at the time that it was just such a honey-suckle-filtered, sunny conversational afternoon that would in years to come, whatever those years might bring, cause her the most sad and exquisite nostalgia. She was sad in advance, and yet at the same time all the happier, doubly happy, for knowing that she recognized her happiness, that it was not slipping by her unheeded, for knowing that she was creating for herself a past. She found Clelia's company extraordinarily entertaining, and bracing only in so far as she liked to be braced: she could hardly follow a word, for instance, of the art references in her conversation, but Clelia managed somehow to combine a great air of erudition and abstruseness with a marked facility for making explanations, so that ignorance was no bar to amusement. She was puzzled only by the unmistakable largesse of the confidence proffered to her, because try as she might, she could not persuade herself that Clelia could talk like this, so wittily and intimately and inquiringly, to everyone; she could not believe that she could talk like this to many. And she even dropped from time to time the odd and flattering hint about the unique nature of her interest. So that Clara, although she found it hard to believe that she herself was thus chosen, had no alternative to believing it. And once she had admitted that it might be possible, she could see that all the evidence pointed clearly in that one direction. So she thought that she might take it on trust. For, after all, it was not humility that restrained her from believing herself to be at first sight infinitely interesting, for she believed herself to be the equal even of Clelia Denham: it was simply a deference to the law of probability. And the law of probability seemed, for once, to have slipped up, and to have permitted her a striking piece of good luck.

Clara's first glance of Candida Denham was through Clelia's high bedroom window. From this vantage point, she could not see much, except the top of her head, and the colour of her clothes. She was sitting on a rug on the long narrow lawn which lay behind the house, with a pile of books and a baby. Her hair was black, like her daughter's, and seemed to be cut in much the same shape, and she was wearing a purple dress. The baby was wearing a pink frilly garment on its top half, and nothing at all, as far as she could see, on its bottom half, but she could not see very well. From the pink frilly garment, Clara would have deduced that the baby must be a girl, but she clearly remembered that it was called James. The baby's father, who was the man called Martin, was sitting a little way off on a deckchair, chewing an unlit pipe, and reading one of the Sunday papers. There seemed to be no signs of a squabble, but Clara was herself familiar with silent domestic altercation, and was willing to believe that the charmingly grouped apparent peace of the scene belied its true character.

'It's quite a nice garden, really,' said Clelia, watching. 'There's another bit, on a lower level – there are some steps going down. And there are steps going down from the drawing room, and up from the dining room. It's because of the steepness of the hill, it's all terraced. People can never get used to the levels. When we were little we were only allowed to play on the lower bit, in case we fell over this top wall, and it was like a dirt track down there, with bikes and trucks and lord knows what. And we all used to climb up and fall over the top anyway. Gabriel had five stitches, and he's still got a scar. But I suppose it kept the bikes off the top bit. They're trying to make the bottom bit look decent now, they keep buying things for it, but it never looks right ... you can't see it from here, we'll go out and look at the garden after tea.'

And as she spoke, Mrs Denham, in the garden below, suddenly leaped to her feet, and started gathering up her things; they could not catch what she was saying, but she seemed faintly agitated, and Martin too got to his feet, though not with any movement that could be described as a leap, and appeared to offer, though ineffectively, to help with his baby. Mrs Denham refused his offer, and tucked the baby under one arm, and started to drag the blanket she had been sitting on after her into the house. Martin offered to have that too, but was instructed to pick up her books instead, so he did. And they all went in.

'I think it must be tea time,' said Clelia. 'I think we'd better go down.'

And Clara, as she went down, felt that perhaps her nervousness was just about to outweigh her anticipation. She hoped very much that it would not, for she wanted to enjoy herself: she hoped that Mrs Denham would not be alarming. She felt suddenly, hopelessly guilty for not having found out all about Mrs Denham before arriving. And she also felt slightly nervous lest the large house should suddenly disgorge many other hidden residents, for what would she do if suddenly confronted, at one go, with Amelia, Magnus, Gabriel, and Annunciata, and all their varying wives and husbands?

But when they reached the drawing room, the only people there were Mrs Denham and Martin, and the baby, which was sitting in a high chair.

'Hello,' said Mrs Denham. 'There you both are. I wondered if you were coming down.'

'This is Clara, mama,' said Clelia.

'Clara, yes,' said Mrs Denham. 'Clelia told me about you. Do sit down, have a cup of tea. I would have called Clelia Clara if I'd thought of it, but I didn't. But I'm sure that that was what I was somehow looking for. To go with Amelia. But then I got led astray, and went and did that awful thing to poor Annunciata.'

'I think Annunciata is a beautiful name,' said Clelia, taking up once more what was quite evidently a familiar theme. 'And she truly likes it, you know, herself. She always did.'

'I think I must have been mad,' said Mrs Denham, taking off the tea pot lid and staring nervously into its smoky silver depths. 'And they went and called her Nancy at school. Like something out of *Swallows and Amazons*. Clelia, give James a crust, he's just about to start to moan.'

And sure enough, just as Clelia ripped a crust from a piece of bread and butter, the baby started to make groaning hungry noises, clenching and unclenching its fists, with histrionic desire.

'I'm not at all pleased with James,' said Mrs Denham. 'He's just peed all over my review copy of that book on Fanny Burney. And I was going to sell it to Harrods, it's such an awful book, I really had decided to sell it to Harrods. But I don't suppose Harrods will want it now James has peed on it, will they?'

'You shouldn't let him lie around without his nappy on,' said Clelia severely.

'Oh, I don't know,' said Mrs Denham. 'I feel so sorry for them, all bundled up and soggy. And when it's such a fine day, for once, one ought to let them kick. It was my fault, I shouldn't have let him be so near. Girls are so much easier, if you put them on a blanket at least all they do is wet it. But boys have such a long range, Clelia, do pick up that crust. No, give it back to him, he won't mind. I'm sure he didn't mean to drop it. Clara, will you have milk or lemon?'

'Lemon, please,' said Clara. And as she stirred her cup of tea, and sipped it, she lost track of the conversation entirely, so engrossed was she in the visual aspect of the scene presented to her: she did not know where first to look, so dazzling and amazing were the objects and vistas and arrangements before her. The room itself would have been enough to efface any human material less striking than Clelia's mother, and it did indeed more or less totally efface the unobtrusive Martin, who sat quietly dissociated, perched on the edge of a gilt-framed armchair, looking as though he did not quite mean to be there. It was a large, high, long room, and so full of furniture and mirrors and pictures and books and chandeliers and hangings and refracted angles of light that the eye could at first glimpse in no way assess its dimensions; it was like some infinitely more complicated and elaborate and intentional version of the hall which Clara had first entered. It seemed to be full of alcoves and angles and small grouped areas of being, though the room itself was a plain rectangle: fish swam in a high globe, a monstrously enlarged goldfish bowl on top of a bookcase, and flowers and foliage stood on small pedestals here and there. Over the marble mantelpiece was a huge oval gold mirror, with an eagle adorning it, and beneath it two gilt and delicate sprays of candle brackets. The floor was wooden, and polished, but most of it was covered by a large, intricately patterned and badly frayed coloured carpet. On one wall hung a large picture of a classical, mythological nature: on another wall was an equally large picture of undulating pale yellow and beige lines.

The third wall was lined entirely with books, and the wall that looked over the garden was not a wall but a window, heavily shrouded with curtains of different fabrics and densities. Clara was astonished; she could compare the room to nothing in her experience, nothing at all, unless it were perhaps to those studiously, tediously visited ancient homes which she had been round on various bank holidays during her childhood. And having arrived at so much in the way of a comparison, she saw, suddenly revealed to her, how much there had been in those other rooms to admire. She had always disliked them, had never for a moment been able to see their virtues; she had been bored by the classical, and had felt a positive, righteous contempt for the baroque and the neo-Gothic. She had thought the quantities of gilt (never did she credit that it might be real gold) an evidence of shocking vulgarity, had sneered at the bad taste of the ornate picture frames, at the ridiculous excesses of the pictures themselves, and had felt a solid, suburban scorn for the frayed and patched tapestry chair seats and the faded hangings : she had wondered why, if so rich, they did not throw out their tatty Persian coverings, and buy themselves a good bit of fitted Wilton or Axminster in a good plain colour. And now, suddenly, stunningly confronted, she saw, if not the details, at least the nature of her errors. For this room was the real thing : so much was unmistakable. Just as Clelia's particular combination of virtues could never have been arrived at by fraud, so this room could never have been created out of ignorance or servile imitations. And if this room was real, so might the others have been. The aristocratic ideal was vindicated. She stared at the golden eagle, so arrogantly and eternally poised, and wondered why she had ever thought birds on furniture were a bit off : why had she never bothered to look, why had she never asked herself what her eyes had told her? Why had she had to wait for such an education? The eagle was so evidently, so ferociously beautiful; one would have thought that it could have impressed itself upon the most unwilling beholder. She wondered how many other such eagles she had blindly passed.

Mrs Denham herself made a fitting occupant for such a room, poised equally between frayed charm and the austere splendour of riches. After the initiation of Clelia, she was to

Clara less surprising than she might otherwise have been, for the resemblance between mother and daughter was marked: the features were the same, though worn and lined by grooves deeper than mere wrinkles: the set of the conscious, curious head was the same, and the hair was the same, though streaked with white, and hanging with the benefits of expense, as well as of style. Clara had never seen such securely straight hair on so old a woman; even the more fashion-conscious of the middle aged lecturers at her college were adorned with the permanent waves of their generation. Nor had she ever seen such a dress on anyone over the age of thirty, but seeing it, she had to admit that it did not even look bizarre: it was a pale purple smock, waistless and bustless, with long, much-buttoned sleeves, and yet it managed to give only the faintest, most delicate air of Bohemia. Mrs Denham wore heavily-rimmed glasses, and she took them off from time to time, restlessly, as she talked: the crows' feet round her eyes were deeply scored, and her eyes without their glasses had a distant, worried look, as though committed to far other fields of concentration. And yet, when she talked, she seemed to be there, and with them; she did not seem to be elsewhere.

She talked of books, from what Clara, in her haze of observation, could hear: about some books that she was, ah yes, what was that word, reviewing? a critic, then? No, not a critic: her attitude to her present undertaking was too anxious, too casual, to be the attitude of a weekly employee. A writer, then, perhaps: and Clara, searching for help, directed her excellent vision at the distant titles of the books on the shelves behind Martin's head. And help was forthcoming, for there was a whole row of somehow familiar books, and the name on the back, she could just decipher it, was Candida something, why yes, of course, Candida Gray, she saw it with a flash of inspiration, for it had never occurred to her to look for a surname other than the one that she already knew. Candida Gray, Candida Gray, a name that she had known for as many years as she had known any such names; she had not read as many of the novels as she ought to have done, but she had read one at least, and that one she actually remembered. In the sudden satisfaction of recognition, Clara nearly cried out, into the midst of the conversation, I read your book, I read that book of yours, I read *Custom and Ceremony*: but she didn't, she kept quiet, she did not want to betray, even directly, the novelty of her discovery. And she thought, a little aggrieved: I do think Clelia might have told me, how could she assume that I knew her mother's maiden name? Or does everyone know such things but me? Of course they don't, and she should have known that if anyone didn't, it would be me. This is what she said to herself, but at the same time she was alarmed, faintly alarmed by the implication that everyone did know such things. She had a long way, still, to go.

Her discovery did, however, although belated, do much to help her understanding of the conversation: references hitherto obscure became suddenly clear. She began to feel that she knew where she was, a little: and after a while she too began to talk. And they talked to her, most politely: the Martin man asked her when she was doing her Finals, and she told him, and he asked her what she was going to do then, and she said that she thought she would do a teacher's training course.

'But will you teach?' asked Mrs Denham anxiously.

'I don't suppose so,' said Clara, 'but it makes a qualification, doesn't it?'

'I used to teach,' said Mrs Denham, 'but I was always so afraid of being boring that I could never talk for long enough. One has to do so much talking, and I don't like talking. Or only to people. I suppose you will probably get married, will you?'

'I never seem to feel like getting married,' said Clara.

'That's what Clelia says,' said Mrs Denham. 'And she has good reason to say so when she looks at what has happened to all the rest of them.'

'Why, what has happened to them?' said Clara, who felt such a question to be not impertinent but positively requested.

'They all got married,' said Mrs Denham, 'all except the little one, and she's still at Oxford. The eldest one couldn't have children, and quarrels with her husband, and has gone dotty because she can't have children, and wanders around in a very odd coat all the time. She lives in the country, it must be a mistake. Then the second one got married, and he's got four children, and the third got married, and he's got three children, and they're both going dotty because they've got too many. Aren't they, Clelia?'

'No more than most other people, I don't suppose,' said Clelia.

'But you must admit,' said her mother, 'that it's put you off.'

'No it hasn't,' said Clelia. 'And look at me, I've managed to pick up a baby without even getting married, haven't I, Jamesie?' And she gave the baby a lump of sugar.

'The maternal impulse in your family tends to run riot,' said Martin, 'don't you think?'

'And a good thing for you that it does,' said Clelia, with a sudden asperity, 'or you'd be out on your ear.'

She said this with a certain violence, and Clara's attention quickened, for she thought she was about to witness the emergence of one of the buried conflicts of which she had heard so much: but Mrs Denham said quickly, 'For goodness *sake*, Clelia, you know how good it is for me to have James around, it takes me back to those lovely days when you were all so small and docile.'

'What rubbish,' said Clelia. 'You know he gets on your nerves.'

'No he doesn't,' said Mrs Denham. 'I like babies, why do you think I had so many? And he's a kind of consolation prize to me, in my change of life.'

'I'm sure you didn't have so many because you *liked* them,' said Clelia. 'You used to shout at us all the time.'

'Why, as a matter of interest,' said Martin, calmly, as though the discussion up to this point had been quite unreliable, '*did* you have so many children, Candida?' and Mrs Denham, strangely, took off her glasses, and frowned, and began to speak as though she had indeed up to this point been talking nonsense.

'I really can't quite decide,' she said. 'Why do you think it can have been? In a way, I think it was a kind of *pride* that did it. I had two, and then Gabriel was an accident, and somehow the thought that he was an accident was so insulting to me that I had to have some more, to prove that he wasn't. Everyone *thinks* Annunciata was an accident, being so much younger than Clelia, but she wasn't, I had to work terribly hard to get Annunciata. So I must have wanted them, you see. For some reason. Or another.'

'You like to tell people,' said Clelia, 'that you've had five children. Because you like to see them gasp in amazement. And then start to flatter you about how thin you are, and how productive you are, and all that. Don't you?'

'I suppose I must,' said Mrs Denham. 'But it doesn't seem a very good reason, does it? I mean, it sounds more like a justification than a reason. And then, you see, it's always such a wonderful excuse. For not having done other things.'

'How vain you are,' said Martin.

'But it's true,' said Mrs Denham, 'that I really do like to have James. Otherwise I would surely have sent you packing, wouldn't I? It must be because I need him. It's nice to have a baby in the house again. Clelia, would you mind making his bottle?'

'Martin, you go and make his bottle,' said Clelia.

'Must I really?' said Martin.

'Yes, you must,' said Clelia.

'Oh, all right,' said Martin, and got up and went.

'He gets worse and worse,' said Clelia, when he had gone. 'Why on earth don't you back me up when I try to get rid of him, mother?'

'It seems so crude, somehow,' said Mrs Denham. 'Just getting rid of him.'

'You might at least ask him to go and make his own baby's bottle,' said Clelia.

'It's all very well, but I'm sure he doesn't boil the milk. I'm sure he just heats it, I'm sure he doesn't actually boil it. I only ask you to do it because I know you'll do it properly.'

'What happened to his wife?' said Clara, not for the sake of asking, but because she really wanted to know. Clelia and her mother looked at each other blankly, and 'We don't know,' they said, 'we never like to ask.'

When Martin returned with the bottle, Mrs Denham picked the baby out of his chair, and settled back with him in her arms. 'Do let me give it him,' she said. 'Do let me, I like to hear him suck. Go and show Clara the garden.'

And they went. They went through the French window at the end of the room, and down the stone steps into the garden. When they got there, Clelia said to Martin, 'You really do get on her nerves, you know. She's not joking.'

'I know I get on her nerves,' said Martin. 'But she likes things on her nerves.'

'Not things like you,' said Clelia.

'Anyway, she likes James,' said Martin.

'Of course she likes James, I mean to say, there's nothing to *dis*like in James, is there? She likes all babies, you can see her outside the fishmonger's peering into other people's prams. But that's no reason for taking advantage of her weak points.'

'She's not a child herself,' said Martin. 'And when she says she wants a baby in the house, I do her the credit of believing her.'

'Well, that's very hypocritical of you,' said Clelia, 'because you know quite well that she only wants to have James so as not to hurt your feelings. She's getting old now, she's fifty next year, she doesn't want to run around making bottles and changing nappies. And she's got quite enough grandchildren without having to borrow other people's spare babies.'

'Why should she care about my feelings?' said Martin.

'Goodness me, don't start taking *that* as a compliment, she cares about everyone's feelings, she's an archetypal victim, she's an absolute fool about other people's feelings, and let me warn you, I may as well warn you, the more she *dislikes* somebody, the more somebody *annoys* her, the more careful she is *not* to hurt their feelings, in fact the only people she is ever rude to are people like me and Gabriel and Papa, I mean people she cares for enough not to worry about being *fair* to. My goodness, Clara, how frightfully boring for you, how can you bear to listen to us. Let's go to the end of the garden and look at the ghastly thing that Martin flogged us.'

'It isn't boring at all,' said Clara, truthfully. 'I find it quite enlightening.'

'Enlightening, enlightening,' said Clelia, 'I don't at all like the sound of that word. I don't want you to find things out about *me*, I don't want you to stop liking me.'

'Enlightenment,' said Martin, reaching for Clelia's arm, 'can only endear you. The more one sees of you, the more . . .'

'Oh, lay off,' said Clelia, and pulled away from him, and skipped a few steps on the green short grass, and then did rather a professional cartwheel. 'Can you do cartwheels, Clara?'

'I can,' said Clara, 'but I won't because my pants would show.'

And she followed Clelia, more decorously, to the end of the garden. At the end of the lawn there was a sundial; they looked at it and it had got the time right. 'I'm always amazed,' said Clelia, 'to find the sun is so reliable.'

Behind the sundial there were a few trees, some of them in flower: a small path led into their deceptive shallow depths, and there, in a hollow a few yards from a high brick wall that bordered the garden, stood a sculpture. The trees grew closely round it, and willow-like fronds drooped upon it; it was made partly of bronze, and the bronze had taken on the colour of green bark.

'We tried to hide it,' said Clelia, and laughed. 'We shoved it down here because we wanted to hide it. It's quite horrible, really. But you can't see it properly here. You can't see how bad it really is.'

'I wouldn't know,' said Clara, 'whether it were bad or not. But it looks quite pretty with all the leaves.' And she stared at it, glad to have been told that it was not good, for she could make nothing of it: it stood about five feet high, on a stone lump, and it had holes in it and stretching arms.

'Look inside,' said Clelia. 'Look inside, through the holes.'

And Clara went and put her eye to the hole, and inside the block swam sadly a drowned lady, some seaweed, and an orange.

'How strange,' said Clara, stepping back from it. 'I think I rather like it. How do they make it look so huge inside? Who made it?'

'It's all done by mirrors,' said Martin, and Clelia said, 'it was made by an awful Frenchman that Martin discovered, wasn't it, darling? Though I will say this for you, my love –' and here she put her arm most affectionately round his waist, 'in the years I've known you, he's been your only *real* disaster.' And, turning to Clara, 'His taste is most remarkable, you know. Really remarkable.'

'He was such a charming fellow,' said Martin. 'And I thought some people might like them.'

'But nobody liked them,' said Clelia. 'Nobody at all.'

'Whyever did you buy it then?' said Clara.

'My mother bought it,' said Clelia. 'He got round my mother. She wanted something for the garden. So he told her how marvellous it was, and how misunderstood this wretched Frenchman was, and she bought it. It was thoroughly unscrupulous.'

'No it wasn't,' said Martin. 'She knew quite well it wasn't worth what she paid for it.'

'That doesn't make any difference,' said Clelia. 'Just because she does it with her eyes open. That doesn't make it any better. It was lucky we had enough trees to hide it in.'

'It isn't as bad as all that,' said Martin. 'It's nothing to be ashamed of ... It's better than that junk she's got on the lower level. And I know what she paid for that too.'

'The trouble with you,' said Clelia, 'is that you don't appreciate the distinction between the decorative and the creative arts. It may be junk, but it looks all right in a garden. You don't understand. Look what a frightful sight your flat used to be. All those white walls and contemporary curtains. And I mean to say, who would want to live in your gallery?'

'I always thought that gardens,' said Clara, as they progressed slowly back along the long stretch of grass, and down the steps to the lower level, 'I always thought that gardens were for growing flowers in. But you don't seem to have much in the way of flowers here.'

'We don't go in for flowers,' said Clelia, displaying with a sweep of her arm the lower level, curiously cluttered with urns, a bench, a dislocated piece of mosaic resting on its end, and a functionless fountain. 'We don't understand flowers, we can never remember their names. And we're too lazy to do any gardening. You don't have to bother with all this stuff, you just leave it, to grow weeds. It doesn't need any attention.'

'I see,' said Clara, descending: and she thought of the square flat patch that extended beyond her mother's house at home, and of the grudgingly mown grass, and the dutifully weeded herbaceous borders, and the complaints about neighbouring cats and dogs that would come and dig in the unrewarding earth. Her family did not much understand gardening either, and took little pleasure in the fruit of their unskilled, social labours; as far back as she could remember, Clara could recollect her mother's perpetual nagging at her father to cut the lawn, her father's occasional outburst of resentment against the boys who trampled on the borders. It never looked very impressive, at the best of times, though in spring the daffodils would lend it a brief colour: all the plants were dirty, with the insidious industrial grime, and the evergreens were particularly filthy. She remembered the leaves of the laurel, a thick, tough, leathery spotted green and yellow: she was obliged, through ignorant association, and through a learning far wider than her experience, to picture poets and emperors crowned with such grim suburban foliage. The garden's sole glory was a laburnum, which blossomed wonderfully each year: but even that she associated more with its dry black fatal pods than with its flowers, so often and so rigorously had she been warned of its poison. When her father died, her mother continued to look after the garden, though Alan would come home at weekends, even after his marriage, to mow the lawn; it gave her so little enjoyment that Clara wondered why she did not let it go to seed. There was a widower, two doors away, whose garden had done just that: he never touched it, and grass grew feet thick all over it, and weeds flourished, and roses climbed the hedge, unpruned, and ramped across the soil. Mrs Maugham would often abuse this garden and the widower's laziness, with a self-righteous, alarming complacency, saying that it was a scandal and a disgrace, and that it ought not to be allowed: and when one day Clara, exasperated, as she sometimes rashly was, out of her usual silence, asked her what harm it was doing anybody, Mrs Maugham had snapped triumphantly that it was harming everybody in the street, because it helped the weeds to spread. 'You can see them,' she said bitterly, 'all those dandelions and thistles, and all that bindweed growing under the fence. It's a blot on the whole neighbourhood, that's what it is.' And Clara, abashed, had retreated into silence, because she could see that it was true. One could not rot peacefully and harmlessly, in such a neighbourhood: the airy seeds of debility would float too easily over the garden walls.

The Denhams' garden seemed to have no walls, so thoroughly were its boundaries screened and disguised. Clara liked it, as she had liked everything that afternoon, but even as she stood there and admired, and heard the history of the lump of mosaic, and listened to Martin's views on Candida's view on the social connotations of goldfish, she began to feel a sense of overwhelming fatigue. Her head ached: she could encompass no more. She felt as she felt at the end of some long and erudite lecture in a foreign tongue; her mind would no longer pay attention. Whole concepts, whole reorganizations of thought swam drunkenly through her head, and lurched and revolved like the drowned woman and her orange: she no longer knew what gardens and houses were for, and their distinctions, once clear, had grown confused. She followed Martin and Clelia into the house, and drank, eventually, a large gin and tonic, and then she went home on the bus, and when she got home she was suddenly and violently sick. She could not assimilate, however hard she willed to do so, such strange food: and she woke in the morning hungry, but with her head still aching.

Chapter 6

The sense of exhaustion which the Denhams produced in Clara took some time to wear away, and she grew accustomed to leaving their house with a headache and with a sense of familiar fatigue, as though she had walked for too long, and made too much conscious effort of application in front of works of art arranged in some peculiarly absorbing art gallery. She wanted to see, but the things that she saw were too much for her; her mind stretched and cracked in an effort to take them in. It was not that they did not make her welcome; indeed, she suspected from time to time that it was the warmth of their emotion as much as the strangeness of their ways that tired her. She was not used to such interest, such demonstrations, such inquiries, such overwhelming faculties of sympathetic recollection. Nor was she used to so large a family. Her own home, even when it had contained, at its fullest point, two parents and three children, had always given the impression of silent pockets of isolated, self-contained, repellent activity: the children had lived as much as possible behind closed bedroom doors. Whereas the Denhams seemed to be perpetually, intricately, shiftingly involved, each with the other, and each with a whole circle of cross-threaded connexions. It did not take Clara long to notice that Martin was as much taken with Clelia's mother as with Clelia, and she thought she once surprised in Sebastian Denham's eye a glance, directed towards herself, that she would never have expected from so old a man. Such mingling of the generations confused her, although it filled her, at the same time, with hope, for had she not always known that life did not, need not end so grimly and so abruptly?

The relationships between the brothers and the sisters were also a revelation to her. The feelings between them were peculiarly intense; their concern for each other was unfailing, and they spoke of each other with absorbed and passionate affection. Only the unfortunate eldest, Amelia, was excluded from the close circle of mutual admiration, and she had cut herself off, had deserted them, had gone away with a dreadful man to live in the country. They mourned over her, and recalled together the happy past before her severance, and discussed her plight with endless solicitude, but to no avail; though constantly invited, she never came. And Mrs Denham, when she spoke of Amelia, which she often did, as though in nervous, restless propitiation, would seem overcast by some real shadow, a shadow that for Clara merely heightened the radiant intimacy of those that remained. She had never in her life seen or heard of such a mother, a mother capable of such pleasant, witty and overt concern, nor had she ever seen an image of fraternal love. She had read of it, in the classics, as she had read of human sacrifices and necrophilia and incest, but she had not thought to see it with her own eyes.

She never met Amelia, but she met all the others. She met them gradually, by means of a photograph album. Had she not been past astonishment, she would have been astonished when Mrs Denham, after supper on the first whole evening that she spent with them (an evening specially arranged, or so they managed to make it seem, to celebrate the end of her examinations) had produced this photograph album, for she had always been taught that such objects were marks of vulgarity, manifestations of the worst possible taste, as fatally revealing as a pet Alsatian dog on the windowsill or ferrets in the back yard. Her own mother had had much to say on the subject of pricey albums entitled 'My First Baby' or 'Our Wedding Day' purchased by other residents in Hartley Road. But the Denhams seemed gaily unaware of the dreadful risk that they were running, and Clara, looking with Clelia and her mother at the strange pages of strange photographs, could see that they had little to lose. The pictures were a weird mélange; some of them were classical family groups, of weddings and christenings and birthdays; some of them were amateur holiday snapshots; some were highly glossy, highly expensive posed pieces, of Mrs Denham at her typewriter, Mr Denham by a garden urn, Mrs Denham with a baby on her knee; and some were photos cut out of newspapers and magazines. Clara stared at them, enthralled. She did not know which amazed her more, the pictures of Mrs Denham holding some lace-trailing infant with all the gravity of tradition behind her, or the pictures of small children disporting themselves in classy sunhats on the beaches of southern Europe. It was by means of these photographs that she finally managed to sort the family out: the two eldest, Amelia and Magnus, closely resembled their father, being tall and heavily built, whereas the three younger ones, Gabriel, Clelia and Annunciata, were all amazingly alike. The same face stared out of all their photographs, the same distinctive face. The similarity startled her, for she had thought that Clelia must be unique. There was one photograph in particular that caught the whole family, in sudden clarity: it had been cut out of a glossy magazine, together with its caption, and the caption said:

Candida Gray, seen here with all the proof of her creativity over the last twelve years, including her newest production, *A Fall from Grace*, published by Walter Bruce and Co. Ltd, and her newest baby, Annunciata. The three youngest children are wearing clothes by Hesther Laprade, whose new shop, *L'enfant gâté*, opens this week.

And the picture showed Candida, sitting in the very armchair in which she was at that moment, sixteen years later, occupying, with a pile of her own books on a small table by her side, a baby on her knee, and four children ranged neatly around her. When Clara exclaimed upon it, and upon the exquisite scowls adorning the faces of the older children, Mrs Denham started to apologize for it, saying that she had never meant to let the children be put in magazines, and that really she did find it a little, yes, just a little embarrassing, to see what she'd allowed to happen, but that she'd only really done it for Hesther's sake, and that it had all been wasted effort anyway, for Hesther was no business woman, and had indeed gone bankrupt, and that all that anyone had profited from it had been her own acquiring of a free set of clothes for Gabriel, Annunciata and Clelia.

'And lovely clothes they were, too,' she said, finally, 'and they wore well too, and I kept them because they were so nice, and Gabriel tells me that their baby looks lovely in Annunciata's dress, though I haven't had a chance to see her in it yet. Pale green, it was, with honeysuckle on, a kind of lawn, I think, rather a bore to iron if I remember rightly, but pretty, quite pretty enough to make it worth it; and if there is anything Phillipa will spend time on, I must admit that it's on clothes.'

The other picture that Clara particularly liked was a posed portrait of Candida with Clelia as a two-year-old, and Gabriel as a small boy by her side. It had been taken on Clelia's second birthday, and it had been taken by one of the very few photographers of whom Clara had ever heard, and who emerged as a friend of the family, as did, peripherally, so many other familiar names, whose faded faces, or truncated limbs, or unintentional back views adorned a large quantity of the holiday snapshots.

'I *think* that must be Eliot,' said Candida, at one point, peering hard at an infinitely receding figure in the pale brown mists at the back of one document from Paris in the thirties: and Scott Fitzgerald, front view, and arm in arm with Candida, was more confidently acclaimed. The posed portrait reminded Clara of paintings that she had seen, with little enthusiasm, in art galleries and ancient monuments, and just as the Denhams' drawing room had reconciled her to so many other dead and empty drawing rooms, so the photograph seemed to breathe life into those tediously scrutinized oil paintings of long aged and dead small children. Candida sat there, her back to the long window, and her hair longer than it now was, and piled upon her head: small Clelia, grave and round, in a short dark crochet-collared dress, sat solemnly upon her knee, and her arm and her mother's arm lay side by side, their gentle flesh most softly parallel, in a lovely heap of human shape. Candida's other arm encircled Gabriel who stood by her side frowning, and holding in one hand a wooden ship. Clara seeing it, understood entirely, as she had never understood before, why one should wish to perpetuate such things, and why generation after generation had endeavoured to fix such moments into an eternity. For love, surely, was at the source of such conventional efforts; there had been love and at every stage.

She liked the look of Gabriel. She looked, anxiously, through the more recent pages of the book, in search of his adult image, but he was rather sparsely represented; there were a couple of snapshots of him at Cambridge, looking indistinctly handsome sitting on a wall in front of King's, but the only revealing picture was one which had been taken at the christening of Magnus's first child. Gabriel was, in fact, holding the baby: a baby elaborately draped and swathed in the ancient lace robe of the Denhams' own childhood christenings. Candida had herself been christened in it, she claimed, and it had been embroidered by her own grandmother. Gabriel was not looking at the camera, but at the child, and he was smiling. He looked very promising. As far as one could tell from a photograph, he looked quite alarmingly wonderful. She wondered if it were possible for him to look as wonderful as the camera promised that he might.

There were no pictures of Gabriel's own wedding. Mrs Denham said that as they were only five years old, she had not yet got around to sticking them in, and that they lay somewhere at the bottom of a drawer.

When the album had been put away, Clara, thinking over the world that it had revealed to her, thought that perhaps it dismayed her a little, although it at the same time so strongly attracted her. It was a small rich world, a world of endless celebration and fame, and a world that was gone and past sharing. Advantages blossomed on its pages, and it seemed at moments as though love (and why not?) might be a forced plant, an unnatural flower that could not grow in thinner soil.

The Denhams led her, quite literally, into areas that she had never visited before. She knew Highgate and Hampstead from earlier days and visits to other friends, but she had never set foot in Bond Street, where Clelia's gallery was, and where, from time to time, she visited her. She had had no cause to go there, having no money to spend. And Bond Street seemed in some way to be but a logical extension of the Highgate house, for there in the windows of the shops, in the embroidered evening bags and jewelled trinkets and silken shirts, she found faint, degraded echoes of the charm of the Denhams themselves, and she wondered uneasily if expense were not after all the key to so much charm. Bond Street tired her, as the

Denham's conversation tired her; the streets might have been paved with gold, but they made hard walking, and the sight of the price tags made her feel faint.

Clelia's gallery exhausted her too, though in a different way. It rigorously eschewed the decorative; it was small, select, and very white, and full of a chilly pale intimacy. It specialized in bleak, expensive, fashionable, non-representational paintings: Clelia said that they were all good paintings, and Clara's eyes and imagination ached from the effort of trying to locate their virtues. It was there that she first met Magnus, the eldest brother, who had dropped in for no other reason than to have a chat with his sister; he was, or so Clara had been told, a political economist, but he appeared nevertheless to know a considerable amount about paintings, and discussed the current exhibition with some finesse, finding causes for preference and dislike where she herself could see only indistinct austerity. She did not make much of Magnus; he was too like his father, he offered little, and spoke so quietly and modestly that it was hard to catch what he was saying. When he had gone, Clelia turned to her eagerly and asked her, as was her manner, her views, and Clara hardly knew what to reply. In the end,

'I didn't make much of him,' she honestly said, and Clelia laughed, and said that he was an acquired taste, and that she should wait until she met Gabriel.

Clara spent much time in Clelia's gallery, over the last weeks of her final term. Clelia seemed to like to have her there, as she had no work to do; there were few visitors, and few of those who came wanted to buy, and when they did want to buy Clelia had to send for Martin. So all the time that Clara was not there, Clelia spent in reading novels under the desk. Clara liked to go, because she liked Clelia, and because she found the Bond Street world compelling, irresistible, uniting as it did so much that she desired and mistrusted: they had lunch together, in different places each day, and listened to the conversations of others when they ran out of breath themselves, and Clelia always, deprecatingly, tactfully, disarmingly paid.

And over their mushrooms, risottos and escalopes and chips they vowed, after a manner, an eternal friendship, each being old enough to recognize the rare quality of their communications. When Clara left London for the summer, and returned to Northam, they wrote to each other, long, intimate, witty letters, the kind of letters that Clara fancied she had for years been casting before if not swine at least less than perfect readers; in August Clelia went to Greece for three weeks, but even from Greece she sent postcards. And when, towards the end of September, they both returned to London, Clelia from Athens, and Clara from Northam, each thought of their reunion with satisfaction, and Clara had to acknowledge to herself, and, indeed, in correspondence, deviously, to Clelia, that the thought of Clelia roused more enthusiasm in her than the thought of rejoining any of the other inhabitants of her emotional domain.

It was on her return to London that she met, for the first time, Gabriel. The very evening of her arrival Clelia rang, and after the excited exchange of news asked her to come round.

'Come at once, come instantly,' said Clelia, 'I can't wait to see you, and if you can come this evening you can see Annunciata. Do come this evening because she's off to Oxford tomorrow.'

Clelia managed to imply that the seeing of Annunciata was the greatest treat she could offer, and Clara wondered what it must be like to have relatives that one could thus serve up, with pride, as ornamental additions to one's own confident self.

'I don't know if I ought to come,' said Clara. 'I'm supposed to be unpacking my trunk.'

'Oh, for Christ's sake,' said Clelia. 'Do come, please come, you must come.'

'All right,' said Clara, 'I'll come at once.'

'I'll tell you what,' said Clelia, 'I'll send Gabriel round for you in his car.'

'Oh goodness no,' said Clara, shocked by such magnanimity on another's behalf, 'oh no, I'll come on the bus, it won't take me long.'

'No, no,' said Clelia, 'I'll send Gabriel, just a moment, I'll go and ask him,' and she went off before Clara could protest any further. And when the receiver was picked up, it was Gabriel that spoke.

'Hello,' he said, in a voice that much resembled his sister's.

113

'Hello, Clara. Do let me come and fetch you, because look, it's raining outside. Let me fetch you. Where are you staying?'

And Clara, looking out of the window at the rain, and hearing his voice, and the risky, familiar use of her name by those unseen lips, and feeling the glass of solitude crack instantly at the faint warm enticements of sociability, said yes, all right, and gave him the address of her lodgings. She had found herself a room off the Archway, and when he heard the name of the street, he said,

'But that's no distance at all.'

'No, it isn't,' said Clara, who had chosen the room for precisely such a reason.

'I'll be round in five minutes,' said Gabriel.

And he was. Clara spent the five minutes by changing out of one jersey into another more or less identical one; all her clothes were the same. And during the five minutes she also considered that she would probably fall in love with Gabriel, because a summer in Northam always reduced her to a state where she was ready to fall in love with a taxi driver or the man in the restaurant car on the London train. She viewed the prospect of falling in love with Gabriel with a fatalistic pleasure; she thought that she would enjoy it. The fact that he was already married was to her merely an added enticement, for she had always fancied the idea of a complicated, illicit and disastrous love. She had up to this point spent much time gratuitously complicating various perfectly straightforward affairs with her own contemporaries, in the hope of discovering the true thick brew of real passion, but her efforts had not had much success; she had lacked the ingredients. And after her acquisition of Clelia, earlier that year, she had detached herself entirely from her one thin, current attempt at intrigue with one of her professors: an intrigue which she had fostered more for its lack of orthodoxy than for any progress that it might be expected to make.

So that when Gabriel knocked upon her door, she was positively waiting for him. And she knew as soon as she set eyes upon him that he was what she wanted. Her certainty, as she saw him, seemed to be what she had thought to be love: she stood there, looking at him, and she felt herself move slowly,

114

inch by inch, inevitably, and then with gathering speed, as she fell (and never had the metaphor seemed real to her before), as she fell in love. He was breathtaking: she stood and gaped. He was not tall, not much taller than herself, and his skin was worn, but the shape of his head had the square, solid assurance of extreme symmetry, and although it did not seem possible that anyone so handsome should also be intelligent, it seemed equally impossible that he should not be. He looked like Clelia, there was no denying that he looked like Clelia, and he wore a woollen checked shirt and trousers that were dangerously low on his hips; watching him throughout the evening Clara found it difficult to take her eyes off the shortness of his crutch, and she had to console herself by telling herself that it was clearly intended thus to rivet her attention. She thought that she had never seen anyone so sexy off the cinema screen in her life, and very few on it, and she was amazed that he should be allowed to wander loose around the world; she had always idly assumed that there was some system, some process which selected such people, and removed them safely to some other place, where they were no longer accessible to normal human need, no longer part of the system of chance and meetings, exempt from human imperfections, reserved for their own like only. She had thought that they would live, these heroes and heroines, in some bright celluloid paradise: a paradise from which Gabriel had perhaps fallen, for she might surely never ascend? She had never seen such a person so close, so near; she had seen others, fleetingly, but a mixture of envy and desire had kept her at a distance, she had kept well away from a closer vision of the locked and pearly gates. But Gabriel stood there in front of her, smiling, accessible, full of good will, as mortal as she was mortal, or acknowledging her too as divine. She wondered, as he helped her on with her raincoat, what blessed, superior creature he might have as his wife, and why he had come to fetch her so kindly in the rain.

They did not talk much in the car. He asked her how she had spent the summer, and she said she had done nothing, what had he done, and he said he had been working. She inquired the nature of his work, feeling that such a question, to a member of such a family, could not be impertinent, and indeed knowing already, from Clelia, something of the answer; he said that he worked for one of the largest of the Independent Television companies, and that he had been doing a documentary on the life of Lorca, a subject which would surely interest her, as he knew that she knew Spanish. She did not accept the offered politeness, but asked him, instead, if he enjoyed his work, and he said that he did not like it as much as he had hoped, and that he had to please too many people. She could not see that this would give him much difficulty, though she did not say so, for he had every advantage, every faculty for pleasing, he was Clelia all over again, but lacking even her faint abrasive edge. She could not see that he would arouse in others any oppositions save the oppositions of jealousy.

He aroused in her, sitting by his side in the small estate car, symptoms that she could not mistake. Her flesh stiffened at his nearness; even the skin of her face, the skin of her right cheek fronting him, grew taut from its exposure to his presence. She seemed to feel a sympathetic response, but she told herself that he too, like the rest of his family, must possess an inherited universal sympathy: for what rejections, what repulsions could he ever have received? Surely his every movement all his life, must have been more than eagerly met: and she sat still and rigid, even a little withdrawn, drawing her legs neatly over to her own side of the car, away from his. In the long pauses in their conversation she stared out of the window at the terraced houses, at the drab shops, at the ornate bridge of the Archway itself, averting her eyes from his too lovely profile.

When they arrived, Clelia met them in the hall, and stretched out her arms to Clara and embraced her most tenderly, as a long lost friend, and Clara returned the embrace with equal feeling, amazed and relieved to find that feeling itself could lead quite naturally to such a gesture. She had not been reared upon embraces. She took her place in the rich, diversely-lit evening of the drawing room with a sense that if she belonged anywhere it was as much here as to those long and silent evenings in front of the derided, loquacious television, and the Denham parents and Martin greeted her with flattering, particular familiarity, as though they knew her well, as though the summer had accumulated knowledge between them, instead of

estranging them; Candida asked her how she had found her
mother, and Martin (no longer, she somehow gathered, resi-
dent in the house) asked her whether she had been pleased with
her respectably pleasing examination results, and whether or
not she thought her sessions in his gallery with Clelia might not
have cost her a few marks, to which she said no, that Clelia
could have cost her nothing, could have brought her nothing
but gain. And Mr Denham himself looked at her with recognition, shook her hand with warmth.

She was, however, somewhat taken aback by the sight of
Annunciata, who looked ridiculously like Clelia, in style, in
feature, and even in manner; the matter was made worse by
the fact that they were wearing the same shirt, though over
differently coloured trousers. She resented such similarity, and
she also resented, though pleasurably, the sisters' expansive,
mutual admiration. They displayed each other, they encouraged each other; they spoke about their impending, transient,
trivial separation with real regret. They put their arms around
each other; they laughed, in the same key, at each other's jokes.
Clara had never in her life seen such a vision of sisterly affection: in her part of the world, in her background, sisters were
expected to resent and despise each other, at least until marriage and the binding production of children. Her acquaintances
in Northam, she thought, would have considered such affection
unnatural, and probably perverted, if not wholly insincere, and
there was something in herself that could not help but suspect
it: and yet at the same time it seemed to absolve a whole area
of human relationship, to rescue it, wholesale, from the scruffy
ragbag of the tag ends of family bitterness and domestic con-
flict. And such affection had, surely, its precedents, for were not
sisters classically intended to love, and not to despise one
another? She thought, unaccountably, of Christina Rossetti's
Goblin Market, a poem which she had learned without comprehension but with considerable interest at primary school: she
had always been strangely compelled by the passionate and
erotic relationship described in the poem, so remote from any
of the petty hostilities that she had ever witnessed. Descriptions
and displays of passion had always compelled her, but she had
considered this particular manifestation to be a fabrication, a

117

convenient lie. She began to think that literature did not lie, after all; nothing was too strange to be true.

Nevertheless, despite the interest of such a discovery, she did not like the fact of Annunciata. She resented her, she took the liberty of resenting her, on Clelia's behalf. She did not like to think that Clelia was in any way thinned or dispersed or diluted by such a close resemblance; she wanted her to be unique.

Nor did she like the look of Gabriel's wife. She had hoped against hope that Gabriel's wife would be somehow, in some way, a non-contender, but Gabriel's wife looked capable of contending with anything. She was a thin, tall small-boned girl, with a great deal of very long, thin, flat blonde hair; she looked far too thin to have had, as Clara distinctly remembered, three children. She was pretty, in a pale, neurotic way; her skin had no colour, and she wore no make-up, and her fingers were brown with nicotine. She sat, most precisely, on one end of the large settee, her long legs crossed, and her body twisted from the waist, as she leant on one arm; her angle had a brittle, deliberate elegance, a conscious threat. She smoked incessantly, tapping non-existent ash from the end of her cigarette on to the carpet as she listened; she did not say much, and she listened with an impatient, alien, critical reserve. But what alarmed Clara most of all were her clothes. She was used to the artistically bizarre, and she was tolerably used to the sight, at least, of the expensive, but she had never before been in the same room with so much accumulated fashion. Gabriel's wife looked as though she came off the front page of *Harpers*. Everything was intentional, and everything was new. Her shoes were so new that Clara had not even seen debased versions of them in the shops or magazines; nothing but sheer contemporary novelty could explain their extraordinary, unfamiliar shape. Her stockings were of a shade that Clara had never seen in stockings, a strange greyish-yellow, which she took to be the newest colour available. Her skirt was three inches shorter than anyone else's in the room, and it was made of a curious quilted material which would have made any other woman look fat; her shirt had a strange floppy neckline, that Clara dimly remembered having seen on a poster for a film at King's Cross

118

underground station earlier that day. The whole ensemble was extraordinarily effective, and not a little intimidating. Clara wilted, revived a little when it occurred to her that Phillipa Denham might be or once have been a model, and therefore professionally informed, and then wilted once more when it became clear from the conversation that she had never been any such thing. She preferred the way that Clelia and Annunciata looked, she preferred the style of their house, but there was an assurance, a wealth of successful calculation in Gabriel's wife's appearance that frightened her. She looked au fait, she looked in touch, she looked knowledgeable; she did not look as though she would relinquish anything very easily.

The conversation turned, finally, after detours, to Gabriel's career. He seemed dissatisfied, and his parents, despite all their efforts to the contrary, seemed merely to reinforce his dissatisfactions. 'It's no use,' he said, 'I know quite well what you think of it, you think it's just an easy life, don't you? Go on, admit it, you do, don't you?'

'Absolute nonsense, Gabriel,' said Candida Denham. 'I don't think anything of the sort. I daresay you work very hard.'

'I work a damn sight harder than Clelia,' said Gabriel. 'Clelia just sits at her desk reading books all day.'

'The only trouble with it seems to me,' said Mr Denham, 'that it's neither one thing nor the other. You never appear to know whether it's entertainment or not. Basically.'

'Talking of entertainments,' said Gabriel. 'Matthews was on at me again today. But I said "no".'

'I think you're mad,' said Clelia. 'I'd love to see you on the telly.' And, turning to Clara, she said in her best explanatory manner, 'Gabriel is engaged in a perpetual flirtation with his boss, who thinks he's so lovely he ought to be in front of the cameras instead of behind them, or whatever the phrase is. What is the phrase, Gabriel?'

'Something like that,' said Gabriel.

'And Gabriel keeps on saying no,' said Clelia, 'because he's more than a pretty face. Isn't that right, Gabriel?'

'What do they want you to do, in front of the cameras?' asked Clara.

'Oh, I don't know,' said Gabriel. 'Interview people about things, I suppose.'

'You'd be marvellous at it,' said Clelia. 'Don't you think he'd be marvellous at it, Nancy?'

'Absolutely marvellous,' said Annunciata. 'Absolutely made for it. Honestly, Gabriel, you can't go on hiding your light under a bushel forever. You must let the world see you. How can you deny them?'

'Why don't you want to do it?' said Clara.

'It doesn't seem a sensible idea,' said Gabriel, 'because I am quite clever, too. And I'd rather think than talk.'

'The trouble is,' said Clelia, 'that Gabriel's boss is passionately in love with him, isn't he, Gabriel, he thinks he's the most beautiful thing he's ever seen, and he never lets Gabriel go away anywhere to do anything exciting because he wants to keep an eye on him.'

'Gabriel thinks it's vulgar,' said Annunciata, 'to let people stare at him.'

'I don't care who stares at me,' said Gabriel. 'I quite like being stared at. But one has to think ahead. One has to think about all those children. And people might get tired of staring at me. Even Matthews might get tired of staring at me. And then where would we be?'

'Nobody could *ever* get tired of staring at you,' said Annunciata. 'One would as soon get tired of staring at Marlon Brando. You'd be made, you'd be a millionaire in a year or two, you could send all your children to Eton. You just daren't give in, that's all, you think it's a wicked seduction, you think you ought to work for your money. It's the effect of Magnus, probably. You probably think you ought to work as hard as Magnus. Or Papa. But there's no need, honestly, there's no need. You couldn't go wrong. People would stare at you forever. I bet you never get tired of staring at him, do you, Phillipa?'

And Phillipa, tapping restlessly at her next unlit cigarette, looked up and stared at them all, and smiled slowly and said, 'No, never.' And there the conversation died.

Gabriel and Phillipa drove Clara home, when she said that it was time for her to go; they said that it was on their way, for they lived in Islington, and she thought that Phillipa was glad of an excuse to leave. Clara sat in the front again, as the car had no back doors. She thought, sitting next to him once more, of how beautifully his name reflected his ambivalent nature: she had always assumed that Gabriel was a girl's name, until enlightened by Thomas Hardy, just as she had always as a child assumed that angels were ladies. So beautiful, and with such long hair, what other could they be? And Gabriel, she felt, was drawn in more ways than one: she felt his nature, uncircumscribed, rich, perpetually blessed by the possibility of choice. She was sure that he attracted men and women equally, and what she had heard of his flirtation with the television powers merely confirmed her view that life was to him a perpetual invitation. She wondered what parts of it he chose, graciously, to accept. The revelation of the fact of homosexuality had come to her comparatively late in life, for she was sixteen before Walter Ash helpfully though not entirely accurately pieced together for her the hints and suspicions that she had hitherto received: she remembered clearly the initial shock, and the immediate, instantaneous recovery. For the notion, once the shock was over, attracted her; she liked the thought that such strange things could be, she liked any promise of the eternal devious possibilities of the human passions. She liked areas of doubt. Houses were not houses, gardens were not gardens: plants grew along picture rails, stone tables stood in the garden, and Gabriel with his three children was much loved by a man called (and how shortly, with what disrespectful honour) Matthews. How infinitely preferable was such a world to the world where Walter Ash had grabbed her, sternly, singleminded, with undeflecting simplicity of purpose, amongst the buttercups.

When they dropped her off at her doorway, she thanked them for the lift, and they said, politely, that they hoped that they would see her again. She said she hoped so too, and then she said 'Good night', and went. She had meant to say 'Good night, Gabriel', she had meant to use his name, just as he, smiling, warm, provocative, had used hers, with that note of deliberate intimacy in which his family so much specialized, and which came from him with a sudden breath of danger: 'Good night then, Clara', he had said, as she turned from saluting

Phillipa in the back seat, and she had replied, losing nerve, a simple good night. She regretted it, for she had meant to use his name, as a recognition, to herself, of the fact that she had accepted it, and the system that had chosen it, and the implications that, to her, it carried. It would have meant nothing to him, had she used it, for it was after all his name, a word to which he might be expected to answer: but to her it would have meant much, as much as the facility of the embrace which she had bestowed upon his sister. For these strange names would not pass, try as she would, her unaccustomed lips; she was not ready for them. They sounded as ill in her voice as the accents of a faultily pronounced foreign language. She could not speak them naturally; generations of harsh restraint prevented her. She would have felt foolish, using such words, however far from detection, however much herself admiring them. She had conquered, on the whole, the flat edge of her birthplace; the tones and accents of others came naturally to her now, but their words and phrases sometimes failed her. Endearments failed her: men found her more lavish with acts than with words, and to call anyone 'darling' would have killed her, for to her the term was buried deep in profound layers of ridicule, soft and dead and rotten. She liked to hear it, she liked others to use it, but for her it was dead. And Christian names, even those less rare than Gabriel's, defeated her. She liked Christian names, she liked those who used them as a sign of easy inclusion and intimacy, but to her the use of a name remained a proclamation, an action, an event. She was not accustomed to names. Her parents, friendless, respectable, disconnected, used surnames only; and they spoke of each other, when addressing the children, as 'your father' or 'your mother'. They never, to each other used any form of address or even of courtesy. If in sight of each other, they would look at each other and speak; if not in sight they would merely raise their voices. Their names, whenever she heard them, took her by surprise; her mother was called May and her father was called Albert, but the names were the names of strangers.

She wondered what her mother would have made of Amelia, Magnus, Gabriel, Clelia and Annunciata, let alone Sebastian and Candida. She hardly knew what she thought of them herself; she could not tell whether they were names exotic to the point of absurdity, or whether they were strange to her alone. She thought it possible, perfectly possible, that many people in the world might hear such names, and be seized by not the faintest impulse to laugh or to admire: and yet on the other hand she had sensed from time to time a certain mockery of the family itself towards itself, and had not Mrs Denham herself expressed a doubt that with Annunciata she might have gone too far? What she could not grasp was the notion that a family might deliberately, and without guilt or irresponsibility, choose for its children names not wholly suitable or conventional, for the sake of a whim or an association, or for the sake of beauty or charm. The use of a singularly beautiful or portentous name had always been derided by her mother; names like Helen, Grace or Alexander had been known to cause illplaced mirth. But how, with so fine a sense of distinction and significance, her own mother could have called her Clara, she could neither understand nor forgive. Carelessness might have been forgiven, but not intention. And yet, at the same time, Annunciata might forgive her mother, had she needed to, because the intention was, Clara thought, so innocent, so lacking in harm. And yet, there again, she did not need to, because she would not have minded, however eccentrically christened; she could have worn such a name, as she could have worn Clara's green dress at that dance so many years ago.

Clara often found herself wondering what her mother would think. Such wonder never prevented her from any course of action – on the contrary, she sometimes feared it impelled her – but nevertheless, when drunk or naked, thoughts of her mother would fill her mind. And with the Denhams, these thoughts pressed upon her intolerably. As she lay in bed that night she could not help comparing this evening, the evening of Annunciata's departure for Oxford, with the preceding evening, which had been that of her own departure from Northam for London. Oddly enough, her mother too had asked the family round, though not, as she from time to time declared, through any sense of occasion; she thought occasions unecessary. The family thus invited had consisted of her brother Alan and his wife Kathie, and they had been asked because Mrs

Maugham had wanted to consult Alan about some problem connected with the rates. Clara did not know whether to regret or to rejoice at their arrival; she did not get on well with either of them, and in many ways they subjected her to precisely the same strains as her mother did, and yet on the other hand their presence did not intensify the difficulty of an evening, but somehow dissipated and confused it, so that at least its burden did not rest upon herself alone. And after several weeks of evenings spent largely à deux, she was glad, quite simply, of a little change.

She had always preferred Alan, the younger brother, to the absent emigrated Arthur, largely because he had always been more kind to her; if she could have felt that he liked her, she would have liked him. He worked at a chemical factory on the other side of town; he and his wife lived on an estate about six miles away from their old home, and the distance and their two small children prevented or excused them from visiting Mrs Maugham often. Kathie, as a girl, had lived in the same road, and Clara had once admired her from a distance, for she had seemed the very essence of desirable, attractive, unattainable normality. She had pale red hair, and blue eyes, and freckled white arms that stayed white in the summer; and this colour scheme had for years seemed to Clara to be the mark of beauty itself. Kathie had always managed to hit the very middle of everything; she was neither clever nor stupid, neither tall nor short, neither fat nor thin, and she always wore rather pretty versions of what everyone else was wearing, and read the comics that everyone else was reading, and played tennis with other people, and when she grew older she went to dances to which all other girls save Clara seemed to be invited. She was good natured and sociable, and once she wrote in Clara's autograph book, when autograph books were obligatory, 'Be good, sweet maid, and let who will be clever': from anyone else Clara would have taken this remark as an act of malice, but from Kathie it came to her as a mere happy lack of invention.

However, two children, and the passage of time, and marriage to Alan had managed to sour Kathie's nature considerably, and Clara now found her both less attractive and less patient

124

than herself. She had grown fatter; her bottom had spread, but she seemed unhappily not to have acknowledged the fact, for she wore skirts of the same size as she had worn when a girl, and they did not fasten properly, and bulged and sagged in the wrong places. She no longer wore make-up, and her hair, though still frequently done at the hairdressers, was now done in a style too old for her years, too formal, too rigorously waved and matronly. And her manner had taken on a scarcely concealed resentment and impatience. She had once treated both Clara and her mother with a kind of superior, assured, charitable kindness, but now she seemed to find their company hard to bear; she snapped at Mrs Maugham when Mrs Maugham tried to persuade her to have another potato with her fish for supper, and reminded Clara more than once that she had forgotten their eldest's third birthday. She did not remind her directly, naturally; she merely repeated, from time to time, the recital of the miraculous way in which Uncle Arthur's present had arrived all the way from Australia on the very day itself. Clara was depressed by such petulance, and wondered that she had not seen the signs of it before.

After supper, a coldly festive meal of salmon, boiled potatoes and wet lettuce, they went to sit in the sitting room. There was one settee and two matching armchairs; Mrs Maugham, as usual, took her chair, and Alan took another, so Clara was left to sit on the settee with Kathie. She hated the settee: she hated the feeling of contact, the jarring stirrings of the springs, the stifled, antagonistic closeness. Kathie smoked, constantly; her mother-in-law did not like her to smoke, and made much show of having no serviceable ash trays, and Kathie muttered audibly that there was no other amusement going, and nothing else to come for. Clara found herself thinking, for the first time, how much a drink would have helped; nobody in that house ever drank. After a few minutes she accepted one of Kathie's cigarettes, though she did not like smoking; even an amusement she did not enjoy seemed momentarily better than no amusement at all. They drank tea, and made remarks, from time to time, about the children, and about the garden, and about Arthur's letters, and about what colour Alan would have his house painted next spring. After a while all conversation died away, and when he had finished his second cup of tea Alan got up and put the television on. The sheer noise was a solace; they gazed at it, all four of them, and their stiff efforts weakened and died, and they sat back in their chairs and relaxed. The programme was a variety show; they sat there and watched singers and dancers and comedians, escaping not from themselves but from each other, paying the programme no attention at all, but relieved by it of the necessity for choosing between silence or talk. Silence was too great, too evident an indictment, and talk too great an effort, so they watched the television, where in larger rooms, on bare and wider floors, people could move and shout and make jokes.

Clara thought of the Denhams, where conversation had flourished, where there seemed to be no end to current and interesting talk, no possibility of silence, so diverse and so rich were the possible permutations, the possible connexions: in such a room as theirs, moreover, there could be and frequently were several conversations carried on at once. Talk is expensive. She thought of Phillipa Denham, Gabriel's wife, sitting at one end of the settee (a settee so long and so sprung that it gave no sensation of indecent proximities) and holding on her knee a small, bright silk-fringed cushion: she was pulling at the fringe, restlessly, all the evening, with long stained fingers, and she was irradiated from behind by some small gold local source of light.

At the Maughams', all the light fell brightly in the small square bow-fronted room, from one central plastic-shaded bulb.

Clara's next meeting with Gabriel took place upon neutral ground. She was delighted by this fact, for it seemed to add to his authenticity; she was also delighted by the evidence, thus innocently and without contrivance presented to him, of her possession of other friends. She had never managed to dispel the everyday threat and terror of contemptible solitude, and was beginning to see now that it would never be dispelled; she would never be able to take society lightly, and the frantic loneliness of Northam would never leave her. And in some way her acquaintance with Clelia had merely impressed upon her the slightness of all other contacts in her life; it had increased her hunger, as well as satisfying her needs. So she felt curiously gratified to meet Gabriel at a party, at a third party's party; she felt herself to be represented in a most satisfactory light. She at the same time felt the light to be unrepresentative, though this feeling was without foundation, for she went to many such parties, though she could never believe, as each one came, that she would be invited to another.

The party was in Swiss Cottage, and it was given by a boy whom Clara had known at college, in conjunction with his elder brother, and it took place about six weeks after her first encounter with Gabriel. When she first saw him, he was talking to a group of his contemporaries, but when he caught sight of her he abandoned his conversation and crossed the room to talk to her. He did not say much; he asked her how she was enjoying education, asked her how she liked her flat, asked her what she thought of Clelia's gallery's new exhibition, asked her, most idly, if Clelia still fancied Martin. Clara answered all these questions save the last, for Clelia's affairs always seemed to be too subtle and delicate and *sui generis* to repay discussion, but she was flattered by the suggestion that she alone might know. He did not press his query, and shortly went away. But his very withdrawal seemed portentous. Clara looked around for his wife, but did not catch a glimpse of her until an hour or so later: she was dressed, as on her last appearance, in all the splendid, ephemeral glory of instant fashion and she looked more vain than gay.

She next saw him a week later, at his parents. She had gone round there to spend the evening with Clelia; all the rest of the family were out, attending a function in south London of some bizarre and dutiful literary nature. Clara and Clelia boiled themselves some spaghetti for supper, and sat eating it in front of the fire; neither of them could cook, and the spaghetti was not quite done, but they did not mind. They talked about their experiences abroad; both had been resolute hitch-hikers, and both had covered most of western Europe. Clara had once lived for a month in Spain on fifteen pounds, and Clelia had been attacked and indeed wounded in a ditch by a man with a knife, and both were proud of their adventures; and Clara thought that on such territory at least their past histories converged. She had to fight for those holidays, herself; they had not been offered to her, as Clelia's had been. But nevertheless, with the excuse of linguistic exploration, and the rigorous saving of and improving on State money, and the precedent offered by that first mild Easter trip, she had managed to convince both herself and her mother of the necessity for such excursions, and she had had them, as much as anyone, she had had them. From the moment of embarkation, each time, there had been nothing to differentiate her from other voyagers. Indeed, her French put that of the middle aged, middle class tourist to shame. Such, she reflected and said, was the Welfare State. And Clelia, agreeing, asked whether the alarmingly increased velocity of progress might not perhaps take its toll, some day: whether one person could achieve, in effect, the travelling of many generations. You think I'll crack up, said Clara, you think they'll win, you think I'll go back: you can't hold back, said Clelia, there is nowhere for you to go. Knowledge cannot be forgotten, no will power can forget knowledge. And then they talked about their affairs abroad, and of the utilitarian, experimental nature of such affairs, and Clelia put forward the view that nowadays girls go abroad for their sentimental education, having nowhere in England to find it, and Clara was just about to put forward her theory about herself, which was that she was incapable of enjoying herself with anyone who had any odour of a long-term, respectable prospect about him, when Gabriel walked in. And Clara's first thought, upon seeing him, was that he had known she was there, for he did not seem surprised to see her: he could well have known it, for the evening had been arranged some days ago, and she knew that all the family were in daily contact; they would ring each other up constantly, all over the country, at vast expense. It seemed dangerous to assume that he might have wished to see her; it seemed to be a notion that verged on madness, as so many of her notions in the past had done, or if not upon madness, then upon some colossal, crazy, optimistic hope. And yet other hopes just as crazy had in the past been fulfilled, so why not this one? Perhaps he looked at everyone in such a way, but she could not believe it; or if he could, he was but the more remarkable.

Clelia offered him some supper, in a very inviting manner, but he declined her offer, saying that he had eaten something at home, and that Phillipa's cooking was marginally preferable to his sister's. But he poured himself a whisky, and sat down.

'I never know what you mean,' Clelia said, when he had seated himself, 'about Phillipa's cooking. Whenever I've eaten anything she's cooked, it's always been absolutely delicious.'

'That's because she always makes a special effort when she knows anyone else is going to eat it,' said Gabriel. 'But she doesn't bother any more for me. She's so lazy, she hates cutting things up, she always cooks everything whole, in lumps, great lumps of meat, whole huge old potatoes, whole carrots, whole cabbages. I don't think it occurs to her to chop them up.'

'She probably gets bored with it,' said Clelia, 'with all those children.'

'She always has to throw all the meals out,' said Gabriel, 'because the children won't eat them. They won't eat anything except baked beans. but she goes on cooking these cabbages, and throwing them away. It's very extravagant. I keep telling her how poor we are, but she doesn't listen.'

'Gabriel, you must be mad,' said Clelia. 'How can you be poor?'

'Anyone with three children is poor,' said Gabriel. 'It's impossible to be rich with three children. I do my best, but it's still impossible. Bits of the house keep falling down, and I have to keep paying to have them stuck on again. The Macadams had dry rot, did you know? And they're in the next street but one. What if it spreads? A spell of dry rot would land me in heavy debt, I can tell you. I went to one of these meetings earlier in the evening, one of these meetings about the preservation of Islington, but the best thing that could happen to us would be an eviction order or a demolition order or whatever it is that people get. I'd like to be forcibly rehoused, that's what I'd like, at the Council's expense.'

'Television directors aren't allowed Council houses,' said Clelia. 'And I don't think you ought to go to preservation meetings.'

'That's what Phillipa says,' said Gabriel. 'But I don't

suppose she says it for the same reasons. I shan't go to any more, I don't fancy the company.'

'You're a snob,' said Clelia.

'So are we all,' said Gabriel. 'What else could we expect to be? What do you think, Clara, what else could we expect to be?'

'I don't know,' said Clara. 'It always seems to me that it must be hard for you, coming from this house, to know where else to go. I mean, what should one do, but try to build it up again somewhere?'

'What's wrong with that?' said Clelia. 'Though I don't bother to do even that, I don't even bother to move.'

'We don't try to do it all over again,' said Gabriel, 'Phillipa and I. You must come and see our house some time. It's very near.'

'You go the other way,' said Clelia, 'which is worse.'

'Nothing is worse,' said Gabriel, 'than living at home, at your age. That's positively unnatural. Don't you think, Clara?'

'I don't know, I always envy her,' said Clara.

'She certainly couldn't afford such a nice standard of living anywhere else,' said Gabriel. 'And she knows what I come round for, I come round to pinch the drink. Once I even took some Stilton and a packet of cornflakes. And that can't be right, can it? They shouldn't lay themselves open to such taking of advantages.'

'They don't care,' said Clelia. 'They don't notice. They're too busy to care. You wish they would notice, but they don't. They don't count the cornflakes.'

'There has always seemed to me to be something inescapably comic,' said Gabriel, 'about the attitude of parents such as ours. All this affectionate uncritical encouragement, it can't be right, can it?'

'What do you want?' said Clelia. 'Do you want someone to tell you what not to think? Ask Clara about how awful that is, she knows all about mothers.'

And Gabriel did ask Clara, and they discussed, for some time, the effects of parents upon children, and Clara conceded that she might have gained somewhere in her total severance (though at the same time uneasily aware that there is no such thing as severance, that connexions endure till death, that blood is after all blood, however fanciful and frivolous such a notion might seem; and that a humble acceptance of this was more elegant than a blunt denial) and then, as it was getting late, Gabriel offered Clara a lift home. Clara had been hoping that he would, and had been enjoying, in anticipation, the ride, for the drawing room of the Denhams, so spacious and so full, left her too much leeway for voluntary evasion; he had come to sit near her, at one point, but she had got up and moved to another chair.

But in the front of the car there was no opportunity for withdrawal. Their legs were side by side, and there was nothing they could do about it. On the way down to the Archway he did not speak, but Clara from time to time wildly expected that he might grab her knee; she thought she knew the symptoms, but feared that she might be confusing them with her own desires. When he reached her doorway, he stopped the car, but left the engine on, and said, 'Why don't you come round now and have a drink?'

'I don't think I should,' said Clara. 'It's getting so late, won't your wife have gone to bed?'

'She may have done,' said Gabriel, 'but then again she may not have done. But it doesn't matter, she wouldn't mind.'

'I'd like to come,' said Clara. 'It's just that it's late.'

'It's not very late,' said Gabriel, and started up the car. As they drove down the Holloway Road and into Islington, Clara wondered whether she ought not perhaps to have asked him in to her flat for a drink instead, and was glad, on the whole, that she had not; for one thing, she remembered that she had no clean cups left, and did not want to start washing up, and for another thing, she wanted to see his house. Judging from Phillipa's appearance, and from the one other converted house in Islington that she had seen, she was expecting something rather spectacularly gay, some prize and choice specimen of London housing, well stocked with Heals' furniture and quickly-dating wallpapers and gleaming wooden floors and white paint and coloured crockery and pricey paper flowers in white Italian vases; even the children, she was sure, would manifest themselves by smart wooden toys and decorated felt wall hangings and well-selected beakers and free-expression paintings on the walls. She was not familiar with the genre, as few of her friends, as yet, had children, but she had visited it peripherally, and knew of it from her Colour Supplements; she knew what she expected, and she wanted, very much, to see. And she was, too, incurably mean and lazy; she would rather any day be guest than hostess, she would rather reach out her hand for a drink than wash out a glass and lift up a bottle to pour one. She never entertained, and could not see that she ever would; her resentment of the notion of entertaining was so deep-rooted that she could never decide its primary cause, and laid it from time to time at the charge of avarice, idleness, or sheer social ineptitude, all of them reasons base enough to be true. It never crossed her mind that others might feel a similar reluctance; she expected to be on the receiving end.

As they drew nearer to Gabriel's house, they crossed a couple of squares with which Clara was vaguely familiar, squares once thoroughly decayed, and now full of the apparatus of demolition and construction; the area attracted her strongly, in its violent seedy contrasts, its juxtaposition of the rich and the poor, its rejection of suburban uniformity. Anything unfamiliar attracted her; the idea of sleeping six to a room, like the Neapolitans, seemed as charmingly far from the memory of her own small square solitude as did the complex associations of Clelia's room, with all its thickly-peopled corners, and its dense photograph-covered walls. She looked at the peeling, cracked façades, and the newly-plastered, smartly painted ones, and she thought that she would like to have lived there, among such new examples.

She was, however, somewhat surprised by the look of the street in which Gabriel finally came to a halt. She had been expecting, she realized, one of the largest and the smartest of the new conversions; indeed, they had passed, a street away, a house which she had been sure must be his, possessing as it did a lovely corner site, some ornate iron window boxes, and a stone pineapple on its corner gate post. But the street in which they stopped had no such houses. Conversion had not reached it, nor was it architecturally particularly inviting; the terraced

132

houses were tall and dark, the paintwork grim, and the stone lintels cracked and scooped by time, neglect and hard weather. Clara found herself telling herself that it might be all right inside, though why it was any concern of hers that it should be all right she could not think, nor what the term 'all right', when used of Gabriel's house, might signify; but when they got inside, it was not all right. He let them in with a key, and they stood in the hall, lit by an unshaded bulb; she was braced to meet Phillipa, for the light of the front room downstairs was still on, and as soon as they entered the house they heard voices. The hall was amazing; it was squalid, in a way that not even the worst of landladies' entrances are squalid. A piece of coconut matting covered part of a bare, broken wooden floor; hooks covered the wall, and from the hooks hung clothes of all sizes. A pram and a push chair stood one after the other, and on top of the pram was a child's tricycle; underneath them was a heap of shoes, boots and old plastic toys. The wallpaper was of a brown, pale, cheap floral design, and it was very old; in one place it hung in shreds, and the children had peeled it off the bottom of the staircase; in another place it had come away to reveal a large hole in the damp, crumbling plaster. The stairs were uncarpeted. Clara stared at it all, though she tried not to stare, and she felt rising in her a whole flood of Hartley Road emotion, which she was obliged to force herself to reject; she was rather annoyed that she should have been taken so off her guard, she had thought that she had got the Denhams' measure, she had thought that her expectations had been safe, she had not thought that it was possible that one of Mrs Denham's daughters-in-law should have kept such a house. Although there was, of course, the mad Amelia: perhaps Amelia's madness and her strange garb were not so picturesque in reality as they were in narration. However it might be, Clara told herself that she must take it that such a house was the most natural place in the world for such a man as Gabriel to live in: but even as she thought this, even as Gabriel pushed open the door of the living room, she found herself thinking that it might be better inside.

And it was better inside, marginally better, in that the room was occupied by perfectly recognizable people: Phillipa herself sat there, not as she had feared transformed into some shabby shadow of herself, but as sharply exclusive as ever, and with her sat two other couples, both in their mid-twenties, both dressed in a perfectly unexceptional manner. And they all seemed to sit there quite happily; they did not shrink from contact with the chairs, nor raise their feet delicately from the threadbare, stringy carpet. Gabriel introduced Clara, and as she sat down and waited for him to bring her a drink she gathered, from the conversation, that the other couples had dropped in idly, and had been waiting, idly, for Gabriel's return. 'If I'd known you were coming,' said Gabriel, his back to the room, 'I'd have come straight back from that meeting, but how was I to know?'

'You weren't to know,' said Phillipa, speaking for the first time, 'and anyway, what does it matter? We were all right, we were just talking, we weren't going to wait.'

She spoke in an extraordinarily cold and nervous tone, as though Gabriel's return had been truly the last thing she had expected; and Gabriel looked round from the hatch at her, and they exchanged glances, and Clara, watching, thought that she saw in their looks some sudden evidence of some appalling, exhausting strain. They looked at each other with something like hatred; they looked at each other with despair. Clara looked round the room, at the old broken furniture, at the stained and grimy ceiling, at the rows and rows of books, lonely evidence of culture, and she drank her whisky very quickly, and did not say no when she was offered some more. She could not tell, for sure, but she imagined that Phillipa Denham must have had more than fifty pounds' worth of clothes on her at that moment, and for an unexpected, an unforeseen evening, if the truth were being told; and yet the carpet must have been bought with the house, and the curtains hung crookedly from old rails, and were a foot too short for the windows.

It soon became clear that both Gabriel and Phillipa were engaged in a struggle to prevent the departure of their guests. Gabriel's efforts were spent largely upon a lavish replenishing of glasses, and an equally lavish expenditure of charm; Phillipa made no effort, no apparent effort, but she made no sign of dismissal either, and her cool and formal smile had a retaining authority, so that the others clearly felt they could not go. Clara was glad they did not go, for she wanted to stay; she drank more than she had meant to, through nervousness, and she could not prevent herself from watching Gabriel, though she tried to, and tried all the more because she felt that Phillipa was, however indirectly, watching her. But her eyes kept meeting Gabriel's across the room.

She could not make him out. She could not understand why he had to be so excessively pleasant, so amusing, so interested and concerned, so much a claimant of all the virtues; he worked hard to make himself agreeable, and yet there was clearly no need for him to do so, as he was quite agreeable enough by nature, by mere presence, so that any hard work on his part was superfluous. There was even something faintly ingratiating in his manner, which she found not at all offensive; on the contrary, it seemed an agreeably appealing weakness, a sign of vulnerability, which the too adequate Clelia lacked. Clara liked Clelia to be as she was, perfect, for she wanted nothing from Clelia: but in Gabriel she was glad to see marks of need. And she wondered whether his charm might not be in some way a recognition of the room's defects; whether he might not, in fact, be struggling against the odds of his décor. The relationship of the Denhams with the two other couples was not at all clear, and Clara could not assess the degree of intimacy between any of the people present; one of the couples, an architect and his wife, seemed to have reached a considerable state of badinage with their hosts, but as they lived in the next street but one Clara could not but suppose that the friendship was one of convenience – and she more particularly supposed this as the wife, a solid cardiganed lady, had a kind of cheerful well-informed attitude towards life which assorted ill with Phillipa's fringe attractions. The other couple were in appearance at least more congenial; the wife was an actress, and the husband a painter, and they were wearing the same excessively ephemeral style of clothes as Phillipa herself. The husband, a bony elegant-looking Scot called Alistair, was wearing a camel-coloured suit such as she had never seen on a real man; she had always supposed such garments to appear only in magazine advertisements for cars and liquors. She was rather glad that Gabriel did not wear such clothes; there was something about his check wool shirt and the way it fitted into the low waist of his trousers that suggested most marvellously the body underneath, whereas the Alistair man's suit concealed him completely.

They talked about art. Clara felt that if she had not been there, they might all have talked about their children, as even the actress had a child, but as it was they talked about art, with only the most casual and deprecating references to the exploits of their off-spring. They talked, rather well, about the desire to imitate and to represent; Clara was impressed by the way they all managed to talk intelligently, yet without strain, without intensity, without affection, and wondered if they could do it so easily merely because they were older than her and her friends, or whether they had been accustomed to talk so all their lives. The cardiganed lady put forward the theory that abstraction in art was a primitive whim, corresponding to the very earliest whims of childhood, and that any true artistic desire was a desire to represent the human form, in whatever medium; she illustrated this, subtly introducing her children, by describing the efforts of the American teacher at their nursery group to make the children paint with free expression. 'And they hate it,' she said, triumphantly, 'they absolutely hate it. The little tiny ones don't mind, they don't mind slapping paint on with their fingers or making blodges all over the paper, but the big ones want to make real things. The older they get, the more they need to imitate the real, free expression bores them rigid. Miss Watson thinks my eldest has got something wrong with him, just because he paints real trees. She says he's got no imagination.'

The painter demurred, and seemed to imply that such a chronological interpretation of artistic development was not particularly valid, and Gabriel told a story about Clelia, who used as a child to have a passion for modelling things out of an obsolete substance known as Glitterwax. She was good at making things, he said, but not good enough; her critical faculty was always better than her creative, and when she was eight or nine she would sit for hours and hours in her room, savagely, persistently trying to create in the obdurate intractable wax the images of her imagination. She made trees, and flowers, and animals; but she was not content, she had to make people. And she could not make people. The human form escaped her. So she took to making sketches for her Glitterwax models, and worked for hours trying to reproduce her own designs. Then one day she did not come down to tea, having been out of sight all afternoon; after half an hour her mother went up to look for her, and found her sitting on the hearth rug in front of the fire, surrounded by the most delightful and talented drawings, weeping bitterly over a shapeless lump of Glitterwax, which she was kneading tearfully in her hands. Her mother inquired, tenderly, the cause for her distress, and Clelia, amidst many sobs, finally confessed that she was weeping because she feared she would never be an artist. Clara listened to this tale with a sense of extreme delight, for she liked to hear people talk of Clelia, as lovers like to bring in the name of their loved ones, and mothers the names of their children; moreover, she liked to hear Gabriel tell it, she liked to hear him speak, and to speak so kindly of his sister, to speak of her with such affection.

It began to get late, and still nobody went home. Clara looked at her watch, and saw that it was after one. Eventually Phillipa told Gabriel to go and make some coffee, and he went through into the kitchen, and five minutes later put his head through the hatch and asked her to come and help him carry the cups. Phillipa did not move. 'I can't get up,' she said. So Clara sprang helpfully to her feet, and went and got some cups from the hatch, and brought them through and put them on the floor at Phillipa's feet. Then Gabriel called that he couldn't find the coffee grinder. 'Oh Christ,' said Phillipa and did not move.

'I'll go and look,' said Clara. And she went out of the room, and through the unspeakable hall, and into the kitchen, where Gabriel was standing looking bewildered, with some coffee beans in a jar, and a coffee pot. 'There's a grinder, somewhere,' he said. He was not trying to look; his eyes were not looking at anything. Clara looked around for a coffee grinder, and noticed as she did so that the kitchen was both better and worse than the rest of the house; worse in its basic structure and materials, but better in its equipment, in that it was full of desirable and well-designed objects, most of which had probably once been donated as wedding presents. There was a new though worn gas cooker, a washing machine, and various fashionable coloured iron casseroles and earthenware pots, though the sink was cracked and ancient, and the linoleum, torn and frayed, showing all too plainly the irregularities of the stone floor beneath. Clara found the coffee grinder without much difficulty, and offered it to Gabriel, who put the beans in it and plugged it in. 'I've never seen an electric one before,' she said, to say something. 'How does it work?'

'You just press the button,' he said. 'Look, go on, press it.' And she did, and the machine whirred and buzzed in her hand, and drowned the faint echoes of conversation from the other room.

The room seemed very small. As she handed the grinder to Gabriel, their hands touched. 'I couldn't see it,' he said, 'I must have drunk too much.'

And he tipped the coffee into a jug, and poured on the boiling water. As he poured it, Clara looked through the hatch; she could see only Alistair Beattie, sitting in the far corner of the room. She turned away, and looked at Gabriel, and he carefully put down the jug. Then he stepped towards her, and took her in his arms. Both of them started nervously at the contact, and glanced, with mutual alarm, towards the square window into the other room, the square opening in the wall, and he pushed her very slightly to one side, so that her head was against the wall, so that they were in the one small wedge of the kitchen that could never be seen from the other room. Then he kissed her. She returned his kiss with ardour, and held on to him tightly; he was hot, and his body under his shirt felt very hard. He continued to kiss her, and to press against her.

When he let go of her, they both glanced once more nervously at the other room, and then he took her hand, and lifted it up, and kissed it, on the palm and on the fingers, and said, 'I'll carry the tray, if you take that packet of digestive biscuits.'

And they went back and joined the others. And she found herself able to converse, as she had not been before, with ease and some point, but for all that she said as soon as she had had her coffee that she must leave. She had hoped that Gabriel might drive her home, but the Beatties instantly and so sincerely offered to take her that their invitation could not be declined.

And as she got into bed, she reflected that perhaps it was as well that Gabriel had not driven her, as he had certainly been drunk. She did not regret this; indeed, she was delighted by it, for without it she doubted whether he would have got round to kissing her so soon, if indeed ever. And she had wanted to be kissed, more by him than ever before by anyone. That secret kiss, in its dangerous angle, with its back to the wall, a few inches from discovery and surprise, was for her the lofty classic height of passion. The suddenness, the danger, the lack of discussion, and the brevity, had but added to her love.

Chapter 7

Gabriel had known for some time before kissing Clara that he was about to kiss somebody. He was on the whole an honourable man, and had not kissed anyone except his wife since his marriage, save in the way of courtesy, so the act was for him a significant one. He was slightly uneasy about the lack of choice and the sense of desperation which had finally pushed him to it, but did not feel that they reflected ill upon Clara; he truly admired her, and the eagerness with which she had returned his onslaught had turned, through relief, his admiration into a kind of love. He had not expected to be so well received, for his vanity, once secure, had been steadily eroded by years of disastrous marriage, and having kissed her, having felt lips more hungry than cold, and a body that trembled with anticipation and not with apprehension, he felt himself to be made over again, to be a new man. He had forgotten the simplicity of such acts, and their lovely associations with the unfamiliar and the unexplored.

Clara seemed to him, in his ignorance, to be everything that Phillipa was not: warm, enthusiastic, easily amused, amusing, and wonderfully, mercifully unexhausted. She listened to everything and everyone, as though she could not hear enough, and her face was mobile and expressive; she smiled and frowned and concentrated in rapid, vivid succession, and her features never set into a civil parade of attention. When she was bored, she inspected, frankly, the furniture. And she wanted him; she had wanted him to ask her round for a drink. In his gratitude, he could have kissed her for that alone. Other girls had seemed to want him, but he had never put them to the test, being unwilling to face the slightest, most minimal coolness, being too unsure of his reception.

Phillipa's receptions he knew, and his knowledge filled him

with despair. He had tried, for years he had tried, and the slow living with his failure had exhausted him nearly as much as it had exhausted her. Half of his effort in life was spent in concealing the truth from the neighbours, a tedious bourgeois occupation which degraded him as much by its nature as by its lack of success. For the neighbours could not help but notice. Phillipa had reached such a point that she no longer knew what she was showing them; she had never much cared, and now she could not even see. She wept in the street; she sat on the front steps and wept. He had come home from work, and found her weeping on the steps, with a baby in a pram on the street by her, and the two others running loose down the pavement. She could not manage the children, a fact which aggravated her condition, but which had certainly not caused it, for it preceded both children, and he devoutly hoped, their marriage. He offered her help with the children, and from time to time they had had girls living in, and women in to clean, but when they were there Phillipa wandered around the house in nervous, silent suffering, unable to sit down in their presence, unable to speak to them, unable to live in the house with others. She liked to be alone, or else she liked to be out; in company, in society, she weirdly flourished, and he had known her dry her eyes after a bout of frightful anguish, and put on her make-up and put on her newest dress, and go out to a party and laugh, and, to all appearances, enjoy herself. Then she would come back, and take off her clothes, and lie rigid upon the bed, staring at the ceiling, uncommunicative, silent, infinitely distressed.

He did not think that he could ever understand her, nor the reasons for her malaise, but nevertheless he knew her, and at times he seemed to stare straight at the springs of her intolerable grief. When he wanted to revive within himself his tenderness for her, and to make his own heart bleed, there was a string of incidents which he would recall, which never failed to cause him an intolerable barb of painful emotion. The first of these dated from the second week of their marriage, when, after lying in bed waiting for her, he had got out, finally, and gone to look for her. He heard her before he saw her; she was in the living room of their small Paddington flat, and she was moaning softly and rhythmically to herself. The light was off, and he did not dare to put it on, but he found her, crouched in a corner behind the armchair, her arms around her knees, wearing her smart trousseau night shirt. Spread before her on the floor was a Durex dutch cap, an instruction leaflet, and various other accoutrements of contraception. She was crying because she could not manage them. She was too narrow, she said, or rather she did not say, for she did not say such things, but this was what he gathered, from her meaningless sobs. He tried to console her, saying he would occupy himself with such things, as he had always done before their marriage, in their quite adequately exciting courtship, but the sight of her, so reduced, had struck him to his heart. And it was too late. Their first child was conceived that week.

Other recollections he had, most of which, like this first, bore witness to a physical sensitivity most tragically pronounced. If she broke a nail, her eyes would fill with tears, and once she bought an unlined skirt which she could hardly bear to wear, for the friction of the cloth of the skirt against her legs would drive her into a frenzy. If there was a wrinkle in the bed, she could not sleep. And yet this neurotic fastidiousness in no way overflowed into her care for the house, which she left to its own squalor, with a fatality unparalleled even amongst their own middle class acquaintances. It was as though, afflicted, she could not bear to lift a finger to help herself; instead she sat suffering, staring the image of her suffering in the face. She was passive, to a degree that was at times dangerous, for she would let the children play with the washing machine and run across the street. Some of her afflictions were at first sight bizarre and out of place; for instance, she cared dreadfully about the shocking conditions in which her neighbours lived, though the conditions were not, as some of her more malicious friends pointed out, so much worse than those in her own home. A social conscience was not something that even Gabriel would readily have credited her with, yet he had to admit that she had one, though it never carried her as far as any kind of action: nothing carried her towards action. She did nothing, and yet she would stand on her front steps and watch the more alarming sights of the neighbourhood, and cry. When questioned, she said that it was injustice that made her weep. And he thought that she suffered from these sights, as she suffered from a broken nail. Proportion had no place in her life: she was so deeply wounded that pain came to her simply, as itself. Once she said to him that she could not bear to have more of anything than anyone in the world and that misery seemed to her to be a duty, but he rejected this explanation, as one too metaphysical to be true.

She did, from time to time, seem to be quite happy. (Sometimes she would laugh at his jokes.) In company she was occasionally even gay, though he never knew how much to trust her gaiety. She loved the children, and would pick them up and kiss them violently, but they did not like such treatment; the eldest of them said, crossly, that he did not like to be squeezed, and whenever he said this she would go into the next room and cry. Sometimes she even cried in front of them; the children were used to the sight of her tears. The only moments of joy that he remembered were the moments of the births of each child; she had sat up in bed, pale and damply gleaming, a smile of triumph upon her face, her fair lank hair sticking to her cheeks and shoulders, transported by the narrow felicity of suffering survived. And the birth of the third was marred by the fact that the third was a girl. He dated the final phase of her impossibility from the birth of the girl. Having two sons, he had wanted a daughter, and whenever the subject had arisen, Phillipa had formally acquiesced, but when she was told, the throes of labour over, of what she had produced, she groaned softly, and said, more frivolously than sadly, that she would not know what to do with a girl. And he had, soon after the birth, caught her staring at the child, at her small girl's body, at the swollen soft red sex of the baby upon the open nappy, so curiously dominant a feature of the newborn, as though sex were the first distinction of nature, and he had seemed to know, with a frightening intimacy, the quality and depth of her anxious, defensive, participating love. For the boys she had no fears, but in the girl, he thought she saw herself and her wounds reborn.

Naturally, the degree of his own responsibility for her state exercised him considerably. At times it seemed to eat up his whole life. There were days when he took the memory of her to work with him, and rejoined it when he got home, without many hours of grace in between. But on most days he managed to forget her for most of the time that he was not with her. He was a sociable man, in a sociable profession (if profession it could be called, which he with his strict inheritance often doubted), and he found it quite easy to fill his time in with people. But he had few close friends: the secret of Phillipa cut him off from the world, he was too scrupulous, too closely wedded to her to abandon her, and she lived with him in some closed and white numb corner of his mind. The people that he saw most frequently were his brothers and sisters, and he was the only member of the family to find such attraction and devotion unnatural. He had learned this sense from his wife, who viewed his background with a profound suspicion, so that he was obliged to feel faintly guilty even about his visits to his own one-time home. His family, for its part, was too delicate ever to question Phillipa's effect upon Gabriel, or his relationship with her, but he suffered enough from knowing that she could not enjoy their company, and that evenings spent with them were evenings of trial.

He often wished he could get rid of her. He thought of divorce, idly, as of a great blessing, but there were the children, and anyway where were the grounds? There was nothing wrong with them, nothing at all. They had people to dinner, they went out to dinner, they slept in the same bed, they even read the same books. Sometimes it seemed impossible that their living could continue, and he thought that he too would sit down as she did, and stare at the wall and weep. He tried to remember when it had started, but he could not remember, for they had never been happy; they had been, at their best, in love. Her beauty had always tended towards the disastrous, and he supposed that he, with his enormous pride, had believed that he could deal with such an ill-fated creature, for he had been brought up to believe in himself, and nothing that he had ever met had shaken his confidence. At school, at University, he had been amongst the most well-equipped, favourably singled out by destiny in almost all his connexions, and his earliest attempts upon girls had been unfailingly successful.

His school reports had remarked upon the way he managed to combine intelligence with modesty and a sense of team spirit, for he had always known instinctively of the best way to ingratiate himself with authority; he had a passion for keeping on the right side of all the world, and the people that he antagonized were rare indeed. He sometimes wondered whether his love for Phillipa had not in fact been some kind of saving lack of grace; he had taken her on because she had not been his measure, because she had been different and beyond him, beyond the scope and range of his charm. He had failed with her, and he consoled himself by thinking that he had needed failure, and that without it he would have been more surely ruined.

She said, repeatedly, that she did not like him, that she did not want him, and that he could go if he chose. She said that it made no difference to her whether he stayed or whether he went. He, himself, thought that it would make a difference; he thought that she needed him, just as much as she needed to say to him that she did not need him. He knew this, though he considered, in his heart, that there was no need for him to know it; after the things that she had said to him, it was his own courtesy that kept him, and not the strict exigencies of honour. He had considered, for a year or two at least, that if he gave way under the strain, then he gave way honourably, after satisfactory efforts to bear it: a report upon his conduct could not have said other than that he had tried hard. He acquitted himself, in advance. Since the conception of their third child, she had not allowed him to make love to her; she had hardly allowed him to kiss her, save for thin kisses of comfort, after hours of tears. He could not be expected to live without a woman forever, he thought; even the law made some concession to such needs. And Clara herself had conceded them most beautifully, and with no faint breath of reproach. He had forgotten the taste of good will.

He thought of Clara's face, and of the way her lips lay, full and pale and gentle, undefended and yet in no way defenceless. They were strongly curved, and the furrow in her upper lip was deep. She looked hard, and yet soft to him: well-defined, and yet not hardened.

Phillipa's body was covered with scars, the blue-white scars of childbearing. And she had been stitched and sewn. She had been too narrow, and they had remade her badly.

Phillipa, on the underground once, tears rolling down her face, for no reason. When she got out, a young man followed her, an Indian, a lonely student. He said to her, Do not cry, do not cry, you remind me of my own sorrows, I think to myself, I have a letter from home, maybe it tell me my mother, my brother, my brother's children, they are ill, and I feel for you, so do not cry, I think I am alone, all alone, and I think no one will come up to me and tell me not to cry.

Phillipa, smiling calmly, said that it was nothing, that she wept for nothing, that she too often wept.

And he followed her, up the escalator, up the stairs, and on to Regent Street, and walked along with her, and they stood there on the corner, and Phillipa stood and stared at the clothes in the window behind the man's head, as he told her of his loneliness, and of his work, and of how he had not gone to work that day, and of the tediousness of his life, and its hardships, and its solitary endurances, and he talked softly on and on and Phillipa stood and listened, not to his words, but to the sound of his words, and to their even grief, and she looked covetously at a grey chenille shirt, and she thought of her incommunicable distress, and his voice continued, and her tears were dried at their source, dried by the cold facts of poverty, by the knowledge that from those who have not even that which they have shall be taken away, and that these dispossessed shall forever meet at street corners, forever uselessly divulging to useless auditors their need.

Gabriel wrote to Clara. She had not known what to expect from him, hardly daring to fear that there might be nothing, and when it was a letter that she received she knew that there could have been nothing more satisfactory. It said:

My lovely Clara,

What can I say to you, what can I say, except to ask that I might see you again? So far I have been content to leave our meetings to chance, but it seems to me that now I must take a step in your direction, even if it is only to allow you to step sharply backwards. In view of the facts, or in view of yourself, either way. I write to you, because I should not like to see you step away from me, with my own eyes. And I will wait for you, next week, on Thursday, at one o'clock, in the Oriental bit of Liberty's (and don't take that amiss, I have spent half an hour composing that sentence) and if you come, I could take you out to lunch, and if you don't come, you don't come. But I hope you will come. And I will be there before you, you will not need to wait.

Yours, Gabriel.

Clara read this letter very carefully, and the more she studied it, the more wholly appropriate it seemed, and with a propriety that was to her the very mark of truth. She had received plenty of invitations in her time, and although the standard of punctuation and syntax revealed in them had risen since those first days of Higginbotham and Walter Ash, it had not risen spectacularly high. She liked everything about Gabriel's letter, from its form of address, sole stroke of colour, to the tender, all-embracing meaningless 'Yours' of its conclusion. She liked the paper on which it was written, official headed paper of the company for which he worked, with an address, she noted, which was close enough to Liberty's, a fact which rendered even more neutral his choice of rendezvous: she liked his writing, small and even, a debased and gentler version of Clelia's defined and aristocratic hand. And she liked the tone of it; its diffident lack of assumption, its confident clarity. He had offered her an assignation which she felt herself competent to accept, and with a quantity of compromise that she felt herself exactly fitted to bear, and he had even, by some truly impressive insight, divined her secret horror, which was a horror of being kept conspicuously waiting in a public place. She did, at times uneasily wonder whether such insight might not be born of much experience, but even the thought of much experience did not dismay her. Indeed, she was not sure that it did not, in a sense, encourage her.

And she thought of Gabriel. She thought of him with the beginnings of a passion: she knew, deliciously, that if she went then it would be too late, for her at least, and that if she did not go, then it would not happen. And yet at the same time, she knew that she would go, so perhaps it was already too late. It was not in her to say no. And perhaps it had been too late since birth, in that she had always been looking for such a man as Gabriel, so endowed, so beautiful, and that if such a man should so much as suggest a possibility of a question to her, then she would answer yes. She knew this, yet did not find her knowledge at all unwelcome, as she had always fancied the idea of involuntary love, and had hitherto found her feelings all too voluntary. She was less happy about the notion that she might be admiring in Gabriel things not personal but generic, but she consoled herself by saying that as she had spent her whole adult life in search of the genre, without success, then the genre must be rare enough: if there were but one Helen, one Alexander, why then hesitate to recognize the heroic stamp?

So she went. Like all provincials she knew Liberty's well enough, and had always known it, as she had not always known the byways of Bond Street, and yet nevertheless when she arrived there, at ten past one, she was forced to face a lurking doubt about the exact nature and location of the Oriental Department. She went in, rashly, from the Regent Street entrance, and immediately found herself waylaid by men's dressing gowns and silk ties, and confusingly ascending lifts and staircases, so that it took her some time to find the main body of the shop. And when she got there, she did not know which floor to look for, and as she was stubbornly averse to asking for directions she spent even more time wandering around looking for Oriental objects. She thought, at one point, that she had found the department, but it was merely a boutique full of Thai silk dresses; she stared at the dresses and at Gabriel's absence in mounting panic, before realizing that she must be in the wrong place, for it was surely not possible for him not to be there. So she went up another flight of stairs, and there, his back towards her, inspecting a nest of blue Chinese dishes, was Gabriel. He turned at her approach, as though he had seen her, and when he saw her, he held out his hand to her, and she took it, and he shook it, as though they were acquaintances, but he held it tightly, and then he kissed her cheek, lightly, as though they were friends, and she inclined lightly towards him, to receive, on a bare and exposed cheek, his lips. Not bred to

such casual embraces, she had never been able to take them
lightly, although she had learned the deft angle at which to
bend her head, and her heart was strangely touched by the
mixture of formality and implication in their meeting.

'I was afraid that you might not come,' said Gabriel.

'Oh,' said Clara. 'You must have known that I was coming.'

'I didn't know,' he said. And he had not known; as he had
waited, her coming had seemed more and more unlikely, and
that solitary kiss more and more of an illusion.

'Perhaps I'm a little late,' she said, standing there, smiling at
him.

'I knew you would be late,' he said. 'But even though I knew
it, I was early. I wouldn't for anything have missed you. And
as I've been here for so long, I had to keep buying things. Look
what I've bought.'

And he took out of his pocket a couple of paper bags and in
them there was a box of matches in a highly decorated box,
and a small sample of flowered silk, and a small horn spoon.

'That proves, you see,' he said, staring down at his collection,
'that I really wasn't sure that you were coming. If I'd been sure,
I might have bought you something. But I wasn't sure, and I
was too mean to spend money on the off-chance. These things
are the cheapest things in Liberty's, you know.'

'They're pretty, though,' she said.

'You can have them,' he said.

'I like the silk,' she said, 'I'd like to have the silk.'

'The silk was free,' he said, and he gave her the small scrap,
and she put it in her pocket. Then they looked at each other
once more, bravely, for the first time since her arrival.

'Shall we go and have lunch?' he said. 'I feel hungry, after so
much waiting.'

'I am always hungry,' she said.

And he took her arm, and they went down the square shallow stairs, and out through the department that sells household
novelties, past ranged layers of such objects as lend a little
mocking charm to so many thousands of kitchens, of which
Gabriel's own, he sadly felt, was merely an absurd, exagger-
ated, neurotic case. He had in his other pocket a gadget for
squeezing slices of lemon which he had bought, idly, for

Phillipa; he rather wished that it was not there. They went east, into Soho, to a little restaurant that Gabriel had first visited, years ago, with his boss; he had never returned and he remembered it chiefly for its furtive gloom, for it was beneath ground level, and inadequately lit. It was still as he had remembered it, dark and warm and not overcrowded. They sat in a corner, he was with his back to the room, and she facing it. He looked at her, and she looked past him into the darkness. They did not know what to say to each other, and after a while Gabriel said that had she known that Martin's wife had returned to him at the weekend.

'No, I didn't know,' said Clara. She did not want to talk of Martin, for she was afraid that they might end up talking of Clelia, but nevertheless curiosity compelled her to ask where Martin's wife had been. Gabriel said that it was generally thought that she had been living with a man in Milan.

'I can't imagine why she should have come back,' said Clara. 'Having gone, how dreadful it must be to go back.'

'Perhaps she was worried about the child,' said Gabriel.

'Oh yes, the child,' said Clara. 'But she'd left it for long enough, why should she come back, having once left it? I could never go back to anything like that.'

And he could see that the thought of a child meant nothing to her, as indeed how should it, and the sight of so much indifference to the most tender points of his life filled him with a sense of liberation, of incipient gaiety. The line was firmly drawn, between one world and another; there were no hands grasping after him, no area of confusion, no grey and trampled, dusty, intermediate terrain. He thought of Clelia's enormous sympathies, of her arms more ready to receive the child than the man, of her studious, elegant denials, and he thought that he saw in Clara a more voracious simplicity, a need that did not pay too much attention to the sources of its satisfaction. And then the soup arrived, and with it the wine, which he was much in need of, and on the surface of the soup there was a most elaborate little trellis-pattern drawn in cream, and Clara, seeing it, exclaimed with delight, and by some fluke of fate their waiter happened not to be disagreeable, and he stopped and most charmingly explained the way to make trellises on soup with the back of a fork, and Clara admired and exclaimed, and the waiter, in an unprecedently archaic way, appeared to take pleasure in her exclamations. And when he went away, glowing with the pride of his profession, Clara picked up her spoon, and looked at Gabriel, and smiled, and waving her spoon gently over the surface of her soup, she said, 'It seems a pity to disturb it, don't you think? Because whatever he said about it being so simple, I could never make it in a hundred years.'

'If you don't disturb it,' he said, 'it will probably melt and fade away all by itself. Look, it's started to spread already. Much better to do it yourself, than to let it go.'

And she put her spoon in, and stirred, and drank.

When they had had their soup, he took her hand under the table. It lay burning in his, dry and quiescent.

Then she looked at him, smiling a little, and said:

'I like that scar,' relaxing suddenly as though everything was settled between them.

'Do you?' he said. 'Do you really? I used to think it was rather fetching myself. But it must be years since I looked at it, since I even looked at it.'

'You did it,' she said, 'when you fell over the garden wall.'

'That's right,' he said. And then he said, 'I'm glad that you like it, I'm glad that you find something to like, because I like all of you.'

And they smiled at each other, tenderly, admissively, securely, their eyes taking on the profound and searching gaze of certainty, their voices mutually sinking and deepening to that tone so much desired, so rarely heard. So rarely ventured.

When they had had their steak, he put one hand on her knee, and she kicked her shoe off and put her foot on his. It felt very soft in its stocking. She had not done at all badly in her effort to drink her half of the bottle of wine, and her cheeks were dimly pink, and her hair fell in her eyes.

'Clara,' he said to her, as she curled her toes on his ankle, 'Clara.'

'My hair gets in my eyes,' she said, for answer, pushing it away, pushing it back with both hands, with both elbows on the table, leaning towards him, her two hands framing a bare white triangle on her high forehead; 'And it's too long, when I eat it gets in my food.'

'Don't have it cut,' he said, 'don't have it cut.'

'I can't afford to have it cut,' she said, 'or not how I would like it, and so it grows.'

'Let it grow,' he said.

And then they had some coffee, and then he looked at her and said:

'We could always go to the cinema, for the afternoon.'

'Shouldn't you be at work?' she said.

'I should,' he said, 'but I shan't go. Whatever you say, even if you say no to me, I shan't go.'

'What would you do?' she said. 'If I said no?'

'Oh Christ,' he said, as the underwash of the dreadful tides of his life washed faintly towards him, from a long way off, from some other sea, threatening the safe and steep-walled inlet where they sat, 'Oh Christ, God knows what I would do, wander around, God knows, I don't know what I would do.'

And she said, quickly, distressed, moved, not as he feared taking this sudden opening as an expression of his desire for her, but taking it for what it was, for a glimpse into the darkness from which he came towards her:

'Oh, I'll come, of course I'll come.'

And so he paid the bill, and they set off together towards the door, towards the stairs up towards the street; the staircase was narrow and dark, and it turned a sharp corner, and on the corner of it he kissed her, and as they stood there another couple, descending, passed them, and he held her in his arms and she buried her face against his. In his arms it was close and private, and he smelled of French cigarettes, and she could feel the hairs of his chest through his shirt. When they had kissed at some length they moved on, up the stairs, and in the street they walked together with their arms entwined, inseparable: they went to the Academy, and sat as each had sat with others in the back row, and as soon as they sat down they turned once more towards each other, turning as they sank into the chairs, mouth on mouth, his arms reaching for her, his hands inside her coat and her jersey, and reaching for so many lost sensa-

152

ꞇions, and finding them there, finding them unfaded as though they had been waiting for him. He had not sat so, in a cinema, for more than seven years, and he felt on her lips the loss of time, and the withering of expectation, and the sudden anxious existence, of himself, so persuasively evoked, and it seemed that in many ways it would have been easier to have kept himself out of the way of such addictive recollections. And yet at the same time it seemed important to be alive, and he remembered, with anguish, that years ago it was such sensations only that he had dignified with the name of life.

The film was an Italian film about an old man, and Clara caught glimpses of it from time to time, and saw as much of it as she would have wanted to see; such a method of viewing films had always seemed to her desirable, and her attention, when caught by the angle of an Italian street, or by the grief of the old man, seemed to be peculiarly intense. When at University, she had read books, voraciously, on her college hostel bed, while her men tried to make love to her; she had read the whole of Adolphe while lying on top of a man called Bernard, and when Bernard had protested she had said, untruthfully, you do not understand, unless I read to take my mind off you, you would be too much for me. She found Gabriel infinitely more disturbing and distracting than Bernard, and the film less interesting though almost as depressing as Adolphe. But she was not depressed: happiness filled her, she thought that she had never been so happy in her life.

They sat through the film twice, and by the time it ended it was almost evening, and they had reached a state where it was no longer possible for them to part. She wondered what he would suggest, as they finally disentangled themselves, at the second raising of the lights, and got up to go: she rested comfortably upon his worldliness, she knew that he would suggest something, and that acquiescence would be all her part. And he, who had for years been dreaming in his office about such an act, could think only of his office. He had feared, in the dim past mists of unformulated anticipation, that she might, if things were ever to reach such a point, find such a suggestion sordid: but from what she had given of herself during those smoky cinema hours, he could see that for such a nature as hers the sordid, if it existed, did not repel, that hesitation only could repel. So he said to her, as they stumbled up the stairs and on to Oxford Street.

'We could go to my office. If you would come.'

'Of course I will come,' she said, 'if you are sure.'

'Sure of what?' he said.

'That there will be no one there,' she said.

And he explained to her that there would be people in the building, but not on his floor of the building, and that he had the key. And she smiled, and said, Oh yes then, that's all right. And so they walked together, south to where his office was, past the bright, cheap, tatty, cobbled clothes in the shop windows, and they held hands as they walked, and kissed once at a corner whilst waiting for the traffic lights to change, and he seemed to be avenging himself upon those lost and bitterly regretted moments, those envied visions of couples kissing on stations, kissing in cars, kissing under bridges and in doorways, kissing on films and on television, kissing in his own head. When they reached his office, they went up in the lift without meeting anyone, and he unlocked his door, and then locked it behind him, and then with mutual good will they lay down upon the floor. And he not ceasing to be astonished by her ease, and she not ceasing to be astonished by her own felicity, they lay there together upon the mock parquet tiles, lit by the band of fluorescent light, their heads in the space under his desk, staring upwards together, finally, at the unknown underside of the desk, amidst the smell of polish, and the unswept cigarette ash of the day, and the small round paper punchings from his secretary's filing activities. Clara's hair, shortly, was full of paper punchings, as of confetti.

After a while, he said,

'Just think, just think, if you hadn't come.'

'I can't imagine,' she said, sitting up and staring down at him, 'how you could think I might not come. How could I ever have stayed away from you? You must be the most beautiful person that I ever saw in my whole life. I would have been mad to have stayed away.'

'And you still see it that way?' he said, still lying flat, his arms crossed comfortably behind his head.

'Why should I not?' she said. 'It was very nice, it's been very nice. I wouldn't have missed it, not for anything.'

And they stared at each other, reflective, hopeful, satisfied.

Then she fished her brown jersey out of the wastepaper basket, where she had dropped it, and started to get dressed again.

'Don't dress, don't dress,' he complained; but she said, 'I'm cold, I must.'

And when she was dressed, she stood up, and started to wander round the office, picking things up, looking at the papers and notices pinned on the walls, inspecting the contents of his cupboard and of his pencil drawer, gazing at herself, in passing, in the mirror behind the door, and reaching flattening, ineffective hands to smooth her hair. She was happy; she felt at home and familiar there, she felt that she had bought herself a right to look, and even the sight of a broken biro on his windowsill was of interest to her. He lay on the floor and watched her; she liked to be watched. And she tried to piece together, from what she saw, the rest of Gabriel's life: but she tried idly, luxuriously, because she did not really want to know. She did not want to know everything about him. She liked the unknown, she liked to feel familiar with the unknown.

Over his desk, on the wall, there were a great many notices and pictures and photographs pinned up, and she looked at these closely, seeing that they were there to be looked at; there were reminders and appointments, and a photograph of Clelia and Annunciata, and a photograph of his two elder children, and there was a whole series of photographs of a pop singer whose fame was currently at its dizzy histrionic zenith. Clara was surprised to find such pin-up photographs: she had thought that Gabriel's world would eschew, somehow, having no need of them, the cheaper glories of the masses, and she turned to him, curiously, and said, 'Why, why on earth do you have all these pictures of Elvera?' and he said, 'Why not? I always thought she was the most beautiful girl I'd ever seen, why, don't you find her beautiful?' And Clara, looking once more at the pictures, of the wide-mouthed, thick-necked singer, throwing her arms up to the heavens wildly, had to concede beauty, had to concede that she had never even troubled to

155

look at such pictures before, so sure had she been that there
would have been no point in looking. And she still did not see
the point in having them there, those cheaply purchasable
photographs: collecting of such things, interest in such things,
had always seemed to her from early school days on to be an
indication of immaturity, of poverty, of lack of resources, of
making do with second best: she had as resolutely and as
puritanically scorned the pop world and its manifestations as
her mother had done before her. But, from Gabriel's example,
she tried to force herself to see the point, to encompass even
this, ready to see in her own disinterest her mother's own
rigidity: because the truth was that everything that Gabriel did
seemed to her to be right. The fact that those pictures were
here upon his wall redeemed all pictures pinned up on all
walls: he had told her that Elvera was beautiful, and so she
was, she could see it now, yes, looking at her, in those thick-
grained overblown photographs, she could see it, and she
wondered what stubborn narrow prejudice had blinded her but
an instant before.

And she felt, as she felt with Clelia, when Clelia opened her
eyes, as she so often did, to some new and unexpected virtue
in the external world: she felt gratitude, and amazement. She
took them on trust so completely, the Denhams, for as far as
she could see they were never wrong. And yet trust was not the
right word for the way that she regarded them, for she did not
humbly and ignorantly echo their judgements in her own head;
she did not say to herself, repeating what she had heard, I like
that advertisement, that house, that film, that book, that painting, that kind of stocking, that man's face. It was rather that
she saw what they saw, once they had told her to see it. They
taught her, they instructed her, as once Miss Haines had taught
her to admire Corneille: and the lesson about Corneille had
been worth while, the object worthy of effort, so why not all
these new acquisitions? She despised in herself the odd, recalci-
trant severity that had condemned Elvera without looking at
her: and yet she knew that without the sanction of Gabriel's
casual approval she would never have bothered to look, just as,
without Clelia's doubtful admiration, she would have seen in
Martin merely a thin, balding, ascetic neurotic intellectual, a

man in no way possibly the object of desire. It was hard work, the acquiring of opinions, and she felt an unresentful envy for those like Gabriel and Clelia, those who had been born with views, those who had known from infancy which pictures to pin up on their walls. Clara's walls were bare, from indecision.

When Gabriel finally roused himself from his floor, and got up and buttoned up his shirt and zipped up his trousers, Clara said to him:

'Do you go in for this kind of thing much?'

'Ah,' he said, 'it depends on what kind of thing you think it is, doesn't it?'

'No, not really,' said Clara. 'What I mean is, do you go in much for the kind of thing that might be taken to be this kind of thing? And to that, you see, you can only say yes or no.'

'No, then,' said Gabriel. 'And what about you?'

'I'm afraid it might be more likely, in my case, to be yes,' said Clara. 'Not that it matters, really.'

'Time alone will show,' said Gabriel.

'Yes, I suppose so,' said Clara.

'We could have another look at the problem on Monday,' said Gabriel. 'I could take you out to lunch on Monday.'

'That would be very nice,' said Clara. 'I should like that.'

Gabriel was late home, but it did not matter, as Phillipa never had a meal waiting for him even when he was on time, and she would never betray the interest in his activities that would have been implied by an interrogation. She was sitting in the living room when he arrived, just sitting, and listening to the radio. He greeted her, and she inclined her head, faintly, in his direction, so he went off into the kitchen and made himself an omelette, and came and sat down with her to eat it. He was faint with hunger, and he ate with the omelette half a loaf of bread. When he had finished eating, he remembered the lemon squeezer in his pocket, and he got it out and handed it to her. She smiled, anxiously, as though willing to appear pleased.

'Why did you buy it?' she said.

'I don't know,' he said. 'I just saw it, that's all.'

Then she reverted her attention to the radio, and he, suddenly desperate before the blank waste remaining hour of the evening, asked her, rashly, recklessly, how she had spent her day. And she told him, very limply and hesitantly, in her flat pale voice, that she had been in the afternoon to the chemist's to buy some Junior Aspirin, and that as it was raining she had not walked as far as her usual chemist, but had stopped at the nearest one, the one on the corner of the next street. It was a shop, she explained, that she always avoided, because of the seedy, flyblown look of the windows, with their ancient out-dated advertisements, and because of the slowness of the service. And this time, she said, she was served by an old man, who had received her request in grudging silence, had spent several minutes looking through the nearest drawers, and then had dragged himself painfully up the steps into the back of the shop to look there. He had not found what she wanted, and had redescended into the shop, unwilling to let her go, mumbling continually that he knew they were there somewhere, and after a few more fumblings the front door of the shop had opened, and his slightly less frail and aged wife had entered. And the old man said to her, as though he were alone with her in the shop, as though the shop were not a shop but a room to live in, it was no good, they couldn't carry on like this, they'd have to close down, and live on their pensions. 'I just can't manage when you're out, Edie,' he had said, plaintively, 'I just can't manage when you leave the shop.'

And Phillipa had stood there, listening, listening to these tragic intimacies, and they had given her the Junior Aspirins, finally, as though she should never have asked for them, as though she should have known better than to ask.

'And the truth is,' she concluded, 'that I had known better. I knew from the look of that shop that I was the last person in the world that ought to go in it. It was written all over their windows, that I ought not to go in.'

'It wasn't your fault, though,' he said. 'They must have needed to sell you the aspirins. Or they would have shut the shop.'

'They needed to. But they couldn't,' she said.

Clara, when she got home, shook the paper clippings from her hair, and smiled at herself in the mirror. She thought that she looked rather well. On the other hand, she was not much looking forward to the night, as she feared she was too excited to sleep. Also, she felt slightly sick, as she had felt after her first afternoon at the Denhams' house: it was the sickness and strain of finding too well what she had been looking for. She had presupposed such a man as Gabriel, such a dark and surreptitious lunch, such an episode upon an unfamiliar floor, and it had happened to her. She felt triumphant, but mingled with her triumph there was a certain alarm. She felt that she was being supported and abetted by fate in some colossal folly: that circumstances were conspiring maliciously to persuade her that her own estimate of herself, that high and grandiose self-assessment of adolescence, was right. She had considered herself too good for such as Walter Ash, and she had got Gabriel. There seemed to be no end to the possibilities of mad aspiration. And yet, she could not feel that this was the way the world should go, she felt that she was breasting, rashly, the marching currents of humanity, and that she would in the end be forced to turn about.

She was so excited that she wished she were still living in college, so that she could call on one of her friends to tell them the whole story. She was not much given to using the telephone, having been bred to use the instrument meagrely and with respect, and anyway the only person to whom she ever told such things, now, was Clelia. And this was one piece of news that she did not think Clelia would much like to know.

But in the end she did ring Clelia. Not to tell her, but to talk to her. And as she talked, the consciousness of practising deception did not distress her, for on the contrary she felt that the possession of a secret gave her an extra dimension, an extra asset. They had all for years had their complications, and now she had hers: it even seemed that Gabriel was another bond between them. It did not for a moment occur to her that Clelia might, in a simple sense, object. She imagined herself to be in a world where such considerations did not exist. And yet she knew that it would be better to say nothing, just as Clelia never said anything about Martin, and indeed now said nothing about the return of Martin's wife. They talked of other things, of Clara's course on Non-Denominational Religion, of a belt that Clelia had lost off her dress that morning on the bus. But behind their conversation lay other shadows, and Clara felt that the thicker the shadows grew, the more nearly she would be approaching the densely forested gloom that she took to be life itself.

When she had rung off, she walked up and down her room for a few times, thinking that she would not sleep, and then she went to bed and straight away she slept.

Chapter 8

Clara found that she enjoyed being Gabriel's mistress. The complications of the liaison, and all its dubious undertones heightened so much her feeling for Gabriel himself that she found herself from time to time on the verge of wondering uneasily whether she did not find more pleasure in the situation than in the man. For she liked the sense of secrecy, the elaborate assignations, the pre-arranged telephone calls in public call boxes, the small, passionate, surreptitious gifts. And yet, at the same time, she was aware, quite distinctly, of Gabriel himself, and could even appreciate, calmly, the impulses that drove him towards her, and the suffering that he had endured. And yet again, on a third level, what she felt for him was need and love, and when he went back to Phillipa, each night, each evening, she felt within herself the dim jealous stirrings of rage. And yet this rage itself she cherished. For to feel jealousy, that classic passion, was in itself a sign of life, and seemed to set a value upon the days through which she was living. She did not see enough of him, did not get enough of him, and felt with the acquired wisdom of her observations that too little was infinitely better than too much, that desire was in every way preferable to possession.

And yet such knowledge did not advise her to refuse him, when he offered her the traditional illicit diversion, a week in Paris. She knew, as she accepted, that perhaps she should have known better, but she also knew herself to be incapable of refusing so dazzling, so delightful a prospect. Paris and Gabriel offered a combination of pleasures that could not be declined. She had visited Paris often enough, since that first school visit, but never with a man, and never with money in her pocket. The money would, in point of fact, be in Gabriel's pocket, not her own, but that would come to the same thing; she had never managed to find in herself the smallest comprehension of Gabriel's complaint of poverty, for he seemed to her to spend money like water. She felt sure that travelling in such company, she would see sights that she had never seen before, sights that had been all her life awaiting her; they seemed to call her, and she said that she would go.

He, for his part, wanted to see her. The charms of deceit did not much charm him, and he lived in London in perpetual fear of surprisal, all the more anxious because he could not tell if his infidelity would be to Phillipa a matter of total indifference, or something more in the nature of a last straw. He did not think she could possibly know, and could not imagine what would happen if she did; and although he managed fine stretches of abandon, in the back of his car, in the cinema, in his locked and viewless office, he could not bring himself to forget. So that when the prospect of a week in Paris was proposed to him, one morning, by his boss, he seized upon it as some kind of answer to his needs, and positively put himself out in order to make it happen. Even his discreet efforts in this direction seemed to him conspicuous, for he had hitherto resisted to the last moment all enticements to foreign travel, and after succumbing to the Spanish trip in search of Lorca had sworn to Phillipa that he would never go again. 'Go if you want,' she said. 'It's all the same to me.' But he had felt himself upon his honour. Now, after so short a lapse, his honour seemed to have decayed, and the thought of Clara was to him so compulsive that he found himself angling, seemingly reluctant, seemingly self-effacing, for the job. Reluctant acceptance was an attitude with which he was invariably successful, and the job was given to him. He had known beforehand that Clara would go, for he felt that she would go anywhere, for the sake of going as much as for his sake, and he did not object to her reasons, for his own were far from pure. He wanted to sleep with her, this was all he wanted, the notion of her obsessed him, he felt that on her body he was trying to regain lost time. And it consoled him to think that her need for him was equally indirect. They met, it seemed to him, in some tender, conniving, amorous bargain; each offered, each took, each acknowledged. Such understanding seemed to him greater,

162

more necessary than love itself. And so he said to her: I have to go to Paris on business, for a week, and come with me, Clara, come with me, you can sleep with me all night long. And she, thinking of hotels, and drinks, and crossed seas, and pale yellow floral stone, and Gabriel as the arms from which she saw these things, said yes, yes, and kissed him most passionately in her gratitude.

She left a message for her Director of Studies, saying that she had returned to Northam for the week as her mother was ill, and left instructions with an obliging friend to corroborate, if possible and necessary, this statement. She felt faintly guilty about taking her mother's name in vain in this way, but she could not think of any other valid excuse for her absence, and felt, in her heart, a faintly pleasurable, guilty revenge, as though she were plucking her pleasures directly from the thorny tree itself. She did not think her absence would cause much disturbance, for there were few people who would even miss her, and the slight element of risk she as ever enjoyed.

She met Gabriel at the Air Terminal: she had had a moment's dismay when she had thought that discretion might oblige him to travel separately, but he had finally decided that there could be nobody on the plane or in the whole of Paris to whom Clara would mean anything at all, and that she could if asked pretend to be his secretary. She was, to his surprise, a little cool about the idea of being taken as his secretary, so he dropped the notion quickly, and said that they might as well stop worrying, because whoever could they meet? Clara was not herself wholly happy about the idea of not meeting anyone, and indeed sometimes suspected that there was nothing that she more desired than compromise, final, decisive compromise, but she took his point and said nothing.

She had never flown before, and the whole adventure of flying was to her a most delightful treat. She liked everything, from the cup of coffee they had at the Air Terminal, to the glassy glittering expanses of Orly Airport, with all its frivolous extravagant facilities for expense. In fact she liked Orly so much that he could hardly drag her away from it; she insisted upon staying there for a drink, although he was nervously anxious to leave his things as quickly as possible at the hotel.

'Why hurry?' she kept saying. 'We have all morning; why hurry? Only people like my mother hurry to get to hotels, why bother about the hotel?' But he, anxious about the devious and complex booking and re-booking that he had been obliged to negotiate, was restless and would not stay, and he bought, to placate her, a bottle of gin in a smart cardboard bag, and a large bottle of perfume, and she clutching these tributes they went and got a taxi and drove into Paris, and to their hotel. Clara, abroad, had never so much as set foot in a taxi; she was absurdly astonished to find that it was possible, so simply, to catch a taxi, for her excursions in Paris had always hitherto been accompanied by exhaustion, aching feet, and the studious recollections of the names of streets. But Gabriel knew a different Paris; he got in a taxi, and told the driver the name of his hotel, and it went.

The hotel reconciled her to the loss of Orly Airport. She had known that it would not be possible to stay in a grand and public, leafy-foyered place, but she had not hoped that Gabriel could so perfectly avoid the shabby. It was a small hotel, on a small and narrow street on the Left Bank, and so discreet was it that they had difficulty in finding anyone to admit their arrival, and yet it made up for the quiet absence of its staff by the glory of its décor. The narrow foyer was lined with mirrors, spotted like the famous hall, so long since visited, at Versailles; Clara now took these spots to be a source of pride and not of shame. On the tiled floor stood suits of armour, heavily reflected, and deeply polished, deeply carved pieces of old wooden furniture; the ceiling was beamed, and the plaster between the beams was painted a deep bright red. Their room, when they finally discovered someone willing to take them to it, was decorated with equally bizarre, consistent verve; the walls were red, the bed was a four-poster of black wood, the bedspread and the curtains were of heavy green velvet. The bath in the bathroom matched the green of the curtains, and the radiators and the frankly exposed pipes of the plumbing and central heating were all painted red. The carpet was thick and green, and from the red walls extended black and gold wooden arms holding lamps. Clara, seeing it, was overcome with delight; she had never seen anything like it, and it seemed to encompass Gabriel and herself, in their momentary solitude, with a peculiarly appropriate, intimate significance. She turned to Gabriel, standing there in the doorway with their two cases, which for lack of offers he had had to carry up himself, up two flights of stairs, and the sight of him struck her once more in all his peculiar beauty, and he put the cases down, and shut the door behind him, and came and took her in his arms. He undressed her, gently, anxiously, and they pulled down the velvet cover and lay on the bed and made love; it was the first time he had slept with her in a bed more than two feet six inches wide: and it was the first double bed of her life.

On the wall at the end of the bed there was a painting, an oil painting of a thin-faced woman, holding in her arms a small dog; the oil of the painting was badly cracked, and the woman stared coldly down upon them, through the stiff wrinkles of age.

On the bed there, Clara said to Gabriel, 'What will happen to me, what will happen if I should ever lose my nerve?' And he did not know what she meant, and she said, 'I am chased, I am pursued, I run and run, but I will never get away, the apple does not fall far from the tree,' she said.

'What apple, what tree,' he said sleepily, and held her as she reared anxiously up from him, sitting up, clutching herself, folding herself in her bare arms; and he said, 'You are all nerve, you are solid nerve, see, I feel you, I hold you, you are firm and hard, all nerve, there is nothing you would not dare,' and she said, 'Yes, I am all nerve, I am hard, there is no love in me, I am too full of will to love.' And he said, hardly listening, 'What nonsense,' and she said, 'Oh lovely Gabriel, I love you, I love you,' and lay upon him and kissed him, her fear and her need combined. Because love, desperately, eluded her; she had not been taught to love, she had lacked those expensive, private lessons.

In the afternoon, Gabriel had to see a man at the television place, so at two o'clock they got up and went downstairs and into the next door café and had some lunch. When Gabriel left her, he gave her some French money and said, when she protested: 'Spend it, spend it, I brought it for you.' And she took it, uneasily, promptly, and put it in her bag. Fifteen

165

pounds, he had given her, to fill in a few hours; without his guidance she did not think she could manage to spend more than ten shillings. And when he had gone, she walked down to the Boulevard Saint Michel, and crossed the river, and looked at the Sainte Chapelle for one franc, and then at Notre-Dame, for nothing, and then she walked on, across the Ile Saint Louis, and up to the Place des Vosges, and on and on, up to Montmartre, miles and miles of stony Paris, stopping once for a small black coffee, which she drank standing, for it was expensive to sit down, and then back again, down the steep hill, and when she reached the big shops fatigue overcame her, and she got on a bus and went back to the hotel, where Gabriel was waiting for her, having returned earlier than he had expected, and she said, sitting on the bed and pulling off her dusty shoes: 'Here, have your money back. I can't make myself spend it, you will have to spend it on me.' And he, most secretly relieved, took it back, and they went out to dinner, to a dark smart place where they sat in an alcove and held hands and ate too much. And when they got back to the hotel, she had a bath, and he sat and watched her, and then she said she wanted a drink, and what about the gin, and he said that there was nothing to put in the gin, and she said that that didn't matter, she would drink it neat. And she did; she got out of the bath, and dried herself, and put on her night gown, and lay there on the bed reading a book and drinking neat gin. The sight of her, thus recklessly ruining her health, her sleep and her digestion, made him feel ill and old; such lack of foresight was quite beyond him. There had been, he dimly recollected, a day when he might have drunk gin for the sake of alcohol, but now he would as soon have drunk liquid paraffin. He wanted her to pay him attention; it was getting late, and he wanted her to look at him, but she went on reading, and he felt that she was reading to shut him out, to prolong, frivolously, their eventual communications, and he was too tired for such frivolity. And yet at the same time he did not want to disturb her, for her happy, false absorption touched him, and he wanted to see on what terms she would turn to him. Because he knew that unlike Phillipa, she would turn in his direction, and that her attention to her book was in some way for his benefit.

After some time, she closed the book, and dropped it on the floor, and rolled over on to her back, and shut her eyes. 'Oh Lord,' she said, as soon as she had shut her eyes. 'Oh Lord, I feel dreadful, I feel simply dreadful, why ever did I drink all that gin? Why didn't you stop me, Gabriel? Gabriel, what a name, Gabriel, did you know that the Italians call their children Paradise and Heaven and such things?'

'Why not?' he said, 'why not?'

'Oh Lord,' said Clara, and got up off the bed, and groped her way to the bathroom, and slammed the door after herself; and he could hear her vomiting violently. He listened, anxiously, to the noise of running water, and after a few moments asked her if she felt all right, and he heard her laugh, and say that she felt fine, much better, and that she'd be out in no time. And she was; she emerged, shortly, her hair tied back with a piece of string, her face shining faintly, smelling of soap.

'I'm sorry, I'm sorry,' she said, as she walked into his arms. 'How dreadful of me, I always do this when I'm unnerved, when I'm happy. Do I smell frightful, can you bear to be near me?'

'You smell lovely,' he said, 'of soap.'

'I was terribly sick,' she said, 'when I got home, the first time I went to your house, with Clelia, it was so marvellous I couldn't take it, I just went home and was sick, and it's the same with you, you're so marvellous I can't take you either.'

'It wasn't me,' he said, 'it was the gin; if you drink like that, what do you expect?'

'I only drank it because of you,' she said.

'If I drank like that,' he said, 'I'd feel ill for a week, and you, you seem to be all right again, how do you recover so quickly?'

And he did not like to think of the answer, although he knew it and she did not; it was because she was so young. In five years, he had entered upon a different generation; her childless, tireless, energy belonged to another, earlier world, and one lost to him forever, however he might try to retrace his steps. She amazed him; she could come to him like that, and Phillipa would turn away to fasten her stockings. And as they embraced, that night, he found himself thinking, I must be at work at ten in the morning, it's all right for her, but I must be at work, and I must, I must get some sleep, and he saw, across the slope of her right breast, the gleaming luminous face of his watch and it told him, in its pale green minatory figures, that it was half past two. But despite his fatigue, she was asleep before him; when he relinquished her she slept instantly on her belly, her face creased up on the pillow, breathing heavily, her arms all folded up beneath her, in a total, exhausted sleep, with all her tautness turned into loose dead weight. And he could not sleep; he lay there restless, thinking of his wife, of his children, of his bank balance, and wondering to himself, irritably, sadly, why he had not arranged to have his car serviced while he was away. He had lost the ability to sleep, as she slept; sleeping and waking seemed to him more and more to overlap, so that he dozed in the day, and dreamed restlessly all night, listening for the cries of children in his dreams.

On the third day, he took her to the television centre with him. Clara had hoped to see, with Gabriel, a different Paris from the architectural, linguistic fortress of her University days, and in a sense she was not disappointed. She saw areas she had never visited before; he lead her to the Faubourg Saint Honoré, as Clelia had led her to Bond Street, and to the bou-tiques of the Left Bank, where all the shop windows were filled with clothes that reminded her uneasily of Phillipa. He bought English newspapers, recklessly, and never thought to stand up when he might sit down, nor to buy two drinks in one bar rather than one drink in two bars for the sake of saving on the service. All Clara's carefully accumulated knowledge of how to live abroad for nothing was to him quite useless, she was glad to note; he took Paris as though it were London, a city to be lived in. She liked the idea that he was here for a specific purpose, on business, though when, once, sitting in a bar out-side Notre-Dame, he tried to explain the nature of his mission, she found her ears closing up with unaccustomed uncompre-hending boredom; but at the same time she found herself possessed, occasionally, by a faint resenting jealousy. If she had been his wife, she could not help thinking, then she would have met people; she would have been introduced. She set great store by introductions, for they fended off from her the
168

fear of solitude. She would have liked to have met a French person. She knew that Gabriel knew people in Paris, and was rather annoyed by the fact that her equivocal status, in other ways so agreeable, should thus cut her off from them. Also, she was proud of being with Gabriel, and the passing acquisitive glances of other women did not satisfy her craving for confirmation, for they saw nothing but his outward graces, not in themselves so rare, and could not assess the more complex graces of his heart and of his heritage. Nor was her presence there with him to them at all remarkable. She wished to see in the eyes of others the dim, narrowing, receding vistas, the arches and long corridors through which she had travelled. She wished to set, through him, a value on herself. The image of a honeymoon, with its close and passionate solitude, meant little to her; she could not keep her eyes or her hands off Gabriel, but other desires and other needs lay deeper in her heart. It was not one man that she needed, but through one man a view of other things, a sensation of other ways of being, she wished to feel herself attached to the world. And once, as she sat with a cup of coffee, alone, it crossed her mind, nervously, uneasily, that it was not Gabriel himself after all that she wanted, but marriage to Gabriel: as Gabriel's wife she would have been irrevocably attached, safe, strapped, labelled, bound and fixed, never to be lost again, and where after all should she find better than Gabriel himself? Nowhere, nowhere, she knew; there was nothing more to look for; he was what she had wanted, and she had him, and he did not belong to her, and she did not want him to belong to her. She did not know what she wanted; she bowed her head, sadly, saddened, staring into her small bitter black cup, seeing there the bitter limits of her own hitherto illimitable designs.

One night, in bed, they talked of Clelia. Clara had always avoided the subject of Clelia, not wishing to spill a drop of her affection, but one night Gabriel said to her suddenly,

'Clara, you remind me of Clelia, at times you even look like Clelia, tell me, why do you look like her, now, at this instant?'

'I look like her,' said Clara, sitting up in bed reading and propped on the pillows, 'because I try to look like her, that's all. I bought this nightdress because it looks like hers, if you want to know. And I went into a shop to have my hair cut like hers, but I came out again, I was afraid she might object.'

'She wouldn't have objected,' said Gabriel, 'she would have liked it. I like you to look like Clelia, do you think I used to be in love with Clelia? I think I probably was.'

'All your family,' said Clara, 'always seem to me to be in love with all the rest of your family. If you see what I mean: it always seems to be rife with incest, don't you think?'

'That's what Phillipa says,' said Gabriel, who had found it easier to talk of Phillipa than not to talk of her; 'she doesn't like it; she thinks we are all self-indulgent, self-erected saints, that we do it all ourselves, that this marvellous world we think we live in is just an image that we impose upon the rest. She hates it, she calls it vanity.'

'I don't hate it,' said Clara, 'I like it; ought I not to like it? I think you are real saints, it doesn't occur to me that you might not be real. Aren't you real? I don't see why people should object to your all being so wonderful; some people are more wonderful than others, they just are.'

'Clelia is the only real saint,' said Gabriel; 'she truly is a saint. My mother always knew she would be the one. The rest of us, well, the rest of us get by, but Clelia has the real thing. Oh, we're all marvellous, we're all polite and delightful and witty and agreeable and all the rest of it, but Clelia is gifted, she's the only one of us who's really gifted, you know. She paints really well, one day she will paint really well. But the rest of us will never do anything. Look at Amelia, she went mad through the shock of waking up in the outside world, out of the golden nest, and she only married to get away from us, you know, to escape from our amorous family clutches, and when she got out, when she breathed the cold air of Essex, she went mad. And Magnus works – he's the cleverest, but they never prized cleverness, they wanted us to be strange and wonderful, so in revenge Magnus works, he kills himself with work; he permits himself to wander so slightly, so discreetly, he lets it be known he's a man of culture, but he works, to prove he can at least do that. And then he must, with all those children. And then there is me, and what can I do? I can do everything and nothing. No, don't look at me like that, because it's true, it's quite true that I can do nothing really well, or rather I can do everything well and nothing well enough, I sometimes think I should have been an actor, because that was the only thing I ever wanted to do, but I didn't do it, and now I couldn't, I know the life too well to want to do it, and so there is nothing left that I want to do. But Clelia, she wants something, I don't know how she can be so singled out, but so she was, and they always knew it, our parents, they recognized the marks. They don't understand what she does, painting since 1865 means nothing to them at all, but people tell them it's good, and since one of their children had to be good then it had to be Clelia.'

'I don't know about painting,' said Clara, 'but Clelia I love.'

'Clelia's nature is perfection,' said Gabriel, 'she is made up of every virtue, and moreover I have never heard her speak a dull word in her life. I could spend the rest of my life with Clelia; I miss her. I've never said this to anyone before, not even I think to myself, but it's true, I miss her, when I married I began to miss her, and Phillipa can tell it, she hated Clelia, she must be the only person in the world who can feel hatred for Clelia. If she *weren't* my sister, I would miss her, and since she is, why should I not?'

'If she weren't your sister, you would probably have married her,' said Clara.

'But she is my sister,' said Gabriel; 'I'll tell you what, why don't we all go and live together, you and me and Clelia? Let's go and live together in the country somewhere.'

'*Mon enfant, ma soeur, songe à la douceur, d'aller là-bas vivre ensemble,*' said Clara, and started to laugh, and said, 'Oh God, if you could just *see* my brothers, you'd see what a refinement it is for you to spend time missing Clelia, Christ, why do you all have such marvellous relatives and wives and husbands to worry about? Why didn't I have a few, just a few?'

'You can worry about me, now,' said Gabriel. 'Me and Clelia, Clelia and me, your family by proxy.'

'What do you think about the ties of blood?' said Clara. 'I believe in them; you know, I could tell my family, if I were an orphan I could go back to my own family, like a kitten, no, I don't mean a kitten, but surely some animal; some insect maybe, that can tell its own blood? My parents were married for five years before they had any children, and it's for that that they look so old, my father looked an old man when he died, and my mother looks twice the age of your mother, but she's not, she's not old at all, she's got years and years and years to live, she isn't even sixty, she might live another forty years, till I'm sixty too,' and at this Clara began to cry, painfully, miserably, propped up against the green velvet roll, against the red wall, the tears rolling down her pale cheeks, cheeks unwontedly pale from sleeplessness and drink and strain and apprehension. And he, too, though he most gently, with soft lips, drank her tears, could have wept himself, for he too felt the weight of those empty, rolling, joyless years, years without hope and without pleasure, for they were his own wife's years unrolling there in Clara's eyes, and rolling down her face. And they sat there together, their backs against the wall, kissing gently, sighing, oppressed, united, related.

The next day, which was their last day, he said that he would take her to work with him, and that she could see the television place, and have lunch there with him. He offered her this partly because he had been touched by her the night before and did not want to leave her, and partly because, it being the last day, he no longer thought it would be dangerous; the man that he was due to see was eminently suitable for introduction to Clara, being a bright young newly-divorced fellow to whom all women promised bright new adventure, and Gabriel thought that he would judge Clara's peripheral presence a complimentary asset rather than an embarrassment. Also, the work that he had come to do had been done; he had purchased a certain amount of film, which had turned out better than he had been given to expect, and also cheaper, and nothing remained of his mission but the final, mutually-congratulatory stages, which he had no objection to her witnessing.

She accepted his offer eagerly; she too felt warm towards him, as he to her, for his reception of her distress the night before had seemed to her peculiarly companionable. She was used to the look of boredom which crossed people's faces when she talked of her mother, and had been grateful not to find it. And the thought of seeing the television place appealed to her as an excursion; she had always liked institution build-

172

ings, and hoped to find in the Maison de la Radio the smart paradigm of all such establishments. The idea of television seemed moreover to her to be instinct with glamour and drama: Gabriel, often profoundly depressed by the prospects of his career, found her enthusiasm and susceptibility an unexpected blessing. She was the perfect audience, the ideal visitor: impressionable, observant, uninformed, and yet at the same time no fool, for the things that she saw were the things that were there, though she saw them with the eyes of indulgence.

They set off in the morning, on a bus, having time to kill, and got off at the Place du Trocadéro and looked at the golden statues and the Eiffel Tower and the inscription on the Palais de Chaillot which said that the artist's well-loved pain strengthens him. Then, to kill more time, they sat on the *terrasse* of one of the cafés and had a drink, and Clara, yet once more, wondered at the way he without thinking sat at the most evident, the nearest, and inevitably the most expensive place, and wondered whether he even knew that by walking a little way off the Place and up a side street he could save himself a few shillings. And she wondered whether the saving of a few shillings would interest him, even if he knew how to do it. She had always been puzzled by the way in which people insisted upon sitting on expensive *terrasses*, and she had imagined them all to be, each time, overcome with shock and irritation when presented with the bill. She had thought the *terrasse* prices to be a vast hoax for the trapping of the innocent and had been perpetually surprised by the never-ending supply of victims, waiting to be duped. And now she saw that those who sat there drinking their expensive beers and coffees and green drinks and pale Pernod were not victims at all; they did not care about the bill, they preferred, they chose to sit upon a *terrasse*, it was worth it to them to sit there and watch the cars screech round the corners and the sun shining on the vast concrete Palais; and it was for such as Gabriel that these places had been built.

They sat there, in the sun, and after a while she said, 'It must be a year now, a whole year, since I first met Clelia. It was last May I met her, a whole year ago.'

And he said, looking at her sitting there under the yellow canvas parasol,

'You know,' he said, 'that whatever may happen to us, to you and me, you can never entirely escape me, you know, nor I you, for you will never give up Clelia, and I can never give up Clelia, so that makes us related for life, that makes you, as it were, one of the family –'

'Why should I wish to escape you?' she said, staring at him, 'on the contrary, there is nothing I want more than to keep – no, not to keep you, but to keep knowledge of you, to know what becomes of you, I should like to be forced to know what becomes of you.'

He took her hand, and they kissed, under their umbrella, and when he let go of her he sat still with his arm around her, and it was as they were sitting there, thus linked, that Magnus walked past.

He walked so close to them, across the front of the pavement where they were sitting, that they all three saw one another, clearly, with recognition, before they had time to turn away. Clara felt Gabriel stiffen by her side, and she too stiffened, in alarm, in pleasure at discovery, and in fear that she would witness in Gabriel some dreadful fall from grace. She thought he would release her, but she felt his arm decide to remain where it was, around her bare shoulders, and she knew that he had taken it, that it would be all right.

'Magnus,' said Gabriel, smiling up at him, with complicity, with charm, with apparent delight. 'Magnus, as you see, we weren't expecting you. But since you are here, sit down and have a drink.'

Magnus, standing there, in his dark suit, and his heavy glasses, looked down at them, at their cosy installation under the parasol, and smiled too, gravely, and said,

'Well, after all, why not?'

'I must confess,' said Gabriel, when Magnus had seated himself, and ordered himself a drink, 'that you were probably the last person in the world that I expected to see. And since so much indiscretion has already taken place, perhaps I might be indiscreet enough to ask you what you're doing here?'

'You might ask,' said Magnus, 'but I wouldn't answer. After all, what the eye doesn't see, as they say.'

'I trust you won't spend too much time grieving over us,' said Gabriel.

'No, no,' said Magnus, smiling at Clara, 'I can't see much cause for sorrow. I don't waste my sorrow.' Then he paused, for a long time, and they were all silent, and then he added, 'I was rather glad to see you, in point of fact.'

Then there was another long silence, and Gabriel finished his drink, and then got up to go, and said that perhaps he might leave Clara with Magnus and that she should come down to the television house and he would meet her in an hour's time. Magnus said that nothing would give him greater pleasure, and that he would walk down with her himself, and so Gabriel left them, and Clara, finding herself alone with Magnus, felt herself to be touching some rare and devious emotion, some refinement of life too delicate to touch, and through sheer nervousness, when Magnus asked her, she ordered another Pastis, her head already beginning to turn from sun and lack of food. And she found herself, as she drank it, staring at Magnus, at silent Magnus, as she had never stared at anyone before, never so evidently stared, and he returned her gaze intermittently, unworried, and after a while he said,

'It's some years now since I've felt it necessary to envy Gabriel. It makes me feel at home, to envy him once more, after all this time.'

'Why did you use to envy him?' she asked, not wishing to pursue the other line of his thought, not knowing where it might lead her. '*Ça ne se voit pas?*' he said, in modest French, and she agreed that it did, and added, generously, that in her view there could not be many people in the world without some cause to envy Gabriel.

And then they were silent once more: she had never in her life felt so little compulsion to chat. As she sat there, a whole new self seemed to be unfurling broadly and confidently within her; nervousness dropped away, and the ease of slight giddiness set in. When he asked her if she wanted to have another drink, she said no, that she wasn't bothered, and he laughed and said that that was the only Yorkshire phrase that he had ever heard her use, and that she must have another drink, so she said that she would, and he ordered her one, and then embarked on some lengthy conversation with the waiter in admirably fluent, pedantic French, and when the waiter went away she said to him that his French was marvellous, much better than Gabriel's, and he said, 'Ah yes, I have advantages that even Gabriel lacks.' And they sat there together, staring out over the Place, with the comfort of conspirators, and as they watched a woman walked along the pavement before them, and Clara idly watched her, she was a large woman with a pink-brown face, and an old flowered print dress, in her forties perhaps, her red-brown hair straight and flat and short and uneven, slightly uneven, not fat, but tall and broad, her face gleaming slightly with what might have been health, a school mistress perhaps, for some reason clearly a spinster, and then Clara uneasily noticed that she was mumbling to herself as she walked, and then, before they had time to avert their eyes, she suddenly squatted down in the gutter, by a parked car, just in front of them, and pulled up her skirts, and Clara saw the bare gleam of her large red thigh, and then she stood up again and pulled down her skirt and wandered mumbling on.

And Magnus said, 'I have seen her before, she is always here, she sleeps, much of the time on the Métro steps, come on, Clara, let's go.'

And they got up and went. They walked together, down the rue Raynouard, and Clara stared at its perspectives, at the steep glimpses of courtyards with clipped bushes and fountains through expensive flats, at Balzac's house, at a house with blue tiles on it, at a priest's house with birds and terra cotta angels on the chimney stacks, and she felt happy in Magnus's company, she felt acceptable, she felt accepting, and when they reached the round block at the bottom of the street she said to him,

'Why don't you come in with me, why don't you come and have lunch?'

And he said no, that he had to go. But she insisted, against her nature and with her inclinations she insisted, she said, 'Well, this evening then, let's meet this evening,' and he said, suddenly, that he would like to, that he would, and they arranged to meet at seven, at the *terrasse* where they had been. And then he said, but it must be your last evening, and she said yes, but that he must come, and he said that he would like to, and so they parted, and she turned her attention to the television house.

She liked the look of the building. It was round, or round in principle if not in fact, as television houses always seem to be, and it had a post office in its basement; she liked places with facilities, and wanted to buy some stamps, but then reflected that French stamps would be of no use to her. So she went in. Gabriel had said he would meet her in the foyer, so she went up to the first floor, where the foyer seemed to be, but it was huge, it stretched right round the whole building, and she could not see him; all she could see were walls of glass sixty feet high, and pillars and vast mosaics and empty grey chairs and acres of fitted grey carpet. She noticed thinking to herself, this ought to frighten me, this is the kind of situation I dislike, but she was not alarmed, she did not care, she was quite glad that he was not instantly there, and she wandered around, her giddiness increasing slightly from the vast grey extensions, but her calm increasing too, with it. And then she saw him, finally, coming towards her from the other end of the expanse, with his friend, and she waited for them unruffled, unperturbed.

The friend, who was called Patrice, suggested that they might go out for lunch, but Clara, when consulted, said with unusual firmness that she would rather eat in the canteen, that she particularly liked canteens, so they went up to the top floor and collected themselves a large self-service meal, and, as she happily noted, an adequate supply of wine. She liked the way that one could pick bottles of wine off the counter, as calmly as though they were milk or Coca-Cola or fizzy orange. When they sat down with their meal, Clara turned to Gabriel and said,

'I arranged to meet Magnus this evening. I said we'd have a drink with Magnus.'

'Did you really?' said Gabriel. 'Why ever did you do that?'

'Why not?' said Clara, starting on her bean salad. 'Why not? I liked him, that's why.'

'I like him too,' said Gabriel, 'but I'm surprised that you do.'

'I like most people,' said Clara, and before the meal had advanced much further she had invited Patrice, whose attitude was most complaisant, to join them too. He accepted with alacrity, and Clara, swallowing steady gulps of *vin ordinaire*, started to look round the restaurant saying, let's ask him, oh look, I like the look of him, and what about asking that woman in that green dress over there. After a while they both succumbed to her mood, and when a colleague of Patrice's stopped at the table to greet Patrice, he too was invited, and he too accepted. When they had finished their lunch they went on to the *terrasse* next door, and there, high up, they had a coffee and stared at the Sacré-Coeur, and Gabriel tried to buy himself a cognac and was told he could not buy spirits, so they went down to Patrice's office, and on the way they passed a stocking coin machine, and Clara stopped and exclaimed at it, and explained that she had not been able to buy stamps, so Gabriel and Patrice put all their spare francs in the machine and bought her three pairs of stockings. Then they went down to Patrice's office and he and Gabriel drank some cognac, and Clara had none, because she felt quite gay enough, for once, without it, and they sat around there talking for some time. And finally Patrice said he had to go down to the studio, and would Clara like to come, so they went, and she wandered around in the dark, tripping over cables, staring at cameras, reading notices on notice boards, while Patrice tried to persuade some men to move some chairs on to a set for a discussion programme. Then Patrice and Gabriel started to have a long and dull conversation with another man about a lens, and Clara, feeling *de trop* and needing the Ladies', walked off to look for one. She had seen them on all other floors but the studio floor, and had to ascend several storeys to find one, and when she came out again she had forgotten how to get back. Curiously, she did not seem to mind; she knew that if the worst came to the worst she could always find Gabriel and Patrice again with Magnus in the Café Malekoff, and so instead of panicking or looking for an exit she decided to walk all the way round the fifth floor, and she set off, on the highly polished pale blue lino, walking very evenly, right in the middle of the corridor, and the names on the doors flowed past her. M. This, Mme That, Mlle This, red doors, blue corridor, round and round, until she noticed on one door a name that stopped her, the name of M. Harronson, and the name brought suddenly back to her so clear, so inspired, so brilliant a vision of the boy with daffodil hair from so many years before that she stopped there, stopped still in her circle, and stood. And then, although she could never in her life have pictured herself doing such a thing, she knocked on the door. She did not really think it could be him, but it was he himself that opened the door to her. He had a small blue office, of his own, and he looked young: her own age, she reflected that he was her own age.

'Hello,' she said. 'You won't remember me, but I saw your name, I was passing and I saw your name.'

He stared at her, and she could see that he remembered her.

'I remember you,' he said, 'I met you in the middle of the Channel, and I danced with you at that dance; I do remember you.'

'You don't remember my name,' said Clara, 'but it's Clara. You'd forgotten my name, hadn't you?'

'I'd have remembered it if I'd seen it written on a door,' he said.

'Ah yes,' said Clara, 'but I bet you wouldn't have knocked.'

'I might not have knocked,' said Peter Harronson, 'but I would probably have wanted to. Come in, do come on and sit down and tell me what you're doing here.'

'Shouldn't you be working?' said Clara.

'No,' he said. 'I've done my work for today. I work too fast for them, I never get given enough to do. Look, I was reading Iris Murdoch.'

And he showed her the book on his desk, which was, no less, Iris Murdoch. So, persuaded, she went in, and she told him, precisely and in detail, exactly what she was doing in Paris, and extracted a similar story from him, and it seemed to her that never had she been so lucid, so perfectly in control of the significance of the events of her own life, so perfectly receptive to those of another's. He was working for French television, he had taken up French, had read French at Oxford, and had

179

been in Paris for a year; his job, he said, was dull, and even to her it sounded duller than Gabriel's, but then, she gently reassured him, he had but to wait, and they would find him something better to do than to read Iris Murdoch under the desk.

Then he asked her why she was carrying three pairs of stockings, and she explained about the machine, and then she asked him if he could help her to find Gabriel again, and looking at her watch discovered that it was five o'clock, so she invited him to come and have a drink with them on the *terrasse* on the Place, and he said that he would, and they set off to look for Gabriel. They did not find him in the studio, and as Clara had forgotten Patrice's surname, if she had ever known it, they did not know where else to look, so they went up to the canteen, and on the way Peter put some more francs in the machine and got her another pair of stockings to add to her collection, and the gesture touched her to the heart, she felt she was very near to some elusive, lovely happiness. Patrice and Gabriel were in the canteen, drinking coffee, and when Clara introduced Peter she thought she surprised upon Gabriel's face a marvellous gleam of alarm.

So they had coffee, and talked for an hour or so about Patrice's divorce, which had been caused, or so he asserted, by his wife's passion for one of his uncles; the conversation was in French, so Clara felt that she was gaining in all ways, in her knowledge of her world, and in her knowledge of the French language. There were a few words that she did not know, but she felt that they were exactly the ones for which she had always been searching, and she recognized them as by instinct. And when it approached six o'clock, Clara, who had never in her life dared to risk asserting her authority on any gathering, suddenly said, 'Let's go, come on, let's go and have a drink.'

And nobody demurred, nobody resisted, nobody fell away; they all said yes, what an idea, let's go and have a drink. And then they all went and got into Patrice's car, and said where should they go, it wasn't time yet to meet Magnus, so they went to the Avenue Gabriel, at Clara's suggestion, who said that she wanted to sit with Gabriel on the Avenue Gabriel, and he sat and held her hand there, before them all, and this made

180

her happy, but at ten to seven, afraid of missing Magnus, she insisted that they should all move once more, so they all got back into Patrice's car and went back to the Place du Trocadéro, and there was Magnus, waiting for them, as he had said he would be, and Patrice's friend waiting at a different table. They stayed there for about an hour, and then Clara began to grow nervous lest they should all go away, and she was not yet satisfied, she had not had enough, she had not had what she wanted, whatever it might be that she wanted, and when Peter said to them, why don't we all go to my apartment, it's just down the road, she heaved a sigh of relief for she knew that they would all go.

Patrice tried to make them all get back into his car, but Peter said that it wasn't worth it, and at first nobody listened to him, but finally they took his word, and followed him, and it was, they found, more or less next door, at the top of the rue Raynouard. Clara was very impressed by the whole installation; the block of flats was large and grand, the lift was made of wood and brass and carpet, and Peter's flat, on the sixth floor, seemed limitless, lavishly furnished, and had an amazing view over the river. She was not alone in her amazement, for everyone else started to make clucking noises of appreciation and wonder, and Peter explained that the apartment was not, naturally his, but belonged to one of his aunts who was never there. At this Clara started a long lecture upon people who had aunts with flats and uncles who ran off with their wives, and broke it off only when Peter appeared with a whole crate of Beaujolais and asked her if she wouldn't like to help him make some supper. No, I wouldn't, she said sharply, I can't cook and I don't intend to try, but having thus stated her position she consented to go into the kitchen with him and opened some tins and cut up some bread. Nobody seemed to mind much what they ate; they sat around eating bread and cheese and tinned asparagus and crême de marron and horrible tinned tomatoes and every piece of fruit in the house, and all Peter's aunt's store of cocktail sausages and cocktail biscuits and olives and packets of Ryvita, and while they ate Gabriel tried without success to make Magnus explain why he was in Paris, and Clara inspected the décor, which, although highly gilt and

181

decorated, was not a patch on the Denhams', and she felt curiously satisfied, to notice its defects. When they all felt less hungry, Peter said, would it be all right if he rang up a few friends and asked them to come round, and they all said why not, so he made several telephone calls, and Clara managed to make herself feel generous about the arrival of other girls, because she was after all herself entrenched beyond all removal, indeed one might say that the whole enterprise belonged to her alone. When Peter had finished on the telephone, he came and asked Gabriel and Magnus and Patrice and Patrice's friend if they would all like to ring up their friends too, and Patrice said he might ring his ex-wife and his uncle, and did, but they were out, and Patrice's friend rang up his girl friend, and Gabriel said that perhaps he might after all ring up Samuel Wisden, who was living in Paris, and he did, and Samuel Wisden said that he would come.

After another hour or so these various guests started to arrive, but Clara found it hard to take them in, and began to think that perhaps she should stop drinking. But she found that she could not stop. A passion stronger than curiosity, or perhaps curiosity itself reduced to a passion drove her. After midnight, the scenes began to take on a truly festive, picturesque aspect; bottles lay all over the floor, Samuel Wisden kept reciting poetry to which nobody listened, and Patrice's friend's girl took off her dress. Peter went out and came back with some bottles of whisky, and tried to persuade Clara to have some, but she declined, and told him instead the story of the Italian man who had taken her to the cinema.

'I bet you fancied him more than you fancied me,' said Peter, when he heard the story.

'It wasn't that, it wasn't that, but what did you offer me?' said Clara.

'We were very young,' said Peter.

'I'm not so old now,' said Clara, and got up, dislodging Gabriel's hand from the back of her skirt, where it had neatly wedged itself; he did not see her go, he was talking to Patrice on the other side. She went to the bathroom, and then into the kitchen, and started to look for some Nescafé, and she had just found it, and was standing holding it to her trying to work out what to do next when Magnus appeared. He shut the door behind him, so she was not, somehow, at all surprised when he came over to her and kissed her. He did not kiss her very seriously, but he held her rather hard and the coffee jar rammed itself uncomfortably into her bosom and his, caught there between them like Tristram's sword.

'Shall I tell you something?' said Magnus, when he let go of her, 'shall I tell you something? Perhaps you won't want to know.'

'I like to know everything,' she said.

'It's about Phillipa,' he said.

'Even about Phillipa,' she said.

'I was in love with Phillipa,' he said.

'Is that all?' she asked him, wanting more.

'Yes,' he said, 'that's all.'

'I don't know,' she said, standing there, and looking for what she was thinking, 'I don't know, but you might almost say that that seems to me to be normal. What I mean is, that it seems to me that I might almost have known it. Though how I should have known it is another matter.'

'One knows these things from birth,' said Magnus.

'Some people may,' said Clara, 'you and all your family may, but I don't know, I didn't know, I've had to find it all out. I think, perhaps, that I am not talking very clearly. Can you hear what I am saying?'

'Yes.'

'You aren't in love with her now, though.'

'Oh no, not now. I don't suppose anyone will ever be in love with her again.'

'You resent me, you resent me,' said Clara, suddenly, seeming to see, through a swaying mist, some new illumination, 'you resent me for wanting Gabriel.'

'No, no,' he said, 'on the contrary, I wish you well, I wish you and Gabriel well, though I haven't very much hope that it will do him much good.'

'I can't stand this conversation much longer,' said Clara. 'I came in here to make myself a coffee, let me make myself a coffee.'

'First of all,' said Magnus, 'give me a kiss.'

And she, acquiescent, confused, willing, stood there and shut her eyes and waited, and he said, patiently, 'No, no, I said give me a kiss. Open your eyes. It is better to give than to receive.'

'You must be very drunk,' she said, 'as drunk as I am.'

'Perhaps,' he said. 'Open your eyes.'

So she opened her eyes, and saw him, and also the truth of what he had said, which was that she had never kissed a man in her life, she had merely allowed herself to be kissed; and she forced herself, she forced herself, she reached up towards him, feeling his height, after Gabriel's, unnatural, and she kissed him, on the lips, and she felt that in doing so she was forcing her nature beyond the limits of its spring, that it could not bend back, that it would break rather than bend so far, or bend so far that it would bear the shape of the curve for life. And then she let go of him, and he, in silence, went over to the gas stove, and put on a pan of water, and got down a cup for her coffee, and another cup for his, and made them two cups of coffee, without speaking another word. Then he said,

'Drink it here, or everyone else will want one,' so she stayed there and drank it, and then she went back to look for Gabriel.

But Gabriel had gone. At first she could not believe it; she sat down and waited for him to reappear, thinking he might have gone to the bathroom, or gone for a breath of air, not beginning to fear that he might not return, but he did not come and he did not come, and as time went on it appeared increasingly obvious that he was not coming, and she could too easily imagine the reasons for his absence. Her conduct, which had hitherto seemed to her to taste of liberation, worsened in her own eyes, worsened with a sickening, dreadful rapidity, and she sat there suffering the loss of faith that she had always dreaded, and all the more bitterly for the fact that the reproach should come from her ally, her lover. She looked back over the day, giddy at the lengthening prospect behind her, and she thought, I thought it was beautiful but it was nothing, I cannot do it, I was not made that way, and all that I have done is to make a fool of myself, and Gabriel knows it, he has found me out, he has recognized that I cannot do it, I am no use to him. And the thought of Magnus filled her with alarm and guilt and misery, and she started to cry, and the thought of being discovered in tears by Magnus pulled her to her feet, and she walked unsteadily through the dining room and through the hall, and started to open the front door, to let herself out, and there Peter Harronson overtook her and asked her where she was going. She said that she was going back to the hotel, and he asked her how, and she said that she would pick up a taxi, which was not true, for she had not enough money on her, and he said that he would come with her, so she let him, lacking the strength to prevent him, and they walked up to the Place du Trocadéro, where she had been so gaily earlier in the day, and there they found a taxi. And she got into it, and then remembered she had no money, and when he said that he would come with her she had to say that he could, and he got in beside her and held her hand, and she cried and cried, all the way across the river, all the way to the hotel. There she thanked him, and he said it was nothing, and that was that, and he went off again, and she had not had to pay.

The hotel door was open; it was always open, and there was never anyone there. She looked at her watch, for the first time for hours, and saw that it was twenty past four. The key to their room was not on its hook, and her spirits rose, slightly, at the thought that he must be there, that his disaffection had not been great enough to remove him to some place where she could not find him; she needed to set eyes on him again. She went quietly up the stairs, and pushed open the unlatched door of their room, and there he lay, flat on the bed, still fully dressed, face downwards, his head buried in the pillow, asleep. He had not even taken off his shoes. She sat down beside him on the bed, but he did not stir. He was sleeping as he had not slept all week, the sleep of total exhaustion. And it occurred to her mercifully, that there was a chance that he had left her because he was so tired. There might have been nothing more to it than that. She sat by him, and she thought of how tired he had been, and of how little they had slept, and of how they had laughed together over their inability to leave each other alone, and of how he had groaned, night after night, into her arms, Oh darling, you're killing me, I'll die of you, I'll die. And these intimate recollections reassured her, and she stared down at his disorder, at the checked cotton shirt escaping from the indecently low waist of his trousers, and at his dangling shoes: she had thought that she would wake him, to hear him speak to her, to see him turn to her, but instead she lay down quietly by his side, and tried to sleep. She thought that it would be an intimate, familiar kindness, to let him sleep, to abandon love and reproaches until the morning: a mark of progress, a sign of unselfish care.

But she could not sleep. The world swam whenever she shut her eyes, so she kept them open and stared at the ceiling, and as she stared she thought of the morning. They were intending to leave together on the nine o'clock plane, as Gabriel had to be back at work. And as she thought of her return, the immense folly of her absence hit her for the first time, and misgivings possessed her; a hundred things might have happened while she had been away, there were a hundred reasons why she might have been found out. She wondered what would happen to her, and whether it would matter, and whether she would mind, and whether it had been worth it. She felt committed: she felt that she had aligned herself. And this gave her nothing but pleasure, for at the heart of all her misgivings there was a small disgraceful gaiety. She had started on a course, and she had gone far enough at last to know that she could never go back.

But, for Gabriel, she was worried. She looked at him, so sleeping, so much himself, so heavily excluding her, and shame renewed in her, for it did not seem that they had used each other well. And she felt that it had ended. She was sure that it had ended; when she had chosen not to wake him, she had chosen not to continue it, but to make an end.

At six o'clock, she got up and put her things in her case. Still he did not move. And it was then that she realized that she was going to leave him there. The thought of walking out on him, as he had walked out on her, occurred to her as though it were the greatest inspiration of her life; indeed, she greeted it with such satisfaction that she was obliged to recognize that she must still be drunk, for it was not the kind of inspiration that came to her often in sobriety. Once it had occurred to her it seemed irresistible. The thought of his missing his plane did not dismay her: she wanted him to miss it. She wanted to shake his faith as he had shaken hers, or this was what she thought that she wanted, as she searched, quietly and anxiously, through his brief case to find the plane tickets. They were not there, so she tried his coat pocket, and his suitcase, and could not find them there either: determination gripped her the more strongly for such opposition to her efforts, and she started to look in his trouser pockets. She could feel them there, and got them out without waking him, though he stirred and murmured and turned over on to his side: she took her own, and left his by the bedside. Then, remembering her total lack of money, she took a ten franc note as well. And then, on the point of leaving him, she stood and looked down at him and she thought: I am not leaving him because I don't want him, but because I do, and because it will prove that I do, because he will know that I want him so much that for his sake I have made myself able to leave this room, for him I have left him, and what I want, I prepare myself most endlessly to leave. For to renounce is to value. And then, leaving no word, she left. It did not much look as though he would wake in time.

She walked to the Air Terminal at the Invalides. It did not take her as long as she had thought it would, and she was there well before seven. She was on the point of buying herself a bus ticket to Orly when she thought of looking at her plane ticket, and discovered that for some reason it was booked from Le Bourget, so she bought one for Le Bourget instead. It all seemed very simple. It seemed too simple. She wondered why journeys had always seemed so significant before, so fraught with possible disaster. She felt strangely clear and light: weightless, almost. Acts that would once have driven her into a panic of hesitation seemed to have become transformed into simplicity itself, and a whole moral inheritance of doubt had dropped away from her; the thought that she might have gone to Orly by mistake did not stay with her, a nagging reminder of human error, an indictment of human effort, but instead it fell calmly away, and drifted off into unnecessary space. She got on to the bus, and sat there with a kind of placid blankness; the night was over, and nothing seemed to be of much importance, it had all grown out into some clear dawn of acceptability.

As the bus moved off, and drove north through Paris to the dreadful outskirts, she realized that she was going to feel ill, and that the night would be in one sense at least paid for, but as she contemplated her growing nausea she found she did not care about it at all, she did not at all care if she was going to be sick all over the bus. It was all the same to her. She stared out of the window, at dirty streets and shabby houses and cemeteries and reaching, unfinished fly-overs, and she thought that she did not care what greeted her when she returned to England, nor what should happen to her, ever, in the future. And yet such carelessness did not pain her; she felt free, the light weight of her limbs, the clear grey spaces in her head, the ebbing of her need, these were merely symptoms of her freedom, and she was in some open early region where despair and hope seemed, as words, quite interchangeable, where she seemed to sit, quite calmly, beside her own fate.

When the bus arrived at Le Bourget, she got off it and went straight to the nearest Ladies' Room and was sick in the wash bowl. She did not give it so much as a thought. Then she washed her face, and her hands, and the bowl, and looked at herself in the mirror, and thought that she did not look too bad; her shirt, which she had been wearing for twenty four hours, was looking a little dirty, but not on the other hand particularly dirty, not dirtier than it had looked on various more innocent occasions, not dirty enough for anyone to know. She did not look as though she had been up all night; she looked no worse than anyone else, at that early morning hour. She put some lipstick on, and she thought that her face took on a positively radiant aspect from so small an addition; she looked as well as she ever looked, after no matter how many hours of preparation. The complete equality of all actions assailed her, solaced her; there was really no difference, it was all the same, Orly, Le Bourget, lipstick, no lipstick, sleep, no sleep, none of it seemed to matter. It would not even matter, she thought, if Gabriel should come. She wandered out of the Ladies' Room, and went to the desk to acquire her flight ticket, and there she was told that she had to pay seven francs tax for the use of the airport facilities. She looked in her bag, and found that she had six francs fifty change from her ten franc note; the bus had cost her three francs fifty. So she looked at the girl behind the desk, the girl in uniform, and said that she hadn't any money, that she couldn't pay. And as she said it, she could not tell whether she cared so little because the question was so totally uninteresting to her, or whether it was the most interesting thing that had happened to her in her life. The girl behind the desk said that she had to pay, and Clara said once more that she couldn't, and gave her the six fifty, and then started to look in her coat pocket, and found a ten cent bit, and another one, and then she opened her hand bag and looked in the bottom of her hand bag, and found another five cents. She handed them over, and stared at the girl in uniform, and said, 'If I owe you twenty-five cents, does that mean I can't go on the aeroplane?' And all the time the extraordinary flavour of nonchalance, a taste stranger than the taste of celebration from the day before, filled her mouth. It satisfied her, to find herself reduced to the small change of life, to find years of in- herited thrift and anxiety and foresight so squarely confronted, with so little disaster in the air. The girl was just suggesting that Clara should look through her bag once more, when a woman standing at the next desk leaned over and gave Clara twenty-five cents, saying *'Je vous en prie, je vous en prie,'* and Clara took them and smiled politely, gracelessly liberated from gratitude, and obtained her boarding ticket, and went and sat down on a plastic covered seat to await, in destitution, the announcement of her flight. And she felt, as she waited, that she had perhaps done to herself what she had been trying for years to do to herself: she had cut herself off forever, and she could drift now, a flower cut off from its root, or a seed per- haps, an airy seed dislodged, she could drift now without fear of settling ever again upon the earth.

She took the flight to London as though she flew to London every day, released from all action by her entire poverty, got off the plane, and collected her luggage, and walked to the bus, as though she had been born to such events. She thought of Gabriel, and she found that her feeling for him seemed to have passed already into the tenuous twilight world of nostalgia; she did not look into the future for his face. She got on to the bus as though in a dream, and took the tube from Gloucester

Road to Finsbury Park, and a bus up to the Archway from Finsbury Park, and when she got home, she found waiting for her a postcard of the Eiffel Tower from her one-time teacher Miss Haines, a letter from her aunt Doris, and a telegram from Northam saying that she was to go to Northam immediately, for her mother was in hospital there and seriously ill.

Chapter 9

When Clara opened the telegram and saw the news about her mother, she trembled as though she had been struck from the heavens. She stood there, staring at the fatal yellow paper, and her first thought was, I have killed my mother. By willing her death, I have killed her. By taking her name in vain, I have killed her. She thought, let them tell me no more that we are free, we cannot draw a breath without guilt, for my freedom she dies. And she felt closing in upon her, relentlessly, the hard and narrow clutch of retribution, those iron fingers which she had tried, so wilfully, so desperately to elude; a whole system was after her, and she the final victim, the last sacrifice, the shuddering product merely of her past.

Then, shaking herself, shaking off these thoughts, she rang up her mother's number, and received as she had expected no reply, and then she rang up Alan, and he told her their mother was in hospital, that she had cancer, that he had been trying to get hold of her for days, and that her mother kept asking for her, and he had not dared to tell her that she could not be found.

'What does she think, then?' said Clara. 'Does she think that I refuse to come? And what does she think is wrong with her, does she know what's wrong with her?'

'No, she doesn't know,' said Alan, 'they wouldn't tell her a thing like that. And I don't know what she thinks about your not coming, I didn't bother to ask her, and she didn't say, she just said she wanted to see you.'

'I'll come up this afternoon, then,' said Clara.

'I think you'd better,' said Alan.

So she went to King's Cross, and got on the train to Northam. She thought that she would sleep on the train, but she did not; she stared out at the increasing familiarity of the landscape, restless, sleepless, wondering what awaited her, what recriminations, what disavowals, what regrets. When she got off the train she took a taxi, Gabriel-style, to the hospital, and tried to find out what had happened, but nobody seemed anxious to help her; it was too late to visit Mrs Maugham, they said, visiting hours were over, and that she should come back in the morning to speak to the specialist. So she went away again, relieved by the delay. She got on to a bus, and went into the grimy town centre, and walked around for a while, staring up at the blackened bricks and the dirty windows and the non-conformist architecture, and thought of Paris, with its angelic cornices and its pale and flowery stones, its classical statues, its draperies and its trees and its gilt. She could not make sense of it. Then she went into a phone box, and rang up Alan, and he said that she should go round to the house in Hartley Road, and that he would come round with the keys and meet her there and let her in.

'You could sleep here, I suppose,' he said, 'but you know what it's like here, it would be much more convenient if you didn't.'

'Oh, all right,' said Clara, 'I don't care where I sleep, I'll sleep at home.'

And she got on another bus, the very same bus that had taken her daily to and from the school, the number seventeen, a number once endowed with proprietory delight, and still familiar beyond all other familiarities, and they went past the school itself, and there was a group of girls coming out of the side door, and she looked at her watch, and noted that it was half past eight on a Friday, and that they had been doing their School Choir rehearsals for the Whitsuntide concert. It was on this bus that she had sat with a boy called Higginbotham, and dreamed of Gabriel.

When she got to the house, Alan was waiting for her; he had driven over in his car. She looked at him, standing there in the back door looking for her, and at the sight of him fatigue suddenly overwhelmed her. She wondered if he would touch her, if he would say anything to her, but he held the door open for her and all that he said was, 'I told you you wouldn't get anything out of them at the hospital.'

'No,' she said, putting down her bag on the kitchen table. 'No, you were right.' And for some time they said nothing to each other, while she went and hung up her coat, and looked in the refrigerator to see if there was anything to eat. He stood around, watching her, and he said nothing, but she felt uneasy under his gaze, as though he could see on her marks and indications. Then, while she made herself a sandwich with some old sliced bread and a piece of sliced processed cheese, he went and sat down in the sitting room and switched on the television. She received its noise with joy, and as soon as it tuned up she asked him, 'Well, do tell me about it, you might as well.'

'They say it's cancer,' said Alan, staring at the flickering set, where two young actors in historical costume were pretending to talk about Charles the Second.

'How did she find out?' asked Clara, seeing that no information would be volunteered and that she would be compelled to demand, rather than be allowed graciously to receive. She had forgotten this stubborn, obdurate refusal to reduce strain.

'About a fortnight ago,' he said. 'She'd been feeling ill for months, she said, but she never saw anyone, and then it got bad, and she went to the doctor. And he sent her to the hospital.'

'How long has she been there?' said Clara.

'Since Tuesday,' he said. 'I rang you on Tuesday, but you weren't there.'

'And is it bad?' said Clara, gazing intently at the television.

'She'll be lucky,' said Alan, with a kind of dreadful satisfaction, 'she'll be lucky if she lasts three months.'

And Clara, hearing it, knew that she had from the first expected to hear it, for what did telegrams mean but death? Not, in her family, births or greetings or weddings or events or excitements, but death itself, quite simply so. Nothing else was worth so extravagant a gesture, so expensive an announcement.

'Oh,' she said.

And warming a little to his theme, Alan continued, 'They say there's no hope, no hope at all, there's nothing they can do for her. It's far too far gone, they said.'

Clara, listening to his tone, felt herself filling slowly with repugnance, for his tone was so grim, so emphatic, so much an inheritance from that dying woman; and she thought to herself, she bred it in him, how can she complain if her death is so received?

'Cancer of what?' she said, knowing that she had got him on to a subject on which he might well be expansive, and thinking that she might as well know; and he told her, he told her everything, with such emotionless self-congratulation that she finally could take it no longer, and interrupted him, and said,

'No, no, that's quite enough, I daresay I'll have to hear it all over again in the morning.'

And so he told her whom to ask for at the hospital, and the number of their mother's ward, and then he left her.

And then she found herself alone in the house. She had not been alone in it, thus, in the evening, for many years, for her mother never went out, and she felt, in her solitude, that her mother was already dead. She walked, restlessly, downstairs, from room to room, opening the cupboards, looking at the sad, much-hated objects of her infancy, the tulip-patterned slop bowl, the plastic mats, the easy chairs, the narrow bulging settee, the tiled fireplace, the plastic pulley in the kitchen, where a few abandoned tea towels still hung. It frightened her to think how much violence she had wasted upon such harmless things. What chance had there ever been, ever, that she would have been condemned to them for life? What immense folly had ever made her fear such a fate? It was nearly over; the house was about to expire, it would be taken to pieces and there would be nothing left of it.

After a while she went upstairs and thought she would have a bath, but the water was cold; her mother, provident even in illness, had switched off the immersion heater before her departure. So she went into her bedroom and started to undress, but anxiousness possessed her so much that she could not make herself get into the blanketed bed, and the sight of the empty room, with its ugly furniture and its bare primrose walls and its small narrow divan disturbed her so much, with so many recollections of the sufferings of her childhood, that she left it, and started to walk up and down the short corridor, up and down, and finally she wandered into her mother's bedroom, and stood there in its emptiness, staring, bemused, at the satin-covered bed. And she felt, as she stood there, that she was facing the room for the first time, no longer averting her own eyes from her own shame before it, no longer blind with vicarious grief, no longer clouded by the menace of her own lack of love. None of it had any longer any importance, and she looked at the bed, and at the wardrobe, and at the flowered, worn carpet with its ill-assorted rugs and mats, and then she went and sat down at the dressing table, and looked at herself in her mother's mirror. Then she started, methodically, assiduously, to open all the little pots and boxes, gazing earnestly at rings and hairpins, at bits of cotton wool and old bus tickets, and then she moved on, to the drawers themselves, to piles of stockings and handkerchiefs, still searching, looking anxiously for she knew not what, for some small white powdery bones, for some ghost of departed life. And in the bottom drawer, beneath a bundle of underwear, she found it. She found some old exercise books, and some photographs done up with a rubber band.

She took them out, and spread them on the dusty glass-topped table, and looked at them. She looked at the photographs first; they were old and brown and faded, and some of them she had seen before, for some were of weddings and birthday gatherings, but there were two that she had never seen. They were both of her mother, her mother alone, her mother aged twenty, and in both her mother sat on a fence in the country somewhere, with a bicycle propped against her skirts, and in one she stared gravely at the camera from beneath her cloche, and in the other she smiled bravely, gaily, a smile radiant with hope and intimacy, at the unseen hands holding the unseen, long derelict camera. She looked thin and frail and tender, quite lacking the rigid misery that seized her face on the wedding photographs; Clara had never in her life seen such a look upon her face. She stared at them with a kind of wonder, and then she put them back in their rubber band, and started to look at the exercise books.

They were stiff backed, and black, and inside they were lined, and covered with thin blue ink, in her mother's hand. She started to read, and at first she could not think what she was reading. One page started: 'It was a bitterly cold day, and

195

Annabella, staring from her narrow attic window, shivered and held her hands towards the solitary candle.' The text was heavily emendated, heavily crossed out, and from time to time there were pages written out as verse; one of them said:

> O let us seek a brighter world
> Where darkness plays no part:

and another started with the verse:

> I wait here for my life, and here I must wait
> While all the world rolls on and passes by;
> Surely my expectations have a date,
> And I will find the answer ere I die?

And Clara, reading this, started to shiver, for she knew that she was reading her mother's life, and that if ever she had needed proof that she had once lived, then this was it. And she turned to the end of the book, and there was the date, 1925; before her mother's marriage, before the end of her hopes. And Clara began to cry, for she could not bear the thought of so much deception, of so much disappointment, of a life so eked and spent and drawn and withered away. She would have preferred to believe that hope had never existed, that there had been no error, no waste, no loss, and yet there it lay, in those faded stilted phrases, in those tenuous and stiffened smiles. It was possible, then, to go disastrously astray; tragedy was possible, survival was no certainty, there was no reason why anyone should escape. And Clara looked back at the writing, and at its shockingly literate echoes of stories and hymns long since forgotten, and she could bear to read no more, and she wondered whether she should fall on her knees and thank Battersby Grammar School and the Welfare State and Gabriel Denham and the course of time, or whether she should reserve her gratitude until more safe and later days.

And she put the exercise books back in the drawer, carefully, where she had found them, and then she went back to her own bedroom, and got into bed between the rough blankets, too tired to look for sheets, and as she fell asleep she noticed in herself a sense of shocked relief, for she was glad to have found her place of birth, she was glad that she had however miserably pre-existed, she felt, for the first time, the satisfaction of her true descent.

In the morning, she got up and went to the hopital, as she had been told, and found the specialist, as she had been instructed, and he told her the whole story, and told it with a kind of bluntness that paid little respect to whatever feelings she might have had. He seemed to be saying to her, beneath his lines: Plain dealing is what you expect, plain dealing is what you will get, we are no fools, you and I, and how useful that neither of us have time for sentiment. She found him offensive, though she could see that he meant to soothe, that he meant to invite her into a dry and stoic world; she wondered how many emotions he had disarmed and strangled at their timid, delicate, hysteric birth. His lack of circumspection pained her, for she had grown used to the circumspect, and she would have preferred a veneer of sympathy, no matter what indifference it might have covered, for she felt herself forever alienated from this world where brutality presented itself as sincerity. She disliked his dreadful suggestion of conspiracy, his suggestion that nobody cared, that death was a necessity, that an appearance of caring would be merely a mockery and a pretence. And when he said, finally,

'She'll be all right here with us, there's no reason to think of moving her, whatever she says, because after all you've got your own life to live, you won't want to be looking after her yourself, let's face it, will you?' She found herself almost forced into revolt, upon the verge of declaring that she could, finally, precisely, face just that, the final, often imagined (and yet how final, and therefore possibly endurable) martyrdom: but she looked at him, at his square face, and his heavy glasses, and his knowing look, and her eyes dropped because of course she could not face it, he was right, he knew the limits of human effort better than she herself had known them, for he had seen them more often than she had.

'No,' she said, meekly, 'no, I couldn't stay here, I have to be back in London, I couldn't stay, I really couldn't stay ...'

And he led her, thus defeated, to her mother. She was in a

197

small ward, curtained off from two other patients, and when Clara was shown into the room she was dozing, her head propped up upon the high mound of hospital pillow, her jaw sagging, breathing through her mouth. She looked appalling; the change was worse than anything Clara had ever imagined, and she could not believe that in so little time so much flesh could have worn itself away. It was only two months since she had seen her, and she had come to this. The bones of the head, once sunk deep, now reached forth through the skin to their final revelation, and the breath disturbed the body, as though it caused it pain. Clara, staring, in the instant before her mother stirred and woke, wondered how she could not have known, how she could have missed the warnings of this imminent decay. And she felt that she was standing there empty-handed, bringing nothing, useless; in a jug by the bedside a few roses withered, and she thought, at least I could have brought her flowers. And she was the more ashamed because she had thought of bringing flowers, she had passed, on the way there, a dozen flowershops, and had not stopped, because she had been afraid, afraid of rejection, afraid of that sour smile with which so many years ago her mother had received her small offerings of needle cases and cross-stitch pin cushions and laboriously gummed and assembled calendars. She had been afraid of the gesture; she had learned nothing, she could not give, and yet she knew that without gestures there was no hope that love might fill the empty frames, the extended arms, the social kisses, the proffered flowers. She had brought nothing, and her meanness dismayed her. She had not wished to be mean.

When her mother woke, she sat up, abruptly, and looked at Clara, evidently forewarned, and looked her in the eye, and said, bitterly, sourly, without interrogation,

'Oh, so you've come then, have you.'

'Yes,' said Clara, standing there nervously, uneasily.

For some time neither of them spoke, and then her mother said, fretfully,

'Sit down, go on, sit down, there's a chair there somewhere, isn't there, you might as well sit down.'

So Clara sat.

'I don't suppose you're going to tell me why you didn't come any earlier,' said her mother, after another long pause.

And Clara, who had been toying with the idea of saying, I was in Paris with a man, as some desperate final appeal to that young woman leaning on a gate forty years ago, found naturally that such an appeal was impossible, against nature; and equally impossible was the only other possible reply, which would have been to answer this dull uninflected demand in kind, by saying 'No, I am not going to tell you.' Freedom abandoned her, the pitiful ineptitude of freedom, and she found herself once more, as of old, basely prevaricating, terrified into deceit, mumbling shamefully on about examinations, and having been away on a course, and not having received messages.

Then her mother, who had been looking down at her sheet, and picking at the hem of it with an unfamiliar feebleness, said suddenly with all her ancient venom,

'If I were on my deathbed, it would be all the same to you lot. What do you care? I work my fingers to the bone, and what do you care? If I were on my deathbed, you wouldn't care. If I dropped dead, you'd walk over my dead body.'

And Clara, telling herself that she had heard these phrases, word for word, a hundred times before, and that hardly a mother in the world had not been driven to them, could nevertheless not restrain a kind of sick shivering, for she knew, then, that her mother knew, and was thus obliquely imparting her terror and her information. For she too was not after all lacking in circumspection: she too could multiply implications. And knowledge lay between them, dourly, without comfort, inarticulate.

After a while they started to talk, laboriously, of other things; of the immersion heater and the laundry and the milk bill. Clara, listening, sustaining her part, dispelled the hope, which had sprung in her the night before, that some reconciliation, some gleams of sympathy or need might show themselves, and she saw, as she had always known, that understanding is never anything but fitful; indeed, she found herself watching anxiously, fearfully, for any sign of feeling, for any chink in the stony front, because it was in truth the last thing that she wanted, the last thing that she could have borne. And there was

199

nothing, nothing at all: with relief she saw that there would be nothing, that she would not be called upon to give, that she could merely answer meanness with meanness. When they started to talk, after some time, of Clara's plans, Mrs Maugham herself like the doctor prefaced her remarks by the assumption that Clara's only desire would be to get back to London as quickly as she could: Clara demurred, denied, postponed, and admitted.

'I'll stay for a day or two,' she found herself saying, 'and I'll come back next weekend, I'll come back on the Friday evening train ...'

She could not bring herself, at first, to ask how the hospital suited her, or whether she would prefer to move, whether she would prefer a private nursing home, but in the end she forced herself to do so, and her mother said,

'Oh no, I'm better off here.'

'Are you sure,' said Clara, feeling herself suddenly called upon to insist, 'are you sure that you wouldn't prefer to go somewhere more private? I mean, I'm not saying it's not nice here, but we could find somewhere else, couldn't we, surely, if you wanted ...'

'Why should I move?' said her mother. 'It's all right here. They'll look after me all right here. And after all,' she said, looking at her daughter squarely in the eyes, 'it's only for three weeks or so, isn't it? Three weeks treatment, they said, and I'll be fit to go home.'

'Oh yes, of course,' said Clara, unable to meet her looks, frightened before such grim mockery, 'oh yes, it wouldn't be for long. But even so, if you wanted to move ...'

'Oh,' said Mrs Maugham, tired, suddenly tired of the whole business, turning her head to the tall white wall, 'Oh, I'm not bothered, it's all the same to me.'

Clara did not know what to do with herself for the rest of the day. It was Saturday; she knew that she had no reason not to stay till Monday, that she must stay until the end of the weekend. She spent the afternoon wandering around town once more, looking in at the bookshop, gazing at the library and the windows of the department stores, walking, walking, tiring herself. The thought of the empty house unnerved her; she did not want to go back to it until she was fit to drop. She bought a sandwich for lunch and ate it as she walked, and in the middle of the afternoon, pleased to find herself hungry, glad to be able to fill in some time by eating, she went to have some tea. She went to the department store which her mother had always favoured, not through perversity, but because it was the only place she knew, and she walked through the counters of haberdashery and gadgets and stockings and cosmetics, and into the lift, and emerged in the tea room, and sat down and ordered herself a pot of tea and some teacakes. All around her, women met and talked and nodded to each other, in their unseasonable tweed suits and their hats and their linen dresses and their unfashionable expensive shoes. It was a nice shop; her mother liked it because it was a nice shop. At the next table there were two women, two middle aged women, both grey haired, and they were talking to each other with competitive pride about their grandchildren; each looked as though she might have been her mother, and yet from them seemed to pour such fountains of innocent, lovely, generous solicitude that Clara, overhearing them, suddenly wondered if her whole vision of Northam might not after all have been a nightmare, and that the whole city might have been filled with warm preoccupations, a whole kind city shut to her alone, distorted in her eyes alone. And she felt once more charitably towards herself, that she had had no wish to hate; she had merely wanted to live.

She visited her mother again in the evening, for the visiting hour, between seven and eight; Kathie was there too, released from the other evil of the children's bedtime, and she and Clara exchanged embarrassed greetings by the bedside, and parted, at the hospital door without having exchanged a word of truthful communication, without even acknowledging their mutual awareness of their visit's purpose. Then Clara got back on the bus and went back to the house and let herself in. It surprised her, to have to unlock the door for herself. She had never had a front door key before.

It was nine when she got back, and she did not think she could go to bed at nine, so she opened herself a tin of soup, then discovered that she was still hungry, and ate a tin of baked beans. There was no milk: she wanted a drink of Ovaltine, but there was no milk. She walked around the kitchen once or twice, and then she went and sat down in the sitting room, and looked at the books on the shelves, at the *Encyclopaedia Britannica*, the school prizes, the Edwardian novels, so well perused, but she did not feel that she would ever care to open a book again. Then she switched on the television, but it meant nothing to her, she had lost the habit of watching, she could not watch it alone. So she went and had a bath and went to bed. She was in bed before ten, and she fell asleep at once, and she dreamed that it was she herself that was dying, that she had been given a week to live, and she was crying in her dreams in despair, but I can't die, there are so many things I wanted, there is so much I wanted to do, things that I can't do now, I can't do them this week, I wanted to do them later, you don't understand, my plans, you don't understand, my plans were long term plans: and yet through her protests ran the fatal certainty that it would happen to her just the same, that it was useless to cry out, for they would never allow her the time that she needed. And then, through her dreams, she heard the telephone bell ringing, ringing downstairs, and she woke herself up and fumbled for the light and went down the stairs, and as she went, as she picked up the receiver, she found that her cheeks were wet, that she was sobbing, that she had been crying in her sleep, and that her throat was still trembling with emotion.

It was Gabriel who was speaking to her. At first, shivering and trembling, she could hardly answer him: his voice sounded as though it was coming to her from another world, after even so short an absence, and it sounded so desired and lovely that she felt relief settle into her, and she said to him, as soon as she could speak clearly. 'Oh Gabriel, you woke me, I was asleep, I was dreaming that I was dying.'

And he talked to her, patiently, with his unfailing ready solicitude, until she had emerged from her night time confusion, and then he started to ask her why she had left him. At first she could not even think what he was talking about, and then it all came back to her, the party, and Magnus, and the taxi, and the hotel, and Gabriel asleep face downwards on the bed, and as she remembered it, as it took colour in her memory, she felt safe and warm once more, back at home in the realm of human treachery and love and infidelity.

'You left me,' she said. 'It wasn't me that left you, it was you that left me. How can you not remember?'

And then, tenderly, bitterly, they embarked upon explanation and recrimination. They went back over it, over the whole night in Paris, over their conflicting jealousies, over his desertion of the party and her silent departure, over his solitary waking in the hotel bedroom, and her return, and her news of her mother's fatal illness. She asked him how he had known how to find her, and he said he had not known, but that he had tried everywhere, and that he had tried, finally, her home.

'Oh God,' he kept saying, 'I'm glad the explanation's so simple. I'm sorry, but I'm glad.'

After a while she said to him, when she had firmly regained her hold upon the situation,

'Tell me, Gabriel, what time did you wake after I'd gone, that morning?' And he laughed and said, 'Oh Christ, don't ask me, I didn't wake till quarter to nine, and serve me bloody well right, I suppose,' and they both laughed, and she could hear herself laughing, and some marvellous indestructible frivolity stirred in her again.

'Look,' he said, hearing her soften, 'let me come up, let me come up and see you. We can't leave it, we can't leave it like this.'

'Oh no,' she said, 'you can't, you can't do that. What will they think, if you go away again so soon?'

'Let me come,' he said. 'Let me come and fetch you back. You can't stay up there, all by yourself. I'll come up and drive you back.'

'I don't know why you should want to,' she said. 'I've finished with you, you know.'

'Well,' he said, seeming to know it, 'then we could have one last glorious ride together, couldn't we?'

'Oh, I don't know,' she said. 'It's a long way.'

'It's only two hundred miles,' he said. 'I've got the map here open in front of me. Let me come up for you. I'll come up in the morning, and we could go back tomorrow night. Think how nice it would be, driving all that way together.'

'It would be nice,' she said, hesitating, completely hooked, as he knew, by the lure of such a treat.

'After all,' he said, 'I've never really driven you anywhere. It would be nice, in the car. So ride together, forever ride, as Browning said, I believe. It would be our last fling.'

'I don't like your driving,' she said, 'you don't go evenly, you accelerate too suddenly, I don't like it. And then there's another thing, I don't want you to see this house, I don't want you to see where I come from.'

'Why not?' he said. 'What does it matter?'

'Ah,' she said, 'it doesn't matter where I come from, but where you come from, that matters to me, you know. All you are to me, you know, is a means of self-advancement.'

'Ah well,' he said, 'I knew that. For all you were to me was a means of escape.'

'I knew that too,' she said, 'but how rude of you to say it.'

'And did you advance yourself?' he asked.

'Oh yes, without doubt,' she said. 'Though others, I suppose, might see it as a decadence. And you, did you escape?'

'After a fashion,' he said.

'I did better, then, than you,' she said. And then said, with sudden certainty, 'And look, I always do best. Look at me, what a fantastic piece of luck my life has been.'

'You've worked hard for it too,' he said.

'Gabriel,' she said, able to use his name at last, luxuriously, expensively, across the long distance miles of wires, 'Gabriel, if you come up and fetch me, which way back shall we go? Shall we go along the motorway and stop at all the all night places?'

'I don't see why we shouldn't,' he said.

'It would be rather nice,' she said. 'I can't deny that it would be rather nice.'

'I'll come, then,' he said.

'Yes,' she said, 'you do that, you come. But you must remember to shut your eyes when you get to this house, I don't want you to remember it, I don't want it in your memory.'

'You're a coward,' he said. 'Why can't I know the worst?'

'Because I don't feel free of it,' she said. 'It's a part of me forever, I don't want it to be a part of anyone else. I can't be free, but there's no reason why I shouldn't be thought to be free, is there? In fact, listen, why don't we make a rendezvous, why don't I meet you outside the Town Hall?'

'No,' he said, 'that won't do.'

'You mean you won't?' she said.

'Yes, I mean I won't. If you want to drive in my car, you must let me see your house.'

'That's fair enough, I suppose,' she said. Then she laughed, and said, 'I can show you a lovely tea set with tulips on, and all sorts of lovely things. After all, why shouldn't you come? Why don't you come right now?'

'I can't,' he said, 'I have to go home.'

'Where are you now?' she said, and then added, 'No, don't tell me, I know where you are, you're at the house, aren't you, you're at your parents', aren't you?'

'Where else,' he said, 'would I dare to run up such a phone bill?'

'I like talking to you,' she said, 'in the middle of the night.'

'It's not so late,' he said, 'it's only eleven.'

'Good God,' she said, 'I thought it was nearly the morning. You will come, then, when it's the morning, won't you?'

'I will come,' he said.

'Promise you will come,' she said.

'I promise,' he said.

'Will you find your way?' she asked.

'I suppose so.'

'I won't give you any instructions,' she said. 'I can never give people instructions. But come, you will come.'

'I'll get there,' he said, 'about midday.'

'I have to go to the hospital,' she said, 'in the afternoon. But then I'll be free.'

'All right,' he said.

'Good night, then,' she said.

And he too said good night, and she rang off. She went upstairs to bed again, and she lay on the bed, looking forward, all of it running into her head, all the years of future tender intrigue, a tender blurred world where Clelia and Gabriel and

205

she herself in shifting and ideal conjunctions met and drifted and met once more like the constellations in the heavens: a bright and peopled world, thick with starry inhabitants, where there was no ending, no parting, but an eternal vast incessant rearrangement: and more close to her, more near to her, the drive in the car, the lengthy devious delicate explanations, the nostalgic connexion more precious, more close, more intimate than any simple love, and the wide road itself, the lanes of traffic, the headlights, the speed and the movement, the glassy institutions where they would eat eggs and chips and put coins in fruit machines and idly, gratuitously drink cups of nasty coffee, for the sake of it, for the sake of amusement, and all the lights in the surrounding dark. Her mother was dying, but she herself would survive it, she would survive even the guilt and convenience and grief of her mother's death, she would survive because she had willed herself to survive, because she did not have it in her to die. Even the mercy and kindness of destiny she would survive; they would not get her that way, they would not get her at all.

More about Penguins and Pelicans

Penguinews, which appears every month, contains details of all the new books issued by Penguins as they are published. From time to time it is supplemented by *Penguins in Print*, which is our complete list of almost 5,000 titles.

A specimen copy of *Penguinews* will be sent to you free on request. Please write to Dept EP, Penguin Books Ltd, Harmondsworth, Middlesex, for your copy.

In the U.S.A.: For a complete list of books available from Penguins in the United States write to Dept CS, Penguin Books, 625 Madison Avenue, New York, New York 10022.

In Canada: For a complete list of books available from Penguins in Canada write to Penguin Books Canada Ltd, 2801 John Street, Markham, Ontario L3R 1B4.